Hello!

A few years ago, my dad said, 'Jenny, have you ever thought of writing a book about a girl who wants to be an astrophysicist?' I snorted – derisively – then pushed his ridiculous idea to the back of my mind. It was ridiculous because:

a) I wasn't entirely sure what an astrophysicist did.

b) Despite Dad having asked me how many miles it was to the sun (every single day of my childhood), I'd somehow grown into an adult who knew nothing about space … except for how many miles it was to the sun (ninety-three million, give or take a few).

So how could I ever write about a girl who wants to be an astrophysicist? Well, I can't resist a challenge, particularly one thrown down by my dad, and slowly the idea grew in my mind. The girl became Meg and her dream got bigger: she didn't just want to be an astrophysicist, she wanted to be an astronaut. She wanted to leave planet Earth and float in space.

In going to understand how Meg's mind worked, I had to learn about the things she loved. I discovered that when we look at stars we're gazing into the past, that our sun is just one of over one billion trillion stars in the universe, that on Mars you can jump three times higher than you can on Earth. I peered into one of the largest refracting telescopes in the world and saw further than I'd ever seen before in my life.

Thanks to Meg (and Dad!), my world has got bigger. About forty-six billion light years bigger.

If you want to join Meg as she reaches for the stars, or just need a little space in your life, then turn the page. Her mission is about to begin!

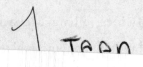

Also by **JENNY McLACHLAN**

FLIRTY DANCING
LOVE BOMB
SUNKISSED
STAR STRUCK

ABOUT THE AUTHOR

Before Jenny started writing books about the Ladybirds (Bea, Betty, Kat and Pearl), she was an English teacher at a large secondary school. Although she loved teaching funny teenagers (and stealing the things they said and putting them in her books), she now gets to write about them full-time. When Jenny isn't thinking about stories, writing stories or eating cake, she enjoys jiving and running around the South Downs. Jenny lives by the seaside with her husband and two small but fierce girls.

Twitter: @JennyMcLachlan1
Instagram: jennymclachlan_writer
www.jennymclachlan.com

STARGAZING
FOR BEGINNERS

JENNY McLACHLAN

BLOOMSBURY

LONDON OXFORD NEW YORK NEW DELHI SYDNEY

Bloomsbury Publishing, London, Oxford, New York, New Delhi and Sydney

First published in Great Britain in April 2017 by Bloomsbury Publishing Plc
50 Bedford Square, London WC1B 3DP

www.bloomsbury.com

BLOOMSBURY is a registered trademark of Bloomsbury Publishing Plc

A CIP catalogue record for this book is available from the British Library

ISBN 978 1 4088 7975 7

Typeset by RefineCatch Limited, Bungay, Suffolk
Printed and bound in Great Britain by CPI Group (UK) Ltd, Croydon CR0 4YY

1 3 5 7 9 10 8 6 4 2

For my brother and sister, Nick and Julia.
I love sharing life on planet Earth with you two.

ONE

On my seventh birthday, Grandad made me a rocket. He used the cardboard box the washing machine came in, put a cone on the top and painted the whole thing white. Then he stencilled *MEGARA 1* on the side with red paint.

Mum took her hands away from my eyes and I blinked. The rocket nearly touched the ceiling. 'Is it real?' I asked.

'Almost,' she said.

Grandad handed me my bike helmet. 'Are you ready for your first mission, Meg?'

I nodded. 'I think so.'

I was already wearing my astronaut pyjamas so all I had to do was put on the helmet and climb inside the rocket. Mum handed me a broken keyboard – my control panel – then shut the door. I ran my hands over the keys. Grandad had stuck labels on the different buttons: fuel boost, disengage, pressure drop. One button was painted green and simply said, *LIFT-OFF*.

'Megara 1,' Grandad said, putting on his smoothest American accent, 'you're good at one minute.'

'Roger,' I replied. Grandad and I were always watching NASA documentaries so I knew exactly what to say.

'Megara 1, this is Houston. You are go for staging.'

'Inboard cut off,' I said, tapping buttons randomly, 'staging and ignition.' At that exact moment a deep growl burst out and I realised Mum had turned on the vacuum cleaner. Its roar filled the cardboard rocket. I felt my heart speed up with excitement and I tightened my grip on the keyboard.

'Megara 1, this is Houston!' Grandad shouted to be heard over the vac. 'Thrust is GO. All engines. You're looking good. This is ten seconds and counting.'

'Ten,' I called out, 'nine … eight …'

Grandad and Mum joined in. 'Seven … six … five …' Then one of them started shaking the rocket around.

'Mum!'

'What is it?' Her face appeared at the cut-out window.

'I'm scared!'

She reached through the window and took hold of my hand. Her silver rings pressed into my skin. 'Don't be scared, Meg. I'm here.'

'Four … three … two … one …' continued Grandad.

'All engines running,' I said, then I slammed my finger down on the green button. 'Launch commit!'

'Lift-off!' shouted Grandad. 'We have lift-off!'

Mum let go of my hand and disappeared.

The vac roared, the rocket shook wildly from side to side and I was leaving Earth and shooting into deepest space!

TWO

Eight years later. Back on planet Earth.

Before I get my breakfast, I make sure everything in my bedroom is just right.

I smooth down the duvet, push the chair under the desk and turn my globe so England is facing the sun. Then I get a red pen and cross yesterday off my homework timetable. Good. If I spend a couple of hours working on my speech tonight then I'll be right on track. I don't believe in luck or superstition, but before I leave the room I take a moment to glance at my picture of Valentina Tereshkova – the first woman to fly in space. Her steely gaze keeps me focused during the day.

I grab some Weetabix from the kitchen then follow the *thud, thud, thud* coming from the front room. Only

4

Mum would play bass anthems at eight in the morning. I find her kneeling on the floor, blowing up a paddling pool. Sitting on the sofa is my sister, Elsa, a jammy crust dangling out of her mouth.

I turn down the music then join Elsa. I start eating my cereal, trying to ignore Elsa's powerful wee smell. Her nappy looks suspiciously bulgy.

There's a hiss of air as Mum pushes in a plastic stopper. 'Looking forward to trying out our new paddling pool?'

'Not really,' I say. 'Mum, we live in a flat. Why do we need a paddling pool?'

'So we can have *fun*, Meg! I thought we could fill it up and pretend summer's here.'

I look around. Toys, clothes and books are spread all over the carpet and Pongo is running round and round the paddling pool, barking at the inflated rings. 'Mum, there isn't enough room for it in here.'

'There's loads of room,' she says, then she jumps to her feet. 'I'm going to start filling it up.'

Elsa takes the crust out of her mouth and holds it out to me.

'No thanks,' I say, but she keeps jabbing it in my direction.

'Da!' she says. 'Da, da!'

'OK, OK.' I take it off her and pretend to eat it. 'Nom, nom,' I say. 'Happy now?'

Elsa smiles, sticks her thumb in her mouth and flops back on the sofa. Then we watch as Mum runs to and from the kitchen with pans of steaming water. She's wearing her Tinker Bell nightie and her bleached-blonde dreads are gathered on the top of her head with a scrunchie. Her bracelets jangle as each pan of water splashes into the pool.

After six trips, the water just about covers the bottom. 'It's going to take ages,' she says sadly, swishing a toe in the water. 'Can you help me, Meg?'

'Sorry. I've got to get to school.' I go to the mirror over the mantelpiece and start brushing my hair back into a ponytail.

'Such beautiful hair,' says Mum. I can see her in the mirror watching me, her turquoise nose stud gleaming on her pale face. We look so different: me with my dark eyes and hair and Mum, blue-eyed and with hair so blonde it's almost white. 'I wish you'd wear it down.'

'It's easier this way.' I smooth a strand of hair behind my ear and button up my blazer. I brush some toast crumbs off my shoulder. 'Shouldn't you be getting ready for work, Mum?'

'In a minute. I'll just put a bit more water in.'

Mum runs the Mencap charity shop in town. That's her paid job, but she's got loads of others, like fundraising for Greenpeace and running the community allotment. She wants to make the planet a cleaner, better place. It's fair to say she doesn't feel the same way about our flat.

'Meg, can you babysit Elsa after school?' Mum dumps another pan of water into the paddling pool. 'You know my friend Sara, the nurse?' I shake my head. Mum's got so many friends I can't keep up with them all. 'Well, Sara's going to do some volunteer work abroad and she needs a lift to the airport.'

'I don't know …' I think about tonight's jam-packed square on my homework timetable. 'I've got so much work to do … Plus I've got to practise my speech.'

Mum looks at me, eyes wide. 'I'll be back around six. You and Elsa can just hang out together until then. It'll be fun!'

I look at Elsa, who's now lying on her back on the sofa, gurgling and trying to get her foot in her mouth. 'You really need to give Sara a lift?'

'It would help her out a lot,' Mum says, then she pulls me into a hug, pressing my face into her hair and I smell the sandalwood incense she loves so much.

I put up with it for a moment then wriggle out of her arms. 'OK,' I say.

Mum's face lights up. 'What would I do without you?'

Over Mum's shoulder, I see Elsa crawl towards the edge of the sofa, reaching for Pongo's tail. '*Mum!*' I say, but already Elsa is losing her balance. She wobbles for a second then tumbles forward, landing on the floor with a thud.

There's this moment of silence before the screaming starts. Mum darts across the room and scoops Elsa up. 'Poor baby!' she says, showering her with kisses. Pongo jumps up and tries to stick his pointy nose between them.

'I'm going now,' I say, but they don't hear me. Now Pongo's been pulled into the hug too and his excited barks rise over Elsa's screams. I slip out of the flat and shut the door behind me.

Immediately, I'm hit by the quiet, the bright cold air and the view.

Our flat might be small and damp, but it's got the best view in town. I stand on the balcony and look from the houses of the estate to my school. Beyond school, I see the hotels, the sea and the pier. Then I look up at the sky, higher and higher, until I find the moon. It's a white smudge that's disappearing fast.

I turn and run down the concrete stairway, my feet ringing out with each step.

I've got to get to school. I've got so much to do.

THREE

School's good. I get one hundred per cent in a maths test, finally learn how to conjugate German verbs and spend lunchtime in the library researching my favourite star, Alpha Centauri B.

When I know the canteen will be quiet, I go and get some lunch. It looks like almost everyone's been chucked out, but some students from my year – Bella Lofthouse and her friends – are still sitting round a table while the lunchtime supervisors clean up. As I walk past, they glance over at me, and I see Bella's lips curve up in a smile. Quickly, I turn away. Bella is always laughing with her friends and she finds me particularly funny. The longer I hang around the more likely it is that she'll say something to me and somehow I'll end up looking stupid. I grab the first sandwich I see – egg mayonnaise – pay for it, then walk straight out of the canteen.

It's at times like this that I miss Harriet. She was my best friend at school. OK, she was my only friend in or out of school, but that didn't matter because we were soul mates, and we did everything together – walking to school, eating lunch, talking for hours on the phone, sleepovers … Harriet even went camping with me and Mum every summer. Then, one day, she told me that her mum and dad were talking about moving to New Zealand. Five months later, she was gone.

When a huge star dies, there is a massive explosion, a supernova, and later, all that's left is a dark, dense black hole where no light can get in or out. From brilliant lightness to total darkness: that's what it felt like when Harriet left.

When I got over the shock of her going and looked around me, there didn't seem to be a place for me anywhere: everyone else was paired up or in groups. I did try to talk to people, wriggle into their conversations, but Harriet had always done the talking for both of us and I was out of practice. Plus, like I said, I was shocked when she went and feeling a bit like a dark, dense black hole.

Who wants to be friends with a dark, dense black hole? No one!

All that darkness has gone now, but the friend-making

10

moment seems to have passed by. Which is why, right now, I'm leaning against the wall by the girls' toilets eating an egg sandwich all on my own.

Like I said. Sometimes I miss Harriet.

FOUR

I get to physics early and find Ms Edgecombe sticking up a poster on the door.

'What do you think?' she says. It's a photo of mission control at NASA and *Houston Space Centre Trip – LIFT-OFF 16th July!* is printed across the top. Ms Edgecombe taps the photo with a blue fingernail. 'You could go there, Meg. In four months, you could actually be standing in mission control for the moon landing!' She laughs. 'Un-bloody believable!'

'Miss, you're swearing again.'

'Sorry, Meg, but some situations call for swearing ... I mean, *mission control*!'

I follow Ms Edgecombe into the classroom. The trip to Houston costs over two thousand pounds and Mum can't afford that. Grandad offered to sell something to pay for me to go, but then he realised he didn't own anything worth that much money, not even his telescope.

'It looks amazing,' I say, 'but I'm not going, Miss, remember?'

She grins at me. 'You might … You just have to win the competition.'

The competition. Two words that have the power to make sweat break out on the back of my neck and my stomach flip over. It's called Reach for the Stars and one teenager from our county has the chance of winning a place on the trip; all they have to do is stand up on a stage and explain what space means to them.

Easy! This should be *my* competition – I'm obsessed with space and know everything there is to know about black holes, exoplanets and our solar system – but, and it's a big 'but', I have a thing about speaking in public. Some people are scared of spiders, or lifts, or clowns. I'm scared of speech. My particular phobia is inconvenient. Let's just say that in your typical day, I'm confronted with speech a lot more often than a coulrophobic is confronted by clowns.

I used to be fine. Back in junior school my hand would be up before the teacher had finished asking the question, but then I started secondary school and I noticed how my hand going up made the other children roll their eyes and snigger. Then, one day in science, Mr Harper said, 'What do we call it when plants use the sun to make energy?' By now, I'd learnt to keep my hand down. 'Anyone?' he said. 'It begins with a "p" … "ph" … "photo" …' Eventually I couldn't bear it any more so I put my hand up and said, 'Photosynthesis.' The word hung in the air for a moment then Mr Harper said, '*Photosynthesis!*' mimicking my voice perfectly. Everyone collapsed laughing. 'Only joking, Meg,' he said, giving me a cheeky wink, but that was it. From that moment on, my mouth was sealed shut.

One to one I can handle. One to two is bearable. But as soon as I have an audience, my words disappear. *Poof!* Even if I'm just asked to read in English my mouth goes dry, my heart speeds up and I feel like I'm going to puke. In fact, just *thinking* about entering the competition is making my egg sandwich creep back up my throat!

'You're worrying about it right now, aren't you?' says Ms Edgecombe.

I nod.

'I can tell because your hands are shaking.'

'They are?' I look down at my wobbling hands and groan. 'How am I going to do it, Miss?'

She laughs. 'Meg, you could talk about space for three

14

hours without even glancing at a piece of paper. Just pick a topic, and talk about it.'

I shake my head. 'I'll only be able to walk on to the stage if I know *exactly* what I'm going to say. I've written the whole speech on cards and now I'm going to practise until I'm word perfect.'

'And how have you found writing the speech?'

'Hard,' I admit, thinking about all the versions I've written and how difficult it is to squeeze my favourite facts into three minutes. 'Space is just too big. I couldn't explain what neutrinos mean to me in three minutes, and they're so small sixty-five billion have just passed through my fingernail.' I hold my finger. 'And that's in the last *second*! I don't know if what I've written is any good.'

She laughs. 'Don't panic, Meg. You've still got three weeks –'

'Two weeks five days.'

'Just try it out in front of some friends. See what they think.'

She says this like it's the simplest thing to do in the world.

'Maybe.'

'Definitely!' she says, then she drops a pile of books in my arms. 'Now be a love and hand these out for me.'

FIVE

Just as I've put down the last book, the other students bundle in. Bella bounces straight up to Ms Edgecombe. 'Guess what, Miss!' She waves a pink card under our teacher's nose. 'We've just got our tickets to the spring ball. We're having it with the Year Elevens at a hotel, which is obviously a massive improvement on Year Nines in the canteen!'

Miss examines the ticket. 'Oh, God ... I think I've got to go to that.'

Bella nudges her. 'You'll love it, Miss. You can show us your wicked moves.'

Miss shakes her head. 'You'd be too intimidated. Now sit down and tie your hair back.'

Bella slips the ticket in her pocket and joins me at our table. 'All right, Megara?' she says with a grin.

'Meg,' I say automatically. Bella Lofthouse is the only

person in the world who ever calls me by my full name. Maybe she's being friendly, reminding me that we've known each other for years … Or maybe she's just laughing at my stupid Disney Princess name. It's really hard to tell.

'Nah, you'll always be Megara to me,' she says, then she starts bundling her hair up on her head. She takes a band off her wrist and fixes it in place. A few strands fall loose and, just like that, she looks perfect, like some girl in a film. Suddenly, she sits up a little taller. '*Hello*, here come the boys!'

I look up to see Raj and Ed strolling towards us, hands in their pockets, their trousers narrow and their hair defying gravity.

'Bella, you troll,' says Raj. He comes up behind her and starts patting her down. 'Give me my phone back!'

'Oh my God!' Bella shouts. 'Get off me, you perv! Miss, Raj's touching me up again!' But Ms Edgecombe doesn't even look up. As they carry on fighting, and Ed starts getting his stuff out and dropping it on the desk next to me, I feel myself almost shrinking into the corner, trying to make myself invisible.

Ed King takes the seat next to me. He's so tall it's like a shadow's fallen over me. 'She's not got it, mate,' he says in his deep voice. 'You're wasting your time.' He shares a quick smile with Bella and she winks back.

Suddenly, Raj's phone is forgotten and Bella's talking about some picture she put on Instagram. 'Show Meg,' Raj says, and Bella's phone is pushed in front of me. I can never stay invisible for long. 'What do you think of Bella's selfie?' he asks, watching me closely and smiling in anticipation about what I might say.

I glance at the photo. From all the bubbles surrounding Bella's face, it looks like she's in the bath. I try to work out the right thing to say, the thing that won't make them a) laugh or b) think I'm weird. I shrug and say, 'She looks clean.'

'*Clean?*' says Bella, bursting out laughing. 'Classic Megara! I'm putting it in the comments.'

OK. I failed.

Raj rocks back on his stool. 'Do I look *clean*, Meg?' he says with a grin.

'Right,' says Ed firmly. 'I want to work, so it's time for you two to shut up,' he points at Raj and Bella, 'and for Meg to lend me a pen.' He holds his hand out, just like he does every lesson.

I find a biro in my pencil case and hand it to him.

Ed studies it. 'Haven't you got a gel pen?'

Across the table, Bella giggles.

With a sigh, I swap the biro for one of my beloved inky gel pens.

'Thanks, Meg,' Ed says, whipping the pen out of my hands and turning straight back to his work.

Halfway through the lesson, Ms Edgecombe starts handing round dominos and ping-pong balls. 'We're going to recreate the nuclear fission process,' she says, 'and I want you to work –'

'In groups,' says Bella. '*Please*, Miss.'

All around the room, students demand to work in groups while I silently beg for 'alone'.

'I want you to work with the person sitting next to you,' says Miss.

'What?' says Bella, scowling at Raj. 'But I want to work with Woody!' This is another of Bella's special names – Ed*ward* – Woody – but unlike my Megara, when she calls Ed 'Woody' you know it's one hundred per cent friendly.

'Well you can't,' says Ed, clicking the lid down on my pen. 'I'm with Meg.'

'As usual,' mutters Bella.

Ed and I are always paired up. It's because we're both clever or, in Raj's words, 'total freaks'. Somehow, Ed manages to be a part-time freak, slipping in and out of the role depending on whether he's in lessons or hanging out with his friends. For me, it's a full-time position. I've often wondered what the difference is between me and Ed, and how he manages to pull off being clever and popular at the same time. Maybe it's because he's a boy, or maybe it's because he's captain of the football team and that sort of counterbalances how clever he is. Who knows. All I do know is that although Ed King and I are both clever, in every other respect, we are a million miles apart.

He shakes out our dominos. 'Meg, you fill in the sheet and I'll set these up.'

Immediately, I say, 'What if I want to do the dominos?' When the other two aren't listening, I manage to talk to Ed. Just about.

'Not sure about the answers?' He looks at me, one eyebrow raised. 'Need me to give you a bit of help?'

'I know all the answers,' I say, pulling the sheet towards me. Ed and I are in competition. Constantly. Our teachers started it but now we do it all on our own. I suppose I should find it annoying, but these 'arguments' with Ed are often the only conversations I manage to have at school.

Ed's shiny gold watch flashes as he places the dominos in the correct pattern. A few seconds later, he mutters, 'U-235 atoms.'

'Sorry?'

'It's the answer to question three. You look stuck.'

20

'Look,' I say, 'are you doing the dominos or the work sheet?'

'I was only helping,' he says with a sideways smile.

'I'm fine, thanks.'

Just as I'm writing down the final answer, something on Ed's science book catches my eye. In one corner, he's drawn an asteroid complete with lines to show it's shooting through space. I glance back across the table. Raj's putting the ping-pong balls in his mouth and Bella's drawing a face on his bulging cheek. They're pretty distracted so, quickly, I say to Ed, 'Have you heard about it?'

His hands pause over dominos. 'Heard about what?'

I point at his picture. 'Asteroid TR7768. It's two miles wide and it's passing close to Earth.'

He studies me curiously and I feel myself blush. I never usually talk to Ed about things like this – we bicker, that's what we do – but seeing the asteroid in his book made me sure he'd have heard of it. 'Asteroid TR7768,' he repeats, a smile playing on his lips. 'Well, my picture is *supposed* to be of a football.'

I look back at the picture. A football? Of course it's a football! My blush hits Mars proportions.

'So tell me about this asteroid,' Ed says.

Across the table, Bella looks up. I turn back to my book. 'It's nothing,' I say.

21

'Hey,' says Bella, banging her hands down on the desk. 'Did any of you see that shark they found near Hastings? It's massive!'

'I saw it,' says Raj. 'Rows of teeth like Jaws.'

'Woody, remember last summer,' says Bella, 'when you swam out to that dinghy?'

He nods, keeping his eyes on the dominos.

'It was probably circling under water, waiting to get *you*.' She shivers dramatically. 'I'm never swimming in the sea again.'

'I heard it could have been a tiger shark,' says Ed. 'They've killed people.'

'It wasn't a tiger shark.' I say, unable to resist correcting Ed.

They all turn to look at me and I realise my mistake. 'It was a porbeagle,' I say quickly. 'They're harmless.'

Bella sighs. 'Please don't make my shark story boring, Megara.' She leans forward. 'Talking of man-eating predators … Woody, do you want to know who's asking you to the dance?'

He laughs. 'Not really, but I've got a feeling you're going to tell me.'

'Chiara Swift! She told me at break.'

Ed shakes his head and smiles.

Raj says, 'Chiara's all right!'

'I told her no way,' says Bella. 'You're my reserve in case I don't get a better offer.' She turns to me. 'Who're you asking to the dance, Meg?'

I straighten up the worksheet. Here we go. I've been expecting this from the moment I saw her pink ticket. For Bella, the spring dance is the perfect opportunity to laugh at me because there is just *so much* I can get wrong: music, dancing, clothes, boys …

Quickly, I say, 'I'm not going.' Best to nip this one in the bud.

'Why not?' Ed says.

'I'm busy.'

'Yeah?' He says this innocently enough, but I'm sure a look flies between him and Bella and I can't shake the feeling that they're laughing at me.

Which might be why I blurt out, 'It's what I was just talking about – the asteroid. It's passing by Earth on the night of the dance.'

Bella says, 'And this rock is more important than the dance, because …?'

My mouth goes dry. How have I been drawn into this conversation? 'Well, it's two miles wide … If it hit Earth, it could wipe out a country.'

'But presumably it's not going to hit Earth?' says Ed.

His 'presumably' makes my next sentence fly out

23

of my mouth. 'No, but we might see a dot of light pass by, and if it does I will see it with my friends at the science centre.'

'And your friends are ...?' Bella asks.

How do I make this sound good? Basically they're my grandad's mates, a group of middle-aged men who meet up to boast about the size of their telescopes. 'My friends,' I say, choosing my words carefully, 'are in the Sussex Stargazers club.'

Bella's eyes go wide. 'Let me get this straight. Instead of going to the dance you're going to watch a dot of light, at the science centre with a bunch of old people?'

She's pretty much summed it up. I force myself to hold my head up high. 'It's called a star party,' I say.

Bella grins. 'Megara, everything you touch turns to nerd!' Then Raj bursts out laughing and Ed joins in too.

SIX

After school, I fit in another hour in the library before I head home. I walk up the hill, through the estate, then climb the three flights of stairs to our flat. As soon as I push open the door, I notice how quiet it is. Usually I'm hit with Mum's Ibiza anthems, or a crazy mash-up of singing, TV, crying and barking, but right now the flat is silent.

Perfect. I can practise reading my speech out loud without anyone listening to me.

I drop my bag on the floor and go into the front room. I know the start off by heart so I clear my throat, focus on Mum's poster of a green Buddha, and say loudly and clearly, 'To me, space means freedom ...' My voice echoes round the flat and sounds so *embarrassing* and Meg-ish that I immediately forget the next sentence. Panic rushes through me and suddenly the Buddha's saintly smile looks like a supressed sneer. This is ridiculous! If I can't speak in front of *a piece of paper*, how can I ever expect to speak in front of human beings?

I take a deep breath. I can do this … But I'll just have something to eat first, something high-energy like peanut butter on toast.

I step round the paddling pool, noticing that Mum's emptied it at some point, then go into the kitchen, and that's when I see the note on the fridge: *Meg, don't forget to collect Elsa and Pongo from Grandad's. Ta! Xxxx Mum.*

I'd forgotten all about Mum going to the airport. Looks like that's the end of my rehearsal time, unless I want to do it in front of Elsa and Pongo. Actually, that's not such a bad idea …

I ring Mum's mobile to check when she'll be back, but as soon as the call connects, 'Let It Go' starts playing from the living room. I follow the sound until I find Mum's phone shoved under the sofa. Then I kick my way through the mess on the floor and grab my keys. I'd better go straight round to Grandad's. I might not want to babysit Elsa, but Grandad can't really be trusted with babies. He's easily distracted and has a love of both bonfires and flammable liquids. Not a good combination.

I find Grandad lying in front of his cooker, surrounded by

tools. 'Hello, Love!' he says, glancing up. 'Come to pick up your sister?'

'Yep … What're you doing?'

'Attaching the cooker to a gas canister,' he says, scratching his wild grey hair. 'I haven't got any instructions, but I think I can work it out.'

I pick up the adapter then sift through the tools in his toolbox until I find the right wrench. 'Pass me the hose,' I say, then I crouch next to him and get to work – no way am I sitting on his filthy floor. Grandad lets his chickens wander wherever they like and Pongo's his only vacuum cleaner. Mum and Grandad are eerily similar in their attitude towards housework. Compared to the flat and Grandad's house, my bedroom is an oasis of cleanliness.

As I attach the adapter, Grandad lights one of his roll-ups then picks up a crossword puzzle. 'Looking forward to Saturday?' he asks, catching my eye.

'Bit nervous,' I say, 'but I'm trying not to think about it.' On Saturday, I'm helping Grandad do a workshop at the science centre. He's done them before and usually I just watch from the audience, but this time I've volunteered to be his assistant. Although I haven't told Grandad this, I'm hoping that passing him balloons in front of an audience will take me a step closer to using my voice in front of an audience. That's the plan, anyway.

'You don't need to be nervous,' he says. 'You'll just be standing at the back and keeping me organised.' He nudges me and grins. 'You and me, Meg, blowing kids' minds about the cosmos ... and blowing stuff up. I can't wait!' He lets the ash from his cigarette drop on the floor.

I stare at the glowing tip of his cigarette and try to imagine me standing in front of all those kids ... Hang on, I'm staring at *the glowing tip of a cigarette*!

'Grandad, tell me you've turned the gas off ...?'

'It's fine,' he says, waving the smoke over his shoulder.

I snatch the cigarette out of his hand and stub it out. 'It's *not* fine.' Just then, I hear a shriek from outside. 'Is that Elsa?'

'She's exploring the garden.'

'Grandad!'

'What? I couldn't keep her in here with me when I was smoking and doing this dangerous job. Anyway, Pongo's looking after her.'

'Pongo's a dog and Elsa's ... what, one and a half years old?'

'No. Wasn't it her birthday a couple of months ago?' For a moment, we try to work out exactly how old Elsa is, but we give up when she starts to cry.

I find her sitting in some daffodils, her hands and hair full of soil. Pecking the ground next to her is one of Grandad's bantams (also covered in soil). When Elsa sees me, she stops crying and starts to laugh and pump her arms up and down, saying, 'Buc, buc.'

Is she being a chicken? Who knows … I pick her up, holding her away from me, and carry her back to Grandad. 'Where's Elsa's pushchair?' I say.

'Your mum dropped her off in the car.'

Great. Elsa weighs a ton. This is going to be one long walk home. Then I spot Grandad's 'funky' Union Jack shopping trolley. Would I be breaking some sort of baby rule if I put Elsa in there? Actually, I don't care if I break a baby rule, I can't let anyone from school see me with a baby in a shopping trolley.

'Looks like I'll have to carry her home.' I pass her to Grandad while I get Pongo's lead.

Elsa stands on Grandad's lap and tries to grab at his crossword puzzle. 'What's "Colourless gas; atomic number eighty-six"?' he asks.

'Radon.' I take Elsa and her muddy fists cling on to me. I shrink away, but she just holds on even tighter. 'You knew that,' I say. 'Stop giving me the easy ones.'

Elsa lets go of my jumper and goes for my hair.

Grandad's hands creep towards his fags and lighter. 'Five letters,' he says. '"Utter confusion".'

'Chaos!' I shout as Pongo drags me towards the front door.

SEVEN

By the time we get home, Elsa and Pongo have both done a poo. Pongo did his by the bus stop – which was very embarrassing because I had to put Elsa on the pavement while I cleaned it up – but Elsa saved hers for when we were going up the stairs. She went quiet, stared into the distance, then turned red. 'Gross, Elsa,' I say. 'We're nearly home. Now I have to hold you *and* your poo.'

'Da,' she says, hitting my face with a sticky fist.

Mum had better get back soon. As far as I'm concerned, Elsa and Pongo both belong to her. I couldn't believe it when she told me she was pregnant. I suppose a part of me thought it might be cool to have a sister, but a much bigger part of me thought, how can we fit anyone else in the flat? Officially, we're not even supposed to have Pongo here. Mum saw him on a website called Hungarian

Hounds and – quote – 'fell in love with his scars'. To get him, she lied and said we had a garden, which meant that when they came to do our home check we had to pretend to live at Grandad's. She didn't need a home check to get Elsa; she just went to Glastonbury, met a Spanish man called Angel and came back pregnant.

I know from the silence when I open the door that Mum's still not back. As if she can sense Mum's absence, Elsa starts to cry, so I put her down in the mess in the living room and open the nappy bag. Time to change my first ever nappy. 'Please be quiet,' I say, trying to remember how Mum does it.

First I take off Elsa's leggings. This makes her cry even more, so Pongo comes over and licks her face. Her screams get louder.

'Not helping, Pongo. Go away.' I push him off, but now he thinks it's a game and starts licking Elsa all over – in her ears and eyes … everywhere. I've managed to undo one side of the nappy when Pongo switches his attention to me, assaulting me with his hot tongue and revolting smell of dog food. 'Stay there,' I say to Elsa, then I drag Pongo into the kitchen and shut him in.

When I get back, Elsa's gone.

'Da!' comes a voice from the doorway.

She's clinging on to the door frame, smiling and

wobbling, her loaded nappy only done up on one side. Any sudden movements and it will fall.

I narrow my eyes. 'Elsa,' I say in my best baby voice. (It's not very good; I rarely use it.) 'Stay. There.' Slowly, I walk towards her.

She takes a step back and sways.

'Elsa!' I switch to my best angry voice. 'Don't you *dare* move!'

Mistake. Elsa slams herself down, clutches her face and starts to cry. As I move closer, she throws herself on to her back and starts squirming. In poo.

I literally don't know what to do. No way can baby wipes sort this out. I need a hose! I grab Mum's phone off the floor. Maybe I should Google 'How to change a very bad nappy' ... There's bound to be a film on YouTube.

'Mama,' says Elsa. She's stopped crying and is reaching for the phone. 'Ma!' Elsa can do lots of animal sounds, but she can only say three words: 'mama' or 'ma' which means Mum, 'na' which means no, and 'da' which means everything else. 'Da!' she says crossly.

'You want Mum's phone?'

'Da! Da!'

'OK. But you hold on tight. No dropping it "down there".' I pass her the phone and she starts to suck it. Then she waves it up and down. Then she sucks it again.

The phone distraction gives me enough time to come up with a plan.

I run a bath then carefully release Elsa from the last bit of nappy. 'Time for a bath!' I say, lifting her up and carrying her to the bathroom.

I hold her over the water. When she sees where she's going, her legs go crazy, pumping up and down, and then her arms join in too. Not only is this going to work, it's made Elsa really happy! Then I remember what Elsa is holding. 'Elsa,' I say, 'don't drop Mum's –' *Splash!* '– phone!'

With a sigh, I lower her in the water, then pick out Mum's phone. It's totally dead. I watch Elsa wriggling around and splashing, my chin resting on the side of the bath, too tired to move out of the way. 'You broke Mum's phone,' I say.

'Da!' says Elsa, then she laughs and slams her hands down in the water.

EIGHT

For the next few hours, I try to read through my speech while Elsa trashes the flat. She pulls crystals off shelves, scatters Pongo's biscuits across the kitchen and throws dirty washing into the empty paddling pool. Pongo follows her around, joining in wherever he can. Basically, they're partners in crime and although I try to tidy up after them and whip things out of their way, they both move *so fast*.

Now and then, they turn their attention to me, which is how I end up with a piece of cold toast mashed in between my speech cards. I peel off the toast, and decide to make a start on my geography homework. I'm describing the impact of erosion on glaciers when Pongo snatches the book out of my hands and runs away with it, hiding behind the sofa. When I try to take it back, he thinks I'm playing tug of war and the book ends up with toothy puncture holes all the way through it.

I run my hands over the ruined cover. I covered it *perfectly* in sticky plastic – there wasn't a single air bubble or crease – and now it's ruined. Mum said this would be fun! This isn't *fun*. It's noisy and messy and chaotic.

'Who wants to watch *Peppa Pig*?' I say. I know I do.

After watching eight back–to–back episodes of *Peppa Pig*, I look up and notice that it's gone seven. That's when I switch from feeling annoyed to worried. Mum's never left me with Elsa for this long before. Usually it's just half an hour while she pops to the shops. I tell myself she must be held up in traffic and that she'll be back at any moment, but when it gets to seven thirty and I see Elsa trying to eat a plastic carrot, I realise I'm going to have to feed her. The only problem is, I've never fed Elsa before and I'm not that sure what she likes to eat …

Beans, I decide. Everyone likes baked beans.

'Dinner time!' I say, putting a bowl of beans down on the tray of the high chair.

Elsa's excited. So excited that her hands slam down and the bowl flips over. Beans splatter across the high chair and the floor – a few even hit the fridge – then Elsa grabs a handful and starts stuffing them in her mouth.

'Hey,' I say, holding out a spoon. 'Ever thought of using this?'

She takes the spoon off me and tosses it over her shoulder. Then she rubs her beany hands into her wispy hair.

I'm starting to get why Mum gives Elsa her bath *after* she's eaten. I've never really paid much attention to what they do in the evening because I'm usually in my room, but I know the order: food, bath, bed.

Elsa starts rubbing bean juice into her eyes.

'Tired?' I say. 'Do you want to go to bed?'

'Na!' she says, shaking her head.

'I'll take that as a yes,' I say, unclipping her from the high chair. I've always wondered why Mum doesn't put Elsa to bed earlier. She'd have loads more free time if she did. All I have to do is change her nappy, get her in her Babygro and pop her in her cot, then the rest of the evening is mine!

'Na!' Elsa screams, as I pick her up. 'Na, na!'

'Can't hear you!' I say. I'm way behind on my homework, but if I go to bed late, I should be able to catch up.

NINE

Why won't she stop crying? I'm sitting with my forehead resting on Mum's bedroom door with my speech cards arranged around me. I swear Elsa's screams are making the door vibrate. It's lucky that Elizabeth downstairs is deaf because Elsa's been crying on and off for three hours. When I go in and see her she stops crying, but the moment I shut the door, the screaming starts again.

I can't take much more of this. It's nearly nine and if Mum doesn't turn up soon, I'm going to have to ring Grandad. The more Elsa screams the more illogical my thoughts become and I start to worry that something bad must have happened to Mum. I imagine car crashes, ambulance sirens, police officers knocking at the door. I even wonder if Mum's been arrested for creating a security risk at Gatwick. This worry isn't entirely illogical.

Mum once stormed the runway at Heathrow dressed as a polar bear. She only got out of going to prison because she was eight months' pregnant with me.

Scream … Scream … Scream …

I shut my eyes and try to remember what silence sounds like. And then, amazingly, after one long massive wail, Elsa stops crying! I hold my breath and press my ear against the door. Could she have fallen asleep mid-cry? I try to breathe as quietly as possible, listening for any snuffle or movement. My heart thuds in my chest.

Now I'm worried that she's *too* quiet.

Then I hear a cough, a whimper, and the screaming starts again, only now it's louder than ever. She was just resting her lungs for the next set of screams!

And that's when I hear something else cutting through her cries: the phone.

I scramble to my feet and run into the front room, grabbing the phone. 'Hello?' I say.

There's no reply, but I can hear muffled voices, laughter, and then a banging sound.

'Mum? Is that you?'

'Meg!'

'Mum!' I sink to the ground, pressing the phone tight against my ear. I burst out laughing. 'When are you coming home? Elsa's nearly puked from crying and I don't know how to get her to stop …' I trail off. On the other end of the line I can hear a rumbling sound and it's getting louder. An icy feeling runs through me. 'Mum, what's going on?'

'You'll never guess where I am.' Her voice is breathless, excited. With a sinking feeling, I realise I recognise that voice: it's the one she uses when she's about to embark on a mercy mission. She's used it before to say things like, 'I'm thinking of adopting a blind cat,' or, 'I've volunteered to come in to your school to talk about teenage pregnancy.'

'Just tell me where you are,' I say.

'On a plane!'

'What?' I grip the phone.

'I'm going to Myanmar!'

For a moment, the words don't make sense to me and I wonder if Myanmar is some music festival. But, then my GCSE geography skills kick in and I remember that Myanmar is a country near Thailand, a country that's *thousands of miles away*. She must be joking. 'Mum,' I say, 'did you say you're going to *Myanmar*?'

'*Yes!* Look, I'm sorry to dump Elsa on you, but when I was picking up Sara she started telling me about how the aid agency she's working for desperately need volunteers and then she showed me these pictures of beautiful children. Meg, *fifty per cent* of child deaths in Myanmar are preventable and I've got nursing training! When I found that out, I knew I had to drop everything and –'

I interrupt her. 'Mum, *please* get off the plane.'

'I can't. It's moving. I've already sorted it out with work. Just take Elsa back to Grandad's and ask him to look after her. You go too. I'll be back in two weeks, that's all.'

With rising panic, I try to imagine us going to live at Grandad's. He's got experiments going in every room, hamsters, chickens, junk piled up in every corner ... 'We can't go to Grandad's,' I say. 'There's no room for us.'

But it's like I haven't spoken. 'Meg, promise me something. Except for Grandad, don't tell anyone that I've gone. Elsa will be fine, but the nursery might not like it. They could tell social services or something.'

'No, Mum, wait ...' I try to find the words that will make her change her mind. 'Grandad can't look after Elsa. He can hardly look after himself and I've got so much schoolwork to do –'

'You worry too much, Meg. Just take some stuff to Grandad's and hang out round there. He'll understand why I've gone.' There's this little hint of criticism in her voice, as if I'm selfish to even say these things to her. 'Tell him I'll be in touch, but that I probably won't be able to ring because we're going to a remote area. Oh … I've got to give Sara her phone back. We're taking off. I love you, Meg. Thank you for doing this, wonderful girl!'

After she's blown me a series of kisses, the line goes dead.

I take a deep breath, then another, the phone still pushed against my ear. Did Mum really just ring me from a *plane*? Did she actually say *Myanmar*? My heart pounds as Elsa's screams drill into my head. Maybe I could ring the airport and get them to stop the plane? I desperately want to speak to Mum and explain why she can't go, that it's nothing to do with being selfish, just that we need her here. I start to dial directory enquires, but then I let the phone fall in my lap. Mum said the plane was taking off. By the time I get through, they won't be able to do anything – the plane will be in the air … And even if it isn't, they'd never stop a plane just because some girl's rung up. I'm being illogical. I'm not thinking straight.

Now Elsa's started coughing as well as screaming. All I want to do is go into my room, curl up on my bed and pretend this isn't happening. But I can't do that. Pongo whines and pushes his nose against my hand. 'I know … I can hear her.' I get up, walk down the corridor and open Mum's bedroom door.

Elsa's standing up in her cot, arms stretched out, her

41

face red and slippery with tears. Pongo trots over and sticks his nose through the bars, but this just makes her cry even louder. I go and pick her up and after a moment of resistance, she flops against me, all hot and heavy. She doesn't stop crying, but she does say, 'Mamama', in between sobs.

'Mum's gone away,' I say. 'She's gone to Myanmar.'

Elsa clings on to me and her yells become little hiccups, and then they stop altogether. She feels so heavy in my arms.

I carry her into the front room, find the phone and ring Grandad. He answers on the fifth ring.

'Hello!' he says, all jolly like he's been drinking his home brew.

'Grandad, it's me.'

'Meg! Are you all right?'

Then, even though I know it's stupid, I say what I always say to Grandad when I need his help with something.

'Houston, we have a problem.'

TEN

At first Grandad doesn't believe me, at least not the bit about the plane and Myanmar. He makes me tell him exactly what Mum said, and I even have to describe the sounds I heard in the background.

Then he laughs. 'Blimey. Alice is a free spirit.'

There are a few words going round my head at the moment to describe Mum, but 'free spirit' isn't one of them.

'Well, you'd better pack up your stuff and come round here.'

'Where would we sleep?' I say. 'Your house is tiny.'

'I could squeeze you in. If I shift the hamsters over, you can both go into the spare room. It'll be just like the old days!'

Is he mad? Me, Elsa and twenty-three hamsters?

How will I sleep with all their wheels going round? How will I ever get any work done?

43

And just like that, I see my chance of going to Houston drifting away from me.

When I was little and Mum went off to rallies or festivals, Grandad's spare room was my second bedroom. Then the hamsters appeared. Grandad wanted to see if he could generate electricity by connecting their wheels to a generator. Turns out he could, but his hamster farm didn't just generate electricity, it also generated loads more hamsters. You'd think that a man with a physics PhD would understand the basics of reproduction.

'Do you know what, Grandad? I don't think there'll be room for us in the spare room, not with all Elsa's stuff.'

'The hamsters could go into the lounge.'

'What about your home brewery?' Grandad's also got quite an elaborate micro-brewery set up in the lounge.

Grandad laughs. 'I'd forgotten about that. Look, I can find room for you somewhere.'

Suddenly, I see that there's an obvious solution to the problem. I'm not sure Mum would like it, but right now I don't really care about that. 'How about Elsa and I stay here, Grandad?'

The line goes quiet for a moment. 'I suppose that could work. I could come and stay with you and just pop home sometimes to check the animals and my beer.'

That's not what I meant. I get why Grandad wants to come round here, but if he does, I'll just end up looking after him *and* Elsa. The flat would just become an extension of his house: taps will be left running, plates will pile up in the sink 'for later', books and newspapers will be scattered all over the floor … It will be like living with Mum, but with added nicotine!

'Actually,' I say, 'I think it would be better if we stay here on our own.'

'Really?' He sounds bemused.

The more I think about it, the more certain I become. With Mum gone, I've got the chance to get things sorted out a bit. Obviously I'll have to keep Elsa here too, but she goes to bed at seven. Once she's asleep, the flat will be mine. No Ibiza anthems, no community allotment meetings, no hot yoga (Mum really whacks the heating up for that), just peace and quiet … at a moderate temperature. I'd be able to work – I could practise my speech for hours. All of a sudden, Houston is back on the cards.

'I can look after Elsa,' I say firmly. 'We'll be fine.'

'Well … I suppose it will make life easier with the chickens.' He doesn't sound that convinced, but I can tell he's going to let me have my own way. Grandad hates arguments.

Elsa tugs at the phone, trying to get it out of my hands. 'It'll work out,' I say firmly. 'You'll see. Before I go to school, I'll drop Pongo round at yours and then I'll take Elsa to nursery.'

'Well … we'll give it a go for a couple of days,' says Grandad. Then his voice perks up. 'Hey, I could make you both dinner when you come back from school!'

'That would be great, Grandad,' I say, trying not to think about the state of his fridge. 'I'd better go. Elsa's nodding off.' She's not. She's very carefully trying to put her finger in my nose. 'Goodnight!'

'Goodnight, love. You girls get a good night's sleep.'

I hang up the phone and look at Elsa. She stares right back at me with her round, blue eyes. A bit of confidence slips away from me. Elsa and I might live together, but essentially we're strangers. Mum's always trying to get me to hold Elsa and 'bond', but I haven't got a clue what to do with her and it's obvious she prefers being with Mum.

As if Elsa can sense my uncertainty, her face crumples and she starts to cry again. A ripple of panic sweeps through me and I wonder if I've just made a very stupid decision. I'm still holding the phone and as Elsa's cries turn to screams, I'm tempted to ring Grandad back and say, 'Move the hamster cages to one side. We're coming round!'

I push the thought away. If I do that, I'll never be able

to enter the NASA competition. I've taken a computer apart and put it back together again; surely I can work out how to get Elsa to stop crying and go to sleep.

I decide to try shushing and patting. I've seen Mum do that loads of times.

'*Shhh*,' I say, and I give Elsa a pat on the shoulder. But this just makes her go rigid and arch away from me. Next, I try stroking her head, but she shakes it wildly from side to side. OK. I'll try swaying. I start to sway my way around the flat, but if anything, this makes Elsa's cries go up a notch. My heart beats faster and I decide to try it all at the same time: I sway, stroke her head, shush like mad and pat her back like it's a drum.

Elsa's screams get louder and my head pounds along with my heart. I'm not soothing her. I'm enraging her! A panicky lump forms in my throat, but I am not going to give up. I hold her away from me. 'Fine,' I say. 'If you don't want me to cuddle you then you can go back to bed!'

I take her into Mum's room and put her down in the cot. Immediately she's up on her feet and shaking the rails.

'Goodnight, Elsa!' I say firmly, then I walk out of the room and shut the door.

I go straight to my bedroom. My duvet is smooth on the bed, my planet mobile is moving gently and everything is exactly where I left it this morning.

Elsa's still screaming, but it's like the volume's been turned down a notch and now I can think about what Mum's done. A few things are bothering me, like how come she had her passport on her if she only decided to go to Myanmar on the spur of the moment? And why did she wait until the plane was leaving to ring me? I stare out of the window at the black sky. I guess she didn't tell me earlier because she knew I'd try to stop her. Or maybe she didn't think about us at all …

I'm not sure which is worse.

Next door, Elsa is still crying. In a slightly crazy way, I wonder what would happen if she didn't stop. Can a baby cry for two weeks? For a moment, I consider going online to see if anyone's done an experiment on babies crying, but then I realise that I'm too tired to open my laptop.

I turn my globe one hundred and eighty degrees, circle today on my homework timetable (I haven't finished it so I can't cross it out), then go back into Mum's room.

Elsa reaches out to me, but I just shake my head and say, 'It's time to sleep.' Then I get on to Mum's bed and pull a pillow over my head. I shut my eyes and squeeze the pillow tight, muffling Elsa's screams.

They're not so bad now. More of a hum than a scream. Almost soothing …

ELEVEN

'Your Mum's got a slipped disc?' Dawn stares at me like she's never heard anything so bizarre in her life.

'It's very common,' I say, 'especially when people have to lift heavy things.' I'm standing on the doorstep of Little Acorns nursery and Elsa's wriggling in my arms. 'Mum's been told to have total bed rest so I'll be bringing Elsa to nursery and picking her up. Just for a while ... Maybe two weeks?'

'A slipped disc?' Dawn blinks.

Grandad said this would be the perfect excuse; I wasn't expecting to have to convince her! I think back to what I read on the NHS website. 'It's when pressure is placed on the sciatic nerve causing severe pain in the leg, hip and buttocks.'

'Buttocks?'

'Mainly her left buttock,' I say. Why can't I shut up

49

about buttocks? I pass Elsa over and start to back away down the path. 'Any problems, ring me or Grandad because Mum needs *total* rest.'

Dawn rubs her nose on Elsa's fluffy hair. 'I guess that's why you're still in your pyjamas,' she says.

Argh! Is she? I just grabbed the first Babygro thingy that I found in the drawer.

'Sorry,' I say. 'I was a bit rushed this morning and Mum was asleep. You know, painkillers …'

Dawn seems to accept this. 'Who's got a poorly mummy?' she says to Elsa. 'Let's get you changed and then I'll give you some honey toast.'

Honey toast? That sounds amazing! Elsa woke me up at around five, jumping up and down in her cot and cackling. Then I had to rush around getting her ready and I didn't have time to eat breakfast or even change out of the clothes I fell asleep in. Right now, I'm wearing yesterday's pants. Not a good feeling.

Just as I'm about to escape, Dawn calls after me.

'So how did your mum slip her disc?'

'Picking up … baked beans,' I say, nodding to show that what I'm saying is definitely the truth. 'She bent like this –' I mime twisting round '– picked up a bean,' at this point I actually hold up an imaginary bean, 'and, bang, it went … or rather, slipped.'

'A baked bean? Well I never.' Dawn forces Elsa to wave at me. 'Say bye-bye to Meggie-pops!'

'Bye, Elsa!' I say, smiling and waving back.

The moment the door shuts, my smile vanishes and I turn and leg it down the road. I am going to be so late for school! I cut through the cemetery, weave round shoppers on the high street and get to school just as the electronic gates are swinging shut. With a final burst of energy, I throw myself through the gap.

I made it!

And that's when I see Mr Curtis, my deputy head of year, lurking by the bushes. 'Meg Clark!' he says, chuckling. 'Are you *late?*'

'Yes, Sir,' I manage to say.

He shakes his head and pulls out a late slip. 'Any particular reason?'

Where to begin? There were the various nappy changes, Pongo stealing Elsa's Weetabix, cleaning up Weetabix number two that landed on the floor, and then cleaning up Weetabix number three that Elsa patted into Pongo's fur – that stuff dries like rock. Oh, and Elsa cried four times and I cried once, but only through pain. Elsa accidentally bit me when I tried to get my keys out of her mouth.

'I overslept,' I say. 'Sorry.'

He laughs again and starts filling in the slip. 'I'm afraid this means break-time detention.' He holds out the slip and raises an eyebrow. 'Now, Meg, you do know what a *detention* is, don't you?'

'Yes, Sir,' I say, snatching the slip out of his hands.

TWELVE

I'm hovering outside the detention room. I can see Mr Curtis inside, but I'm not sure if I'm supposed to walk straight in or wait for everyone else to turn up. Quickly, I check my phone. I've been glancing at it all morning, hoping there'll be a text from Mum saying she's changed her mind and she's coming home. So far, nothing.

'You just take your time,' says a voice behind me. I spin round and see Annie Demos staring at me with her pale green eyes.

'Sorry.' I step to one side and hold the door open. Annie sweeps past me in her wheelchair and goes to a desk at the back of the room. Annie's got a type of cerebral palsy that affects her legs. She can walk, but often she uses crutches and other days, like today, she goes round school in a green wheelchair.

I follow her inside and Mr Curtis's eyes light up. 'Meg! Take a seat at the back.'

He really is getting a lot of pleasure out of this.

'Annie, Meg is here because she was late for school, whereas you are here because you called our head teacher … What was it again?' He makes a show of searching through the slips in front of him. 'A massive dick.'

'Only because he is one,' she says with a shrug, moving from her wheelchair to a chair.

'And yet,' carries on Mr Curtis, 'both of you have a break-time detention. Seems a bit unfair, doesn't it?'

'If you say so,' she says.

I glance across at her. Today, her wild dark hair is pulled in a ponytail on the top of her head and she's wearing bright pink lipstick. If she were anyone else in the school she'd have been made to wipe it off, but Annie Demos has what Mr Curtis describes as 'an assertive personality' – basically she doesn't do anything she doesn't want to do. If Annie Demos wants to wear pink lipstick then she's wearing pink lipstick. She pulls a book from her bag and starts to read, her hair flopping over her face.

I turn back to Mr Curtis. 'Um … do I just …'

'Sit there? That's right, Meg. You don't even have to do any work, I just want to waste your time.'

I'm not wasting any time. I get out my English book and start doing my homework. Gradually, the room fills up. It's quieter and warmer in here than in the library. If I wasn't so hungry I'd actually be enjoying this detention. After twenty minutes, the bell goes. Just as we're being dismissed, Mr Curtis asks Annie and me to stay behind.

'A little bit of news for you, girls,' he says, handing us each a folded piece of paper. 'These were going to be delivered to you in your lessons, but as I have the pleasure of your company right now, I thought I'd give them to you personally.'

I take my note and stare at it, suddenly convinced that it's something to do with Mum. Could Dawn have found out that Elsa and I were on our own last night and rung the school? I did a bit of research during IT and found out that parents have been sent to prison for going away and leaving their children home alone. With slightly shaky fingers, I pull open the note:

Megara Clark, please attend Student in the Spotlight mentoring with Mr Curtis today, 12.30, H4.

Relief sweeps through me. Student in the Spotlight is just some mentoring thing everyone in Year Ten has to do.

'Urrgh!' says Annie, crumpling up her note. 'Are you serious, Sir?'

55

He smiles at her. 'Deadly serious. I'm afraid this is non-optional, Annie, even for you.'

'I don't care how "non-optional" it is,' she says, throwing the screwed-up note in the direction of the bin. 'I'm not going.' She gets back into her wheelchair and heads towards the door. 'I'd rather stick needles in my eyes … blunt needles … hot blunt needles.'

'Annie,' says Mr Curtis, 'are you going to pick up the note? It missed the bin.'

She drops one hand over the side of her wheelchair and makes a half-hearted attempt to reach for the piece of paper. She smiles at him. 'Sorry, Sir, can't reach it.'

'As you're *choosing* not to pick it up,' says Sir, 'shall we see you back here in detention tomorrow?'

'Why not?' says Annie, then she shoots out of the room. There's a crash as a door slams open further down the corridor.

Mr Curtis looks over at me. 'Meg,' he says, 'pick up the note on your way out.'

THIRTEEN

I actually manage to forget about Mum and Elsa during maths. We're doing simultaneous equations and my brain is blissfully occupied with numbers. Soon my book is filled with sums and green ticks (I always mark in green) and as soon as I finish the first lot of work, I start the extension task.

As Sir passes me another sheet, Ed King glances at my book. Just like in English and science, he's sitting next to me.

'You've given yourself a tick, but number twelve is wrong,' he says, tapping *my* pen on my book.

I check my answer again. He's right ... How could I have made such a simple mistake? With an annoying smile on his face, Ed watches as I correct it, then he says in a low voice, 'You don't want to be making mistakes like that when you do your NASA speech.'

'Oh, I won't,' I say. Then I put my Tippex away in my pencil case and do up the zip with a decisive tug.

Ed laughs. I move my book slightly away from him, write *Polynomials* at the top of a new page, switch to a new, sharper pencil and get started.

Next thing I know, Ed's got his hand up. 'Sir.' His voice is loud in the quiet classroom. 'I need more work. I've finished the extension.'

After maths, I head off to H4 for Student in the Spotlight. Even though I know the group will be small, I still feel nervous. The word 'mentoring' tells me we're going to have to talk in a sharey way as a group and I just know that my words will vanish from my lips when it's my turn to speak. Before I go in, I check my phone and see that I've got a text from Grandad: *Hope Little Acorns was OK. All good here except Pongo killed a chicken! (Don't worry, it was a mangy one.) Grandad* ☺

Before I can reply, the door of the classroom opens and Mr Curtis ushers me in. 'Ah, Meg,' he says. 'Nice to see you made the effort to get here on time.'

Two other students from Year Ten, Jackson and Rose, have already arrived and are lounging on beanbags. 'Hi, Meg!' says Rose and I sit down next to her. Jackson raises his eyebrows by way of a greeting, but he doesn't look up.

He's distracted by some polystyrene balls he's managed to get out of his beanbag. I think he's trying to stick one ball on each finger.

'I borrowed beanbags from the library to make things a bit more intimate,' says Mr Curtis.

'*Intimate!*' snorts Jackson.

Mr Curtis rolls his eyes and slips off his pointy shoes. 'OK, guys, I think we'd better get started.'

But before he can sit down, the door flies open and Annie comes in on her crutches.

'Couldn't find any hot blunt needles?' asks Mr Curtis.

She smiles and shrugs. 'Kieron Webber told me you give out biscuits.' She walks into the room then stares down at the spare beanbag. 'I'm not getting down there,' she says.

Mr Curtis thinks for a moment. 'Fair enough,' he says. 'The beanbags aren't essential.' He tosses the offending beanbag aside and gets Annie a chair.

'And I'm not sitting on that with everyone staring up at me.'

Mr Curtis sighs. 'Up you get,' he says, waving his hands at us. 'Grab a chair. Annie's right: we should all be on the same level.'

I move to a chair and so does Rose, but Jackson stays where he is. 'Nope,' he says. 'I like it down here.'

'Fine,' says Mr Curtis. 'Jackson's on a beanbag; the rest of us are sitting on chairs.'

'Cheers, Sir,' says Jackson. 'Hey, look at my specs. It's snowing!' Now he's covered the inside of his trendy black glasses with polystyrene balls. 'Once my cat got in my beanbag,' he continues. 'It was so funny. Actually, I put her in there. Did any of you see the pictures on Facebook?'

'No,' says Annie. 'A, I'm not Facebook friends with you for obvious reasons, and B, it sounds cruel.'

'It wasn't cruel. It was funny and Mindy loved it. You can tell from the photos because she's basically smiling.'

'I'd really like to see them!' says Rose.

'In what way is she smiling?' Annie sounds a bit interested now.

Mr Curtis clears his throat. 'If you've all finished talking about Jackson's cat, I'd like to welcome you to your first Student in the Spotlight session. Now, you're all students who show great promise for your GCSEs, and hopefully these mentoring sessions will help you to realise your potential.'

'Why us, though?' asks Rose. 'I mean, *cool*, I'm missing assembly so I'm glad I'm in this group, but why have the four of us been put together?'

'As a punishment?' asks Annie.

Mr Curtis ignores her. 'As you know, everyone in your

60

year will do this at some point, but you were put together because you're predicted similar grades,' says Mr Curtis. 'Similarly *high* grades, might I add. You are the exceptionally gifted mentor group!'

Quick as a flash, Annie says, 'So if this is some special group for brainiacs, how come Ed King isn't here?'

That was exactly what I was thinking.

'The group is limited to four,' says Sir. 'I couldn't invite everyone.'

'Or Kani Nadar, or Elizabeth West ...?' continues Annie.

For a moment, Mr Curtis doesn't say anything, so Annie leans forward on her chair and says, 'I think I know why the four of us are here. It's generally accepted that Kani, Ed and Elizabeth are all perceived to be a bit more "socially adjusted" –' she pauses here to draw a couple of apostrophes in the air '– than us.'

She's right, I think, looking from shy Rose to mouthy Annie. Just like me, I'm always seeing them on their own around school. I feel a prickle of irritation that, once again, Ed King is one step ahead of me, but this time it isn't because he's cleverer than me, it's because he's more 'normal' than me, and school has officially recognised this fact!

'No,' says Jackson, shaking his head and sending the

61

polystyrene balls flying. 'That can't be why we're here. I'm really popular.'

He's right. He is. Everyone loves Jackson. He's so good natured even *I* feel quite comfortable with him.

Annie's eyes narrow. 'You *are* popular, aren't you ...' She looks directly at Mr Curtis. 'Sir, I'm just going to come out and say what we're all thinking: what's Jackson doing in a group for "gifted" students?'

Rose's eyes widen in alarm and down at our feet, Jackson abandons his polystyrene balls and looks up. 'Because he's a gifted student,' says Mr Curtis, who is starting to look a bit irritated with Annie, 'just like you.'

'Nah, I'm not,' Jackson says. Then he grins. 'Is it because I'm exceptionally gifted in the *looks* department?' He uses both hands to point at his face.

'Unlikely,' says Annie.

'Jackson has a talent for languages,' snaps Mr Curtis.

'No he hasn't!' Annie bursts out. 'Jackson *Woods* has a talent for languages. He can speak Cantonese. You've invited the wrong Jackson, Sir!'

Mr Curtis has gone pink. 'Look, you're here because Mrs Kinney handed me a list of names and told me to start mentoring you. It was that or I had to take 10E for sex ed. So I chose you lot.' He stares at Annie. 'Jackson *Wood* was on the list so he's staying. Got it?'

Anne bursts out laughing like she can't believe it. 'So just because Mrs Kinney gave you some list I'm stuck here once a week –'

'Three times a week,' says Mr Curtis.

'– I'm stuck here *three* times a week with a space cadet, an uber-nerd and a cat abuser?'

'Am I the space cadet?' asks Rose.

Annie laughs even louder. 'Yes, you are!'

I feel my head start to ache. That must make me the uber-nerd.

'Annie, you've gone too far,' says Mr Curtis, tapping his folder on his knee.

'I'm going to go now, Sir,' Annie stands up. 'Thanks for the invite, but unlike Uber-Nerd and Space Cadet here, I really don't need any *friendship* mentoring. I've got loads of friends, they just don't come to this school.'

And that's when my tiredness and hunger overwhelm me and something inside me snaps. 'Well, at least I'm not an uber-*bitch*, Annie!'

Rose gasps, Jackson laughs and Annie turns round to face me, her eyes glittering and a smile playing on her lips. 'The geek speaks! Did you just call me an *uber-bitch*?'

'Sorry,' I mutter. 'I shouldn't have said that.'

Annie smiles and does a little shake of her head, then

63

she goes to the door, pulls it open and leaves us sitting in silence.

After a moment, Jackson reaches up and pats Mr Curtis on the shoulder. 'Don't worry about it, Sir. She does that in most lessons.'

'I know,' he says, then he pulls a briefcase on to his lap and snaps it open. He disappears behind the lid, reappearing with a red box. *Budgen's Broken Biscuits* is written across the front. 'Who wants a biscuit?'

FOURTEEN

Despite the biscuits, by the time I get to my last lesson, science, I'm running on empty. As we queue up outside the classroom, I rest my head against the wall and drift in and out of the conversations taking place around me. As usual, everyone is speaking a language I don't understand, a language that today involves the words 'contouring', 'jacking', 'TPU tips' and someone – or something – called 'Devo'. Harriet used to be my teen-speak translator. She had two older sisters and always knew what this sort of stuff was. Without her, I'm lost.

Ed and Bella are leaning against the wall opposite me. Bella's sucking a lolly and Ed's telling her something that's making her laugh. When she sees me watching them, she pulls the green lolly out of her mouth with a pop. 'I heard you've been a naughty girl,' she says with a smile.

I swallow and try to prepare myself for whatever Bella's about to say.

Ed looks up. 'What's she done?'

'She only went and got a detention!'

'Really?' Ed frowns and laughs.

'I was just late to school,' I say, but I'm drowned out by Ms Edgecombe coming out of the lab and shouting, 'Who's ready to get physical?'

We're working on our own at the start of the lesson so I get to zone out. I spent lunchtime in the library – sneakily eating a baguette and trying to revise the life cycle of stars – but I didn't get much done. I should have just found a radiator, curled up next to it and gone to sleep.

Sleep ... beautiful sleep ...

'Meg!' A bit of rubber bounces off my forehead and I look up to see Bella staring across the table at me. 'I know you've gone all badass on us since you got your detention, but are you actually going to help us with this?'

It looks like Miss handed round a worksheet without me even noticing.

I pull it towards me and read it through. 'The answers are "copper", "attract" and "molecules",' I say. 'Ed can do the rest.' I push the sheet to him then take a big drink of water and press my fingers into my eyes. I need to wake up.

Bella and Raj look at me curiously.

'What's up with you?' says Raj. 'You look –'

'Super-hot?' suggests Bella. 'Bootylicious?'

Weirdly, I'm too tired to be bothered by these comments.

'Rough.' Ed says this without looking up from the worksheet.

OK. So I'm not too tired to be bothered by *that*. I feel my cheeks start to burn and Bella shrieks, '*Woody!* You can't say that.'

'What? She does.' He turns to me. 'What's the matter?'

'I've got a headache,' I say. It's actually starting to hurt to talk.

'It was going to happen one day,' says Raj, shaking his head.

'What?' Bella says.

'Meg's brain has got too big for her head. It'll be coming out of her nose soon.'

'I can see it!' shrieks Bella.

'Please be quiet,' I say. The pain in my head is so bad that I haven't got the energy to tiptoe around Bella. 'Your voice is really loud.'

Raj throws his head back and laughs. 'You have got a big voice, mate.'

Before Bella can reply, Ms Edgecombe slams her hand

down on the buzzer she keeps on her desk. She keeps on pressing it until everyone stops talking … It takes a very long time.

'I just wanted to remind you that your homework for the next two weeks is to work with your partner on your "What Space Means to Me" speeches. I know only Ed and Meg are representing the school in the actual competition, but I still want the rest of you to do it.'

'Seriously, Miss?' says Raj. 'What's the point?'

'The *point* is that you'll be sharing your knowledge about space with your peers and developing vital speaking and listening skills … not to mention learning how to work with others. Basically, this homework is going to make you a better person, Raj.' She presses her buzzer a couple of times to emphasise her point. 'Now, you all know who you're working with so spend the last five minutes of the lesson explaining to your partner what space means to you and arrange a time to meet up and practise.'

Talking breaks out across the room.

'Urgh,' says Bella, looking at Raj and wrinkling her nose. 'I can't believe I'm stuck with you again.'

Raj stretches his arms behind his head. 'Stop moaning. You love it, babe.'

'Er … no, I don't.'

Ed turns to me. 'So what does space mean to you, Meg?' He says this casually, but I know he must be curious about my speech.

For a moment, I consider coming up with some vague answer like 'improved technology' or 'solar energy research', but I'm feeling so tired it just seems easier to tell him the truth. 'To me, space means escape,' I say. He frowns, so I carry on. 'Somewhere in space there might be a new Earth, a habitable planet that hasn't been mucked up by human beings.'

'You mean a Goldilocks planet?' Ed asks.

They're called 'Goldilocks planets' because for humans to live on them everything about them needs to be *just right*: the right amount of water on the surface, the right climate, the right distance from the sun – not too hot and not too cold.

I shake my head. 'No, not a planet *like* Earth, a planet *better* than Earth.' Just talking about this is making me feel more awake. 'Our sun has a lifespan of up to ten billion years, right?'

He nods.

'Smaller suns live for longer and might support a planet richer than Earth.'

Ed's got a half-smile on his face, and I know why: I

never normally talk like this, but suddenly I can't stop the words from tumbling out of me. 'When you think about it, Earth isn't that great. Around ninety-eight per cent of its surface is uninhabitable. We can only live on *two per cent* of it.'

'So you're not that impressed by Earth?'

I shake my head. 'It's too crowded.'

We fall quiet, then Ed says, 'Now's when you're supposed to ask me what I'm doing for my speech, Meg.'

'Oh, right. So … what does space mean to you?'

'Space will be the saviour of Earth!' he says, spreading his hands wide, then he sits back looking pleased with himself. 'I'm going to talk about how satellites and space research will help us sort out all our environmental problems.'

'Right,' I say.

'Adults love it when young people talk about the environment. It makes them feel like they're leaving the planet in safe hands.'

'You've thought this through,' I say. Honestly, I hadn't even considered what adults might want to hear. Once again, I have that worrying feeling that Ed King is just one step ahead of me.

Ed shrugs. 'I've thought it through because I want to win.'

'Time to pack up!' calls Ms Edgecombe, and I turn away from Ed and start stuffing my books in my bag.

As we're filing out of the room, Ms Edgecombe reminds us to bring in our permission slips for the Sussex University trip next week. As I'm jostled and shoved in the corridor, I try to run through what I'll do with Elsa. We'll be getting back too late for me to pick her up from nursery. Suddenly, every single aspect of my life has become more complicated – even this trip that I've been looking forward to for so long.

Outside school, I see Bella go off with her friends and Ed climb into the back of a black Range Rover. I get a glimpse of a cream leather interior before the door slams shut with a heavy clunk. Then the engine purrs into life and the car pulls smoothly into the traffic.

I check my phone: I've got ten minutes to get to Little Acorns. I grab hold of the straps on my rucksack and start to run.

FIFTEEN

'I need eight pounds, Grandad.' I'm curled up on his sofa watching *In the Night Garden* with Elsa. 'Little Acorns charged me a fine for being late.'

In the kitchen, a pan bangs down on the stove and I hear pasta splash into water. 'But you're *never* late!' Grandad shouts back.

'Well, I am now. All the time. I was six whole minutes late.'

Grandad appears in the front room and hands me a cup of scummy tea. 'Your mum's been caught out a couple of times.' He nods at the tea. 'I put three sugars in there to keep your energy levels high.'

I look up and see Elsa standing by the TV, bumping her face into the screen and leaving snotty marks everywhere. 'What's she doing?' I ask.

'Kissing Makka Pakka. He's her favourite.' Grandad

goes back into the kitchen, leaving Elsa smacking the TV (I don't think she likes Iggle Piggle) and me trying not to fall asleep. It's hard. Grandad's homebrew is bubbling away in the corner of the room and along with the piano music coming from the TV, it's making a very soothing sound.

Soon, Grandad calls us in to dinner and while we eat our macaroni cheese, we talk about Mum.

'Alice went to Myanmar just after she had you,' Grandad says. 'She was looking after elephants ... No, hang on, I think it was Thailand.'

'She never told me she went away when I was a baby.' I thought Mum told me everything: the graphic details of Elsa's birth (she tried to get me to watch; I refused), about her adventures volunteering abroad, tales from her wild teenage years ... She'd even told me about meeting my dad in Vietnam – 'the most beautiful man she'd ever seen' – and then moving on to Australia before she realised she was pregnant.

'Well, she was only gone a couple of weeks,' says Grandad. 'She had the baby blues and needed to get away.'

'Plus she does love elephants,' I say, thinking about the troop of rainbow elephants that Mum's painted all through the hallway of our flat.

Grandad nods. 'You're right. Elephants, animals, people ... It doesn't really matter who it is, Alice is a carer.'

Suddenly, I don't feel like eating any more of my macaroni cheese. The sauce is lumpy and Grandad didn't cook the pasta for long enough. 'I think I should get Elsa home.'

'Sure you don't want to stay here tonight?'

I glance at the cage on the kitchen worktop. A chicken is sitting inside watching me with her beady eyes. If an avian flu pandemic ever broke out, this is *exactly* where it would start. 'We'll be fine,' I say. 'I've just got to be organised. Stay on top of things.'

'You're welcome here any time.'

'Grandad, honestly, I've made up my mind!'

Something about the way I say this makes him laugh and raise up his hands in mock surrender. I've seen him do this loads of times before with Mum when she's arguing a point with him. 'I suppose it'll be a bit of an adventure staying on your own,' he says. 'You can think of it as a mission!'

I laugh. 'I think I'm a bit old to play "missions" now.'

'Nonsense. Let's talk logistics. Have you got a pen?'

I pull one out of my blazer pocket. I've always got a pen.

'Right, you find some paper and I'll give Elsa an orange. That should keep her busy for a while.'

Grandad and I spend the next half-hour making lists,

drawing tables and working things through. When I was little and we played rockets, it was all about the mission. I'd put on one of Grandad's shirts as a lab coat and we'd plan a trip to orbit Mars or land on Venus. We'd work out fuel supplies, distances and trajectories. I was so into the planning bit that sometimes we never got round to take-off. Plus, I was a bit scared of aliens.

Soon we've written a plan to cover the whole two weeks Mum will be away. Everything's on there, even little slots for me to rehearse my speech for the competition. Just looking at it makes me feel more in control. I remind Grandad that we need some money; Mum didn't leave any and she took her bank cards so I can't take any money out of a cash machine.

'I got my pension the week before last,' Grandad says.

'That's good.' Grandad's pension comes in once a month so it should cover the time Mum's away. 'I guess you've got most of it left?'

'Ah, well ...' He looks a bit sheepish. 'I did buy something on Saturday: a white silky bantam.'

'Really, Grandad? Another chicken?'

'A *beautiful* chicken.'

I shrug. 'I suppose we can always eat it.'

This makes Grandad laugh. 'Not until we've eaten the one Pongo killed. I've got her all ready in the freezer.'

I remember that's the 'mangy' one and make a mental note not to eat any chicken at Grandad's for a while.

After we've taken the new bantam into account, we discover we've got one hundred and twenty-three pounds to keep us going until Mum gets back. The three pounds is leftover from the pocket money Grandad gave me last Saturday.

'Loads of money!' he says.

I'm not so sure. Sometimes Mum gets me to buy Elsa's nappies and they cost a lot. I point at the first square on my mission plan: 'Tues Evening'.

'I'm up to here,' I say. '"Elsa – bath and bed." Easy.' I push what happened last night to the back of my mind. 'I'll type this up later and laminate it.'

'That's my girl!' says Grandad. 'Now, do you want Pongo to stay here?'

We both look at Pongo: he's standing in the corner of the kitchen, growling at a cupboard door. Pongo might be terrified of everything, even the wind and moths, but he looks scary. It's not just the scars. His teeth are permanently bared and he has wild eyes. 'I think I'll keep him,' I say, 'for protection. Come on, Pongo.' I clip his lead on to his collar. 'Let's get this mission started.'

SIXTEEN

Back in the flat, I follow every stage of the plan. I give Elsa her bath, do up all the little poppers on her Babygro, then hold her on my lap and stick a bottle in her mouth. Straight away she goes quiet, and just sucks her milk and gazes up at me, holding on tight to one of my fingers. I, meanwhile, gaze at my physics textbook and learn about kinetic energy.

The moment Elsa's finished her bottle I look at the clock: bang on seven o'clock. I am so on schedule!

'Time for bed!' I say.

'Na!' She shakes her head.

'Yes,' I say, nodding.

'NA!' she screams, then, like a bar of soap in the bath, she slips out of my hands, off the sofa and crawls across the living room. Elsa can walk, but when she wants to move really fast, she reverts to crawling because she's awesome at it.

Three seconds later, she's disappeared into the kitchen.

With a sigh, I put down my book and haul myself off the sofa. 'I'm coming to get you!' I call out and I hear Elsa squeal with delight followed by a bang and a clatter.

What is she up to?

I walk into the kitchen expecting to see the bin or Pongo's bowl tipped over, but what I actually see is nothing.

Elsa has vanished.

'Elsa?' I call.

Pongo trots in and starts sniffing his way round the room. I look behind the door. Pongo looks under the table. She's nowhere to be seen.

'Elsa!' I shout again, louder this time.

Then I hear a muffled 'Da!' coming from one of the cupboards. Straight away, Pongo shoots to the corner cupboard and starts tapping at the door with his paw. I pull it open – and there she is, curled up behind the carrousel thingy that's full of herbs and baking things.

'How did you get round there?' I say. 'Come on. You need to get out.' I reach towards her, but she just laughs and wriggles wildly from side to side, trying to get away from me. The clock on the cooker tells me it's five past seven. I haven't got time for this. I'm supposed to be doing my IT homework! I get my hands under her armpits (more squealing) and pull her forward, knocking over a bag of sugar. Immediately, Pongo sticks his nose into the cupboard and starts licking it up. I push him out of the way and pull Elsa again, this time even harder.

'Na, na!' she says, shaking her head.

I sit back and look at her surrounded by bags of flour and pots of cinnamon and oregano. 'Looks like you're stuck, Elsa.'

Her face crumples and she starts to cry.

'Don't cry. You're the one who got in there and did all that wriggling!'

She reaches out her arms to me, and with a sigh I start to take everything out of the cupboard. Soon jars, packets and bottles are piled up around me. Pongo is loving it, and Elsa has calmed down now that she's found a bag of raisins.

When everything's out of the cupboard, I can see that the trailing foot of Elsa's Babygro is stuck in the carousel mechanism. After pulling it and twisting in every direction, I have to accept that it's not coming out. So I do the only thing my tired brain can think of: I get a pair of scissors and cut the foot off the Babygro.

'No sudden movements,' I tell Elsa as the scissors go snip, snip, snip.

Finally, I can haul her out.

Elsa throws her arms round my neck and rubs her sticky, raisiny face into mine.

'Mama,' she says sleepily.

'Still in Myanmar,' I say, carrying her to Mum's room.

I put her in her cot and she lies on her back and stares up at me. 'Da?' she says, pointing at her exposed foot.

'I know. Your foot's sticking out ... Remember how you got stuck in that cupboard and I had to cut you out?'

'Da ...'

'Well, no way am I putting you in another Babygro and doing up all those poppers again. I'm just too tired. Plus, I've got to go and put fifty jars of cumin back in the cupboard.' That's an exaggeration. There were only six jars of cumin.

'Da!' she shouts, sounding kind of outraged.

'Goodnight, Elsa,' I say, backing out of the room.

Even though I know she's exhausted, she jumps to her feet and starts to shake the bars on the cot. 'Mama?' she says, and then she starts to cry.

I feel a lump in my throat. 'Elsa, I'm so tired. Just ... go to sleep.'

Her screaming starts before I've even shut the door.

Then, in a horrible rerun of last night, I sit outside the room, my forehead resting on the door, listening to Elsa cry. She just won't stop. She cries and cries and cries. After a few minutes, I try to do some coding for IT, but I find it impossible to concentrate on algorithms when my brain is being stuffed full of screams.

When I was getting Elsa ready for bed, I didn't have time to think about Mum, not properly. But right now, she's all I can think about. It's two in the morning in Myanmar. I wonder where she is: if she's already asleep or if she's sitting up late in a bar somewhere, chatting to her fellow volunteers. Or maybe she's dancing on a beach … Mum once told me that nothing makes her happier than dancing under the stars. It makes my chest ache to imagine her happy to be free of us while Elsa and I are stuck here on our own.

The ache in my chest grows as Elsa's screams get more desperate. Pongo comes and stands next to me, putting a paw on my knee. A tear runs down my cheek. Angrily, I brush it away.

'Pongo,' I say, 'if I can't get her to go to sleep, how can I last until Mum gets back? There's no way I can complete my mission. I might as well just go round to Grandad's and give up on going to Houston!'

Pongo barks, runs to the front door then runs back

again. He nudges my hand with his nose. I rub my eyes with my sleeve. 'You want to go for a walk?' I say. And then I think, why not? Because I know just what will make me feel better, and, who knows, maybe it will make Elsa feel better too.

Plus, anything's got to be better than sitting here and listening to her scream.

I open the door to Mum's room and Elsa blinks up at me, her face red and furious. 'Guess what?' I say. 'Let's put a sock on that foot. We're going stargazing!'

SEVENTEEN

I t's probably hard to get a happy baby in a sling, but when the baby is angry and fighting you, it's almost impossible. Elsa wriggles like an octopus, but eventually I manage to squeeze all of her limbs into what I think are the right holes and I head out of the flat with her strapped to my chest.

I don't know if it's the cold, or just how dark everything is, but as soon as we get outside Elsa stops crying, sticks her thumb in her mouth and looks around. I don't think quiet has ever sounded so good.

Pongo drags us down the stairs and towards the communal garden that rises above the hill behind the flats. We climb up, following the path that winds between the trees. Most evenings, Pongo and I come here for a walk before bed. Pongo chases rabbits and I look at stars through my binoculars. Even though loads of kids play here during the day, it's deserted at night. I know most parents wouldn't let their teenage daughters roam around in the dark, but Mum's keen on 'women living fearlessly' – plus I've got a really big torch.

In a few minutes, we come out of the trees and reach the top of the hill and I stand looking down over our town. 'Do you like it?' I ask Elsa, my voice loud in the silence. From up here, we can see all the way to Hastings: curving rows of houses, cars moving along the roads, even the swaying strings of light that line the seafront.

Elsa pulls her thumb out of her mouth and stares around her. 'Da,' she says, kicking her legs.

'Now look up.' I lean back so she can see the sky. 'That constellation is Crux and that's Pleiades.' Elsa's eyes follow my finger as it draws a line through the sky towards the cluster of stars. 'They're babies, just like you, around one hundred and twenty million years old. Dinosaurs might have watched them burst into life.' I look down and notice Elsa's eyes are starting to close. Am I boring her to sleep? I start to sway from side to side as I list the Hercules constellations, and I watch her eyes narrow to thin slits, then shut completely.

Amazing!

'Pongo!' I hiss into the darkness. He shoots out of a

clump of bushes and skids to a halt in front of me. 'She's asleep. Let's go.'

We scramble back down the hill and creep up the echoing stairwell to our flat.

In Mum's room, I ease Elsa out of the sling and start to lower her into her cot. The moment her back makes contact with the mattress, her eyes shoot open and her face starts to crumple.

'Sagitta,' I whisper, holding her close again, 'Aquila, Lyra, Cygnus …' I put Elsa on Mum's bed and lie next to her. 'Vulpecula, Hydra, Corona …' Even though I'm still wearing my school uniform, I reach down and pull the duvet over us. 'Corvus, Ara, Serpens …' The mattress dips as Pongo jumps on the bed, turns twice then flops against my back. I manage to mutter, 'Lupus,' before my eyes close and the three of us fall into a deep, deep sleep.

EIGHTEEN

'What did you do?' whispers Annie. It's break time and we're both sitting at the back of the detention room again.

'I was late to school,' I say. It was having a shower that did it. To keep Elsa safe, I strapped her in her pushchair and put her in front of CBeebies. At some point, Pongo must have stepped on the controls because when I came out of the bathroom they were both watching Jeremy Kyle. Now I'm in my second ever detention, but that shower was so worth it: I smell lovely.

Annie shakes her head. 'No, I mean what did you do at Mr Curtis's Biscuit Club after I left?'

'We ate the famous biscuits and looked at pictures of Jackson's cat.'

She narrows her eyes. Overnight she's cut her fringe so that it comes to a point between her eyebrows. With her pale eyes and black eyeliner she looks a bit like an alien. 'So, basically a massive waste of time.'

'Jackson had photoshopped teachers' faces on to every cat picture.'

'Yeah?'

'And put hats on them.'

'Oi, you two!' Mr Curtis is glaring at us. 'This is a detention, not a coffee morning.'

'We're working on our supportive brainiac network, Sir,' Annie calls back.

'I don't want any networking in detentions, Annie,' he says, 'just an uncomfortable silence.'

She smiles sweetly at him and mimes zipping her mouth shut. Mr Curtis gives her a thumbs up, but the second he turns back to his computer, she whispers to me. 'Annoyingly, I really want to see those cats with hats.' Then she rests her chin in her hand and goes back to her book.

Which is why I'm not surprised to find her sitting in H4 when I arrive before lunch. Once again, Jackson gets a beanbag while we sit round him on chairs. 'It's like I'm a king,' he says, stretching out, 'and you're my peasants!'

'Or you're our dog,' says Annie, 'lying at our feet in the dirt.'

Mr Curtis interrupts them. 'I thought we'd start with

an energiser called Grab the Finger. Basically, you stretch your hand out to the side and –'

'No way,' says Annie, shaking her head. 'I'm not grabbing anyone's anything.'

'OK, how about Fear in the Hat?' says Mr Curtis. 'You write down one of your personal fears and put it in a hat. It's great at creating group cohesion.'

'Sounds good!' says Rose.

'Nope, sounds terrible,' says Annie.

I'm with Annie on this one – I've just got too many personal fears right now.

'Is there anything else we can do, Sir?' she asks.

'Well, you could write dictionary definitions for each other. That's something that's worked well with other groups. So I might be: Curtis, Tristram –'

'Tristram?' bursts out Jackson. 'Are you having a laugh, Sir?'

Mr Curtis ignores him. 'Curtis, Tristram. Proper noun. 1. Only child, born in Norwich, East Anglia. 2. Aficionado of history with a passion for the First World War. 3. Ornithologist.'

'A horny-whaty?' says Jackson.

'An *ornithologist*,' he says, scowling.

'Someone who studies birds,' I mutter.

'That's what I said!' laughs Jackson.

Annie sighs deeply. '*Sir*, when do we get the biscuits?'

Mr Curtis puts his hand protectively over the box. 'After you've written your definitions.'

'All right,' she says. 'We'll do the dictionary thing. I'm working with Meg.' Then she leans over and gives me a little punch on the shoulder. I surprised to realise that I'm not that fazed by the idea of working with Annie. In some ways she's got an even bigger mouth than Bella, but at least she's honest and I can tell if she's laughing at me or not. Bella's a lot trickier to work out.

Mr Curtis explains that we need to interview our partner before we write a definition that sums them up.

'I'm actually looking forward to doing this,' says Annie, smiling at Mr Curtis. She's using a voice I've never heard before, a sweet, gentle voice. It's a bit creepy. 'But do you know what would make this even better, Sir?'

'What's that, Annie?'

'A cup of tea to go with those biscuits.'

'Two sugars for me,' says Jackson.

'Do you have soya milk? I *love* soya milk!' says Rose.

Mr Curtis shakes his head. 'I'm not allowed to make you drinks.'

'Yes, you are,' says Annie. 'The head makes them for me all the time.' Then she gives him a look, a look that tells him his life will be so much easier if he just goes to the staffroom and makes us all a cup of tea.

He sighs and tears a sheet of paper off the pad in front of him. 'I'd better write down what you want.'

After he's left, I say, 'Do you think he'll get in trouble?'

'Nah,' Annie says. 'Anyway, it's not like you tried to stop him.'

'I guess I really want a cup of tea,' I say, fighting a yawn. Last night I may have had a couple more hours' sleep than the night before, but Elsa still woke me up stupidly early. 'Shall I interview you first?'

'If you must,' says Annie.

I go through all the usual 'getting to know someone' questions and Annie gives the briefest possible answers, occasionally saying, 'Next,' if she doesn't like one of my questions.

After I ask her what her favourite colour is, she rolls her eyes and pulls a pen out of her bag. 'My turn, I think. Clark, Meg. Proper noun,' she says as she writes. 'Let's get the boring stuff out of the way. Any brothers or sisters? Where were you born? Got any pets? Blah blah blah.'

'One half-sister,' I say, 'Australia and a dog.'

She taps the pen on her lip. 'Interesting … I mean the bit about Australia. Are your mum and dad Australian?'

'No.'

Annie continues to look at me, just waiting for me to say more.

'Mum was in Australia when she had me,' I finally say. 'She was travelling.'

'And your dad ...?'

'Never met him.'

After a second, she says, 'Most beloved object?'

Annie has this way of speaking, like she expects to be obeyed, which is why instead of saying 'my phone' or 'my laptop', I go with the truth. 'My Orion binoculars.'

'Are you an ornithologist too?'

'No. I look at stars and the moon.'

'Through binoculars? I didn't know you could do that.' She jots down a few more notes. 'Where would you go if you were invisible?' She asks this without looking up.

'I couldn't be invisible.'

'Just answer the question, Meg.'

'If I was invisible, which I never could be, I would board a space shuttle and fly to galaxy NGC 660, although that's also impossible because it's forty-five million light years away and –'

'Stop,' Annie says, holding up a hand. 'What is your life's ambition?'

'To become an astronaut.' The words fly out of my mouth.

Annie bursts out laughing then stops when she sees my face. 'Hang on,' she says. 'You're not joking?' I shake my head and her eyes widen. 'But unless you're five, that's a terrible ambition because you're never going to achieve it! Why set yourself up for failure?' She's starting to enjoy herself now. 'I mean, how does one even become an astronaut?'

I know the answer to this. 'You get a first class degree in a suitable subject – engineering, maths, physics – then a further degree, then you either train to be a pilot or an engineer. I'm going to train to be a test pilot, and then –'

'*You*, a test pilot?' Annie throws her head back and cackles. 'No offence, but you're not exactly action hero material, Meg!'

I shake my head. 'You need to be technically minded, controlled, calm. I *could* be a test pilot.'

Something about the way I say this makes her stop laughing. 'You're really serious about this, aren't you?'

'It's all I've ever wanted.'

My words hang in the air for a moment, then she says, 'Don't you think it would be lonely, up there in space?'

I think about how I feel when the bell rings for break or lunch and I know I'm going to be on my own, and the hours I spend alone in my bedroom over the weekend. 'I don't think loneliness will be a problem,' I say.

Annie's eyes narrow. 'What happened to that friend of yours? The one with all the red hair?'

'Harriet? She moved to New Zealand.'

'Bummer … So, do you still hear from her?'

I'm not sure if Annie's still interviewing me. I think about the emails that used to arrive from Harriet every day, and how we would Skype most evenings; I'd be in my pyjamas ready to go to bed and Harriet would be about to go to school full of stories about 'crazy Kenzie' and 'hot but boring Ethan'. But then her emails got shorter and shorter, and I'd send two or three before I got a reply and when we last Skyped I could tell from her face that it had become a chore for her, like speaking to her nan or something.

I sent her an email a month ago, but I haven't had one back. 'I still hear from her,' I say. 'She's loving it over there.'

Annie nods, then says. 'Last question: tell me a secret.'

'That's not a question.'

She points her pen at me, narrows her eyes and says, 'Meg Clark, do you have any secrets?'

I know I could say anything. Tell her I once stole a Twix or that I'm scared of the dark, but for some reason I don't want to do this because I can tell Annie is genuinely interested in my answer. She's genuinely interested in me. I glance around then say, 'I'm on a secret mission.'

'What is it?'

'If I told you, I'd have to kill you!'

Annie smiles, then Mr Curtis is backing into the room, sloshing tea over his hands and yelping. As he passes round the drinks and broken biscuits, we finish writing our definitions. I notice that as Jackson and Rose read theirs out, Annie is still writing mine, crossing words out and frowning.

'Lovely!' says Mr Curtis in response to Rose's description of Jackson. 'Now, let's hear what an Annie Demos is.' He looks expectantly at me.

'Demos, Annie. Proper noun,' I say. '1. Born in Watford. 2. Only child. 3. Avid reader with a dislike of human beings, tuna and school. 4. Owns two pet rats, called Alice and Mabel.'

'Yep. That's me,' says Annie.

Mr Curtis turns to her. 'And how do you define Meg, Annie?'

She clears her throat and sits a little taller. 'Clark, Meg. Very proper noun. 1. Born on a journey and in possession of half a sister. 2. Cosmic explorer whose feet are stuck firmly to the ground in sensible shoes.' She pauses and her eyes flick from my lace-up shoes to the badges on the lapel of my blazer. '3. A blazer-wrapped, award-studded human computer whose friend went down under. 4. A fan of facts. 5. A geek with a secret.'

For a moment, no one speaks. Rose's eyes flick between Annie and me.

'That's it,' says Annie, crumpling the piece of paper up just like she screwed up the note in detention. I see it fall to the floor.

'Thank you, Annie,' says Mr Curtis. 'That was powerful stuff and I think we can all agree that the ice is well and truly broken.'

'Smashed to pieces,' laughs Jackson.

'I liked it,' I say quickly.

'Really?' says Jackson. 'You like being called a geek?'

I shrug. The way Annie just said it, it didn't sound like an insult. 'I'm used to it,' I say.

'I'm afraid our time is up,' says Mr Curtis. 'We'll be building on what we've achieved today on Friday ...' He trails off. Annie's already leaving the room. '... And perhaps then we can do some trust exercises.'

'Any possibility of getting us Party Rings?' asks Jackson, heaving himself off his beanbag. 'They're my favourites.'

As Rose thanks Mr Curtis for 'the delicious cup of tea', I pick up Annie's definition of me and slip it in my pocket. I might be feeling painfully aware of my shoes right now, but everything she said was true, and, as she pointed out, I am a fan of facts.

Plus, since Harriet left, that's the first time I've felt like someone actually *gets* me … And what makes it even better is that I think I'm starting to get Annie too.

NINETEEN

I manage to avoid a fine at Little Acorns by being the first out of French and running all the way across town. I dodge nimbly around disability vehicles and scooters, and force myself to keep running even when I get a stitch. Thanks to athleticism (and a shortcut I've discovered through the Co-op carpark) I manage to get to Little Acorns with one minute to spare.

After I've picked up Elsa, I buy food and nappies. Just one bag of shopping takes our money under a hundred pounds. I nearly buy a Crunchie but decide I can't waste a single penny, just in case we have an emergency.

Over dinner, Grandad declares that I'm totally in control of my mission and tells me to cross out today's square on the chart. I can't tell him I've still got to get through the worst bit of the day – Elsa's bedtime – just in case he insists on coming home with us.

'Just a few days to go!' he says.

'Twelve,' I say. Ever since Mum left, Grandad's been acting like she's just popped out to the shops. I stir my beans into my potato. 'Grandad,' I say, 'did she text you today?'

He shakes his head.

'Email? Anything?'

'No,' he says, squeezing ketchup over his potato, 'but I'm sure she's fine.'

'I thought she'd at least want to know how Elsa is.' Grandad might want to pretend everything is perfect, but I don't feel like doing that right now.

Grandad scratches his wild hair and his collection of leather bracelets slip over his arm. 'She knows that we'll look after Elsa. She trusts us. You're both full, you're clean, and I can't see any noticeable injuries!' He laughs when he says this, but somehow he manages to frown at the same time. 'This is fun, Meg, like the old days.'

'I guess so,' I say, thinking about when Mum used to go off on one of her trips and I'd stay round here. It was fun, but I'd still get this Christmas-morning feeling when Mum walked back through the door and pulled me into her arms. She'd always smell a bit different and be buzzing with news. She'd dump her rucksack on the floor and I'd curl up on her lap as she talked to Grandad, her hands waving madly in the air as she described the children or animals she'd helped. I loved hearing her voice, but part of me always felt a bit jealous that I had to share her.

At the end of the table, Elsa drops the spoon and starts drawing patterns in her baked beans. Grandad nods at the mushy food on my plate. 'Now, are you going to eat your dinner or do I have to feed *you* as well?'

I take Elsa home straight after dinner, pushing her up the hill then bumping the pushchair up the three flights of stairs. She tips her head back and watches me. 'Mama … ma?' she says.

'She's not back yet,' I say, but as I put the key in the lock I can't stop myself from imagining – hoping – that we find the flat lit up with candles and fairy lights, and that Mum's inside, waiting for us.

But just like last night, the flat is dark, cold and empty. I take Elsa out of her pushchair and kick my way through toys and balled-up nappies. I can't believe how messy the flat is. Since Elsa was born it's got worse and worse – that's one of the reasons I spend so much time in my bedroom. Right now, Pongo can't even find a space to lie down. After sniffing at a half-buried bowl, he goes and curls up by the front door.

I put Elsa in the empty paddling pool. 'Time to tidy up,' I say.

At first, I think it's going OK. I dump the plates and mugs in the sink and I start to see glimpses of carpet, but then Elsa escapes from the paddling pool and tips out a jigsaw puzzle. She throws the pieces around the room and while I'm picking them all up, she tugs a spider plant off the windowsill, spilling soil all over the carpet and her hair.

I feel the muscles in my body tighten. 'Elsa!' I snap, as I go over to her. She looks up with big, innocent eyes. 'Stop it. I'm trying to make everywhere look nice.'

'Da!' she says, holding out some soil.

'I don't want any soil. I just want you to stop doing crazy stuff.'

She shrieks and crawls away from me, spreading soil across the room.

While I sort out the plant, she pulls herself up on the bookcase. 'Da!' she says, grabbing a book off the shelf and tossing it over her shoulder. 'Da, da!' Book after book is thrown on the floor.

'Stop it!' My voice is so loud and angry it makes her jump. But she's not worried: she looks at me, smiles, and drops another book.

Suddenly, I feel so tired that I want to scream. I go to

the bookshelf and grab a handful of books. 'There!' I say, dropping them. 'Is that better? Why don't we throw *everything* on the floor, Elsa?' I take another stack of Mum's fairy and astrology books, only this time I throw them as hard as I can. They spin through the air, pages fanned out, and crash into the wall. Now I've started, I can't stop. Elsa shrinks back as more books fly across the room. Then I run to the mantelpiece and sweep my hand across it, sending candles, incense cones and Mum's entire collection of Disney Pop! figures tumbling to the floor.

Elsa's hiding behind her fingers. When I pull Mum's wind chimes down from the ceiling, she throws herself on the floor and starts to sob and I stand there watching her, my heart thudding, rage still prickling my skin. Elsa looks so pathetic lying on the carpet with her bottom stuck up in the air, but something inside me – a mean feeling – stops me from going over to her.

With trembling fingers, I pick up the Thumper Pop! and put it back on the mantelpiece.

The flat is a mess … I'm a mess.

I hate Mum right now.

I stare at Thumper's bobbing ears until my heart starts to slow down. I force myself to take slow, deep breaths. In 1970, the astronauts on Apollo 13 were two days into their mission when there was a catastrophic explosion and they started to run out of oxygen. Did they scream and throw stuff? No, they used *tape* and a *sock* and made a machine that saved their lives. Their heart rates probably didn't even increase! How can I dream of being an astronaut when I can't even stay calm looking after a baby?

Slowly, my rage fades away and I'm left feeling shaky and embarrassed that a bit of soil and some books made me lose control.

I step over Elsa and go into the kitchen where I get a rice cake and a roll of bin bags.

I hold the rice cake out to Elsa. 'Here we are,' I say. She lies there, sucking her thumb and staring at me. 'Sorry I shouted.' I put my hand on her warm back. Slowly, her hand reaches out and she takes the rice cake. 'I'll give you a bath, but first we're going to play Chuck Everything in the Bag, OK?'

She sucks on the rice cake.

'Plastic fruit?' I say, holding up some grapes. 'Chuck it in the bag! Peppa Pig? Chuck her in the bag!'

Elsa sits up and watches me. After a moment, she gets one of my school shoes, crawls over to the bin bag and drops it in.

'That's it!' I say, resisting the urge to take it straight out. She smiles and grabs hold of Pongo's ankle. 'No, not Pongo. He's too big.' I pass her a brick. 'Do this instead.'

While she throws in the rest of the bricks, I get all the books back on the shelf. Soon we have three bulging bin bags, a pile of dishes on the kitchen table and, yes, I can see carpet!

'Let's get rid of this,' I say, pulling the stopper out of the paddling pool. Air starts to hiss out and I throw it behind the sofa along with the bin bags. Now we have a big, beautiful, empty space! I lie down in it, too tired to do another thing. Inspired, Pongo and Elsa start doing circuits of the room, occasionally crawling over me. This is lovely, I think, shutting my eyes.

Then something hard and slimy drops on my forehead. I ignore it, but Pongo paws at my shoulder and then the slimy thing hits me again. I open one eye and see that it's Pongo's Kong – the big rubber ball he chases on the Downs. I roll over and force myself to sit up. 'Walkies?' I say.

TWENTY

Thursday passes by in a daze of trying not to fall asleep and resisting the temptation to buy a Crunchie. As usual, we have dinner at Grandad's, then it's back to the flat for a mini meltdown (Elsa decides she hates baths) and up on the Downs for our sleepy walk. Tonight I tell Elsa about the different types of stars – red dwarfs, white dwarfs and hypergiants – and soon her head falls forward and she's sleeping in the sling. On the way back, I make a detour to the all-night garage. It's an emergency. I need a Crunchie to get me back up the stairs to the flat. Once again, we both crash out on Mum's bed. *I really should get her back in her cot*, I think, as I drift off to sleep … *Maybe tomorrow …*

The first thing I see when I wake up on Friday is my phone. It's hard to miss because Elsa's pressing it into my eyeball and having a pretend conversation with me. 'Ah, uh, babab, ah?' she says.

I push the phone away and that's when I see I've got a message. I sit up, snatching the phone off Elsa. She makes a grab for it so I move to get away from her and stare at the screen. It's an unknown number. I open the text. *Am fine and miss u all. Namaste! Xxx Mum*

It's so good to finally hear from her that I smile. Then I read the words again, trying to find something I've missed, some clue about exactly where Mum is and what she's doing. Elsa thumps my back. 'Da!' she says, and my smile fades away. How can Mum say she's fine and then not ask *a single* question about us? And if she misses us so much, why doesn't she just come home?

Elsa latches on to me, pulls herself up and stands there, holding my arm and wobbling in her Winnie the Pooh Babygro. 'Mum's OK,' I say, because I have to tell someone, then I give her the phone and she clamps it upside down against her ear.

'Mamama,' she says, and she starts chatting away in a strange alien language.

And that's when I glance at Mum's clock and realise how late it is. Somehow we've overslept! Quickly, I run through everything I have to do (change Elsa, give her breakfast, feed Pongo), and what I can drop (brushing my

105

hair, feeding me). At the same time I try to work out if I have any hope of getting to school on time. Maybe. If I run.

I grab a nappy and the baby wipes. Then I remember I have PE and that my kit is somewhere in the wash basket. I pull out my mouldy-smelling T-shirt. *'Am fine'*, I think. That's great, Mum … I'm just thrilled for you.

TWENTY-ONE

'I've been told,' says Mr Badal, 'that when I let captains pick teams it makes some of you feel left out. According to one of your mothers,' he pauses here to stare hard at Richard Gardner, 'I should find a different way to do it.'

We're standing in a huddle on the top field, wind whipping up our shorts, icy drizzle misting our faces. *Thank you, Richard's mum*, I think. *Finally!* Mr Badal must be the only PE teacher in the country who still lets popular kids pick teams like this. Usually the only students left standing are me, Richard and Nasma Khan (who has chronic asthma).

Mr Badal thuds his hockey stick down in the grass. 'But I say, "Man up!" Bella and Jackson, you're our captains. Get up here and pick your teams!'

My heart sinks. Here we go …

'Woody!' says Bella (obviously).

'I'll take the one and only Andre Jaquet,' says Jackson, pointing at his best friend.

'All right!' says Andre, and the two of them bump chests. Then, one by one, the students standing around me are selected by Bella and Jackson.

'Excellent!' says Mr Badal, rubbing his hands together, before going off to sort out the pitch.

Soon there are only seven of us misfits left. Bella studies us, nose wrinkled, like she's having to choose between an unappetising selection of sandwiches. 'Ummm … this is hard …'

'Just pick, Bella,' says Ed. 'We're freezing out here.'

'Heidi!' she says.

Oh, *come on*. Heidi? Heidi screams if a ball comes within two metres of her and she's wearing wedge-heel trainers that do up with zips! I go mountain biking and I walk all over the Downs, but just because I can do sums in my head everyone assumes I'm hopeless at sport!

Heidi drifts towards Bella's group. 'Thanks, babe,' she says.

A gust of wind slams against me. I cling to my hockey stick for support, and that's when I hear my name being called. 'Meg!' shouts Jackson. 'Wake up and get your brainy arse over here.'

'Me?' I say, glancing over my shoulder.

'Yes, *you*. And I'll take you lot as well.' He points at the three students standing nearest to him.

'Hey, it's my go,' says Bella.

'Richard's mum's right,' says Jackson. 'This is a stupid way to pick teams.'

'Finally,' says Ed. 'Let's go.' He picks up his hockey stick and heads across the field. Bella follows him.

'Grab a spoon, Bella!' Jackson yells after her.

She turns back. 'What?'

'You're about to taste defeat!'

'Idiot,' she mutters, then she jogs after Ed.

'Yeah, you run away because we're the *whup* and you guys are the *arse*!' Then he screams, holds his stick above his head, and starts sprinting across the field. 'Come on, team!' he shouts over his shoulder. 'Let's *murder* them!'

Maybe it's Jackson's inspirational speech, or maybe it's because I'm so tired and angry with Mum, but I really throw myself into the game. At one point I'm running so fast for the ball that I don't notice Mr Badal until it's too late. I slam into his solid bulk and we both fall smack down into the mud.

Ed, who was racing me for the ball, narrowly avoids crashing down with us by jumping to one side. Sir scowls and rubs his elbow.

'Man up, Sir!' shouts Ed, before whacking the ball and flying after it.

I may be playing with a mad energy, but I'm also hopeless – I blame Mum for this too: I score an own goal, get a penalty for 'using my stick in a dangerous way' (I didn't: my hands were so slippery the stick just shot towards Heidi's face), and I even manage to trip over a crisp packet. Bella's team beats us seven–two.

As we trudge back to the changing rooms, Jackson slaps me on the shoulder. 'You're my player of the match, Clarky.'

'But I got two penalties – *and* an own goal!'

'Sorry, I should have said, "You're my *funniest* player of the match."'

'Oh … Thanks.'

'See you at Biscuit Club,' he says, then he lifts up his hockey stick, has a quick fight with an invisible enemy (I'm guessing a ninja from the sounds he's making), and runs into school.

I'm about to follow him when I hear someone call my name. I turn round to see Ed strolling towards me. Even though he's been running around on a muddy pitch for forty minutes, he's somehow managed to keep his kit pristine, although I do notice that his hair has gone a bit floppy.

I wrap my arms around my musty T-shirt; I really need to get changed.

He stops in front of me. 'We've got to do our homework,' he says, and somehow it sounds like an order. 'I don't really want to do it at lunchtime. Can you stay behind after school?'

I shake my head. 'After school's no good for me.'

'What? Never or just today?'

'Never.'

This throws him for a second. 'OK. How about tomorrow?'

'Tomorrow's Saturday.'

'Right,' he says. 'I forgot.'

Bella appears next to him. 'What did you forget?' she says.

'Nothing. Just talking about our science homework.'

'Me and Raj met up last night. Raj's done this rap about all the different planets called "Space in Your Face".' She gives us a little demonstration, rapping 'Uranus, Uranus, what colour is *Uranus*?' She stops abruptly and points at me. 'Well,' she says, 'what colour is Uranus, Meg?'

'Blue,' I say with a sigh.

She throws her head back and laughs while Ed watches her, one eyebrow raised. 'What?' she says. 'It's funny!'

'Finished?' says Ed.

After a final giggle, Bella nods, then a silence falls over us. Bella looks from me to Ed. 'Well, this is awkward.'

'We could email our presentations to each other,' I say in a rush. 'Read each others' through and suggest changes.'

'I think the point is,' he says, 'we're supposed to practise saying them *together*, but if you've got more important things to do then that's OK. I can always ask Miss for another partner ... Maybe someone who actually wants to win the competition?' Even though he says all this with a smile, it still makes a flutter of worry run through me. The school could only enter two students for the NASA competition and I know how lucky I am to have been chosen.

'Ohhh ... She doesn't like that!' says Bella, seeing my face.

Quickly, I try to work out when I can find the time to meet up with Ed, but my mind is as numb as my freezing fingers and I'm so tired I can't think straight. But then I remember a tiny window in my schedule. 'The science trip!' I say. 'We'll do it then, at lunchtime.'

'Or on the bus?' says Bella. 'You two could curl up on the back seat and talk nerdy to each other.'

'Fine,' says Ed. He looks annoyed, but I can't work out if it's me or Bella who's bothered him. 'We'll do it then.

'Come on, Woody.' Bella starts walking away. 'I want a cheese croissant and they always run out.'

Ed starts to follow her, then turns back. 'One other thing,' he says. 'You've got a bit of mud –' he points at my cheek '– kind of there.'

I rub at my face. 'Gone?'

He shakes his head. 'You need to look in a mirror.'

'It's a massive splat!' Bella shouts. '*Come on*, Woody!'

TWENTY-TWO

When I arrive at the Biscuit Club, Mr Curtis has already made our cups of tea and Annie and Jackson are arguing over the biscuits. 'Mr Curtis actually *broke up* some Party Rings and put them in the box,' explains Annie, 'but I found one that wasn't broken.'

'I saw it first,' says Jackson, trying to snatch it out of her hand. 'You just moved faster than me.'

'Seriously?' says Mr Curtis, staring at them. 'OK, I say Annie gets the Party Ring, but Jackson, you can have these two really rather large bits of Ginger Nut.'

'Yes!' says Annie grinning and sticking her finger up at Jackson. Rose looks aghast and Mr Curtis pretends not to have noticed.

Jackson doesn't care. He's already sucking tea out of a Ginger Nut. He shrugs. 'Actually, they're all right.'

Today, for some inexplicable reason, Mr Curtis wants us to make origami animals. Jackson and Rose get stuck straight into it and soon cats, giraffes and frogs appear on Jackson's beanbag.

'I'm not doing it,' Annie says to me. 'It's pointless ... And before you start feeling sorry for me, this has nothing to do with my cerebral palsy.' She wiggles her fingers in my face. 'See? These puppies are fine.'

I shrug. 'It's better than assembly.' I pick up a piece of white paper and start making a crane.

Annie watches what I'm doing and can't resist pointing out the tiny mistakes I make. 'Fold *backwards* not *forward* ... That's a *beak*, Meg, not a *tail*!' When I finish the crane she takes it from me and examines it. 'Not bad. If you fail in your attempt to become an astronaut, you could make paper animals for a living.' She takes a piece of brown paper. 'I suppose I'll do a bear.'

'I'm doing a penguin,' I say. I fold a black square in half, and then in half again. 'I'm not deluded,' I say. 'I know the odds of becoming an astronaut aren't good – I've got more chance of being struck by lightning than becoming an astronaut – but every day I'm improving on those odds.'

She glances up. 'How do you mean?'

'If I do some work today that helps me get an A*

in maths, then that's bringing me a tiny bit closer to going to a good university and closer to becoming an astronaut.'

'And making an origami penguin helps how?'

I press out a miniscule wing. 'I'm improving my fine motor skills. One day I'll be on a spacewalk, spinning round the Earth at seventeen thousand miles an hour and trying to tighten a bolt, and I'll think back to this moment. This penguin –' I hold the finished model up '– is definitely helping me to get to space.'

She looks critically at her bear. 'So what's the big attraction with space?'

'Have you ever been to a zoo and thought the animals looked sad?'

'I suppose so. Once I sat staring at a gorilla, and he sat staring at me, and I think we shared a moment.'

'Well, I know how they feel. Earth is too small. I want to explore as far as I possibly can!'

I guess this must have burst out of me because Annie draws back and laughs.

'And being weightless would be amazing,' I add. 'Doesn't everyone want to fly?'

Annie looks right at me. 'I dream that I'm flying.'

'Me too.'

'Have my bear,' she says, passing me her squishy

model. 'I know it looks more like a paper poo, but it's the thought that counts.'

Soon we've made a small zoo of animals and Mr Curtis tells us we can pack up.

'Thanks for the wonderful waste of time, Sir,' says Annie as she heads for the door.

'Not a waste of time,' he says. 'You were learning to break down a task into easy steps. Before you go, Annie ...'

She's already halfway out of the room. 'What?'

'You've all got some homework.'

'No.' She shakes her head, making her wild hair fly. 'No, we haven't.'

'Yes, *you have*.' Mr Curtis says this just as firmly and they stare at each other, eyes narrowed.

'What is it?'

'One of the main objectives of Student in the Spotlight is to encourage supportive networks that bridge existing friendship groups.'

'*What?*' says Jackson.

'He wants to force us to become friends,' says Annie, visibly sagging over her crutches.

'No, I want this wonderful group that's forming before my eyes to last. I'd like you to connect out of school, socially, just for twenty minutes or so. I think it would be an extremely powerful experience for you to see each other as individuals, without the barriers of uniform, timetables and social groups.'

'Are you serious?' Annie blinks at Mr Curtis and down on his beanbag, Jackson starts to laugh. 'It won't be an extremely powerful experience,' Annie says, shaking her head. 'It will be an extremely awkward experience!'

'We could go bowling,' says Jackson. 'Or to Laser Quest! Oh my God, Annie in Laser Quest! We'd all be dead in two minutes.'

'It's not happening,' says Annie. 'I want to hang out with my real friends out of school.'

'I think it would be totally cool,' says Rose. She's been smiling since Mr Curtis mentioned the idea. 'How about tomorrow?'

'Obviously I can't force you to do it,' says Mr Curtis, 'but I think you should give it a go, just once ...'

'I'm busy tomorrow,' I say, thinking of the science workshop.

'Sunday?' says Rose.

Rose is small and has plump cheeks and round brown eyes. There's something about her that reminds me a bit of Elsa: her feelings show on her face immediately, and right now her face is showing hope and excitement. I guess no one wants to wipe that look off her face because Jackson says, 'Three o'clock. McDonald's?'

Annie scowls and I know why. McDonald's is at the top of the hill in town. Possibly the worst place to get to if you're using crutches or a wheelchair.

'Fusciardi's,' I blurt out, thinking of the cafe right on the promenade. 'It's by the sea and it has the best ice cream.' What am I talking about? I'm not even going! 'And they give you a little biscuit if you get a coffee or hot chocolate.'

'I *love* Fusciardi's,' says Rose. 'It's covered in mirrors and you can get hot fudge sauce and wafers with bear faces on them.'

'I'll see you there, ladies,' says Jackson, jumping to his feet and throwing a 'maybe', over his shoulder as he leaves the room.

'Yeah "maybe" I'll see you there too!' says Annie, following him out.

'Thanks for suggesting Fusciardi's,' says Rose as we head down the corridor. 'I love it there, but I'd feel stupid going on my own.'

'Right,' I say. I'm starting to get a bad feeling about this.

'I'm going to get there extra early so I can get us a table facing the sea!' She grins at me then dashes off towards art.

I watch her go, her big rucksack bouncing up and down, her bobbed hair flying. I've got enough to do this weekend looking after Elsa, Jackson didn't exactly commit and Annie's obviously not going. Is Rose going to be sitting in the cafe on her own, nibbling a bear wafer and looking around for us? I try to push the thought away, but I can't seem to get rid of the image of her wide, hopeful eyes.

I walk towards the library. This is why I want to go to be an astronaut: life on Earth is way too complicated.

TWENTY-THREE

On Saturday, Elsa wakes me up at five, giving me plenty of time to lie in bed, stare at the ceiling, and worry myself sick about the fact that today Grandad and I are doing our Cool Cosmos show.

I *am* excited too. We've been planning this show for months and the experiments are going to be good. Actually, they're going to be better than good: they're going to be messy and funny and possibly even a bit amazing. The children watching are going to love it, and when I focus on this – on their happy faces – I can't help feeling excited too.

But this excited feeling is nothing compared to the all-consuming power of the pukey feeling. The thought of all those people – OK, those *children* – staring up at me makes my heart race and my skin prickle ... But I keep reminding myself that Grandad will be doing all the talking and that I'll just be standing next to him, handing him ice cubes and fruit. Yes, I'll get some stares, but I can do this. No, I *have* to do this because it will take me one step closer to standing on the school stage and delivering my speech at the NASA competition.

'Let's do this thing!' I say to Elsa, jumping out of bed. 'Right after I've changed your stinky nappy.'

I keep busy and distracted all morning, getting Elsa ready and then going round to Grandad's house and helping him to load up Pete's car. (Grandad doesn't have a car so he's roped Pete, one of his Sussex Stargazer friends, into giving us a lift.) When we're finally packed up and on our way to the science centre, the sickness creeps back in. I wind down the window and take deep breaths. Next to me, Elsa is screaming at the top of her lungs.

'Remind me. Why are you bringing Elsa along?' asks Pete.

'Alice is away at the moment,' says Grandad. 'Elsa won't be a problem.'

'Right,' says Pete. He doesn't sound convinced. Elsa's been crying solidly since we left town. Right now we're driving down a winding county lane with David Bowie blaring out of the speakers and Elsa screaming along to 'Heroes'.

'Here, Elsa,' I say, handing her a carrot puff. She stuffs it in her mouth and the screaming stops. I go back to staring queasily out of the window, the wind whipping my hair. Suddenly, I get a glimpse of the turquoise observatory domes rising out of the trees. 'There they are!' I say.

'Just like spaceships,' says Grandad, turning round and smiling at me. When I was little, Grandad told me the telescope domes really were spaceships and that all the staff at the science centre were aliens. Every time we visited, he implied that there was a good chance we could end up in space. I worked out that he was lying years ago, but I still get this thrill when I see the domes. I love this place.

'Maggie was saying she might give you a job soon,' says Pete.

'Maybe,' I say, glancing at Elsa. 'If today goes well. Maggie is the manager and she knows how much I want to work here. I've got to wait until I'm sixteen, but after that it's up to her.'

'It'll go well,' says Grandad. 'You wait until you see it, Pete. We've got eggs, explosions, costumes … Meg worked it all out.'

'You thought of the costumes,' I say.

'You do love a good costume,' Pete says to Grandad. 'Remember when you dressed up as Halley's Comet?'

'And it caught fire?' Grandad laughs. 'I couldn't get away with smoking in front of the kids these days.'

Pete turns off the road and into a bumpy car park. 'There you are,' he says, pointing at the noticeboard by the entrance:

Cool Cosmos, 11.30. Discover just how miraculous our universe is in our hands-on, family-friendly show. Warning: will contain nuts!

Pete laughs and slams his hand down on the steering wheel.

'Oh, God,' I say, taking an extra deep breath of calming air.

'Do you like the bit about the nuts?' asks Grandad. 'That was my idea!'

All the workshops are run in marquees and while Grandad and I set up, Elsa plays in a cardboard box. Whenever we find something she might like we drop it in the box; a piece of bubble wrap keeps her quiet for ages and she goes crazy when Grandad bats in one of the balloons we're blowing up.

Maggie appears just as we're putting the finishing touches to our flour tower. 'That's big,' she says, eyeing the enormous floury mountain.

Grandad adds a final spoonful. 'It's ten-bags-of-flour

big! We're going to drop a watermelon on it. *Poof!*' His hands mime an explosion. 'We're recreating the impact of comets striking the moon.'

'We're dropping a pea on it too,' I add. I don't want Maggie thinking we're about to trash her tent.

'Sounds intriguing,' she says. 'I'll be watching the second half.' And this is when Elsa decides to pop her head up over the side of the box and scream, 'Da, da!'

Maggie jumps back, a horrified look on her face. 'It's a baby!'

'My other granddaughter,' says Grandad. 'We're dropping her in the flour as well!'

Maggie laughs weakly and Grandad must realise she needs to be reassured because he adds, 'You don't need to worry about Elsa getting in the way. Pete will look after her during the show.'

Somehow I doubt that. In the car Pete tried to give Elsa his Homer Simpson lighter to play with and when we arrived he offered her a king size Mars bar. I don't think he's had much experience with babies.

Maggie frowns down at Elsa, then her eyes flick to me. 'Well, just as long as you'll be supervising both your granddaughters the *whole time*. Meg's not old enough to do this on her own yet.'

'I won't let either of them out of my sight!' Grandad promises.

Just then, Maggie's walkie-talkie buzzes and she backs out of the tent. 'Make sure you don't.'

The moment she's gone, Grandad turns to me. 'You watch Elsa. I'm going to buy a sausage roll.'

TWENTY-FOUR

'You're one hundred per cent sure about this?' I'm wearing a lab coat, a curly grey wig and black specs. I'm a mad scientist. Grandad's wearing something similar, only he doesn't need the wig.

'Definitely,' he says. 'Kids love costumes. Now hold still while I do your make-up.'

He dabs black face paint all over my face. It's supposed to look like something's exploded. Grandad's already done his and it does look quite good, especially with his back-combed hair. 'You're so pale it looks extra effective!' he says, putting a final smudge on my forehead.

I'm pale with fear: there's a constant rumble of voices coming from outside the flaps of the tent and every now and then a curious face peeks in.

Pete wanders by. 'It's mad out there. I'm going to have to let them in. Are you ready?'

'Born ready!' says Grandad, and I swallow and think, *Stay down Shreddies, stay down!*

Pete holds back the flap and children start to pour in, shrieking and pushing each other as they race for the positions at the front. They're followed by their parents – real, live grown-ups. I hadn't really thought about them … They're so *big*!

'Look at the clown, Mummy!' shouts a boy, pointing at me. 'He's scary!'

'It's a *lady* clown,' says his mum, giving me a smile.

I try to smile back, but it's a shaky smile, and I decide to go and check on Elsa rather than just stand here being stared at.

I grab a handful of carrot puffs and pull back the flaps on her box. I peer inside. Everything is quiet and still. 'Are you hiding?' I say, pushing the balloons and cuddly toys to one side. 'Elsa?'

The box is empty!

I see that some of the tape has peeled away, leaving a baby-sized gap. '*Grandad,*' I hiss. 'Elsa's gone!' Then I get down on my hands and knees and start searching under the table and around the various boxes.

Grandad double-checks the box. 'Whoops!'

'*Whoops?*' I say. 'Grandad, this site is basically a baby death trap: there are ponds everywhere, not to mention gigantic telescopes, moving floors, lasers, rocks …'

'Don't forget all the concrete steps,' he says. 'Well, she can't be far away.' He walks towards the exit. 'She's probably crawled under the tent. I'll find her while you start the show.'

'While I do *what?*' I say.

'Start the show!' he bellows, as he strolls out of the tent.

Immediately, children are shushed, the audience falls quiet and everyone turns to look at me.

'Yay, it's starting!' shouts a girl on the floor, bouncing up and down.

I stare down at her, my mouth slightly open. Did Grandad plan this? Knowing how nervous I feel, did he actually let Elsa escape so he'd have an excuse to throw me in at the deep end? My theory sounds mad … but Grandad is a bit mad!

I look up and face the audience. Sweat prickles under my arms and my mouth goes dry. There's a cough, some more shushes and then the yay-girl says, 'Who are you?'

'Ummm …'

'Your face is funny!' she adds.

'I … ummm …' I swallow and grab Grandad's notes, scanning the introduction. A lump has formed in my throat and I know that I can't talk. I just can't do it.

129

Suddenly, Yay-Girl shouts even louder, 'WHO ARE YOU?'

'I am the granddaughter of Copernicus,' I say in a rush, 'the man who just ran out of the tent. Well, he's Copernicus and he's an amazing man and –'

'Why's he so amazing?' The boy who's just interrupted me is sitting by my feet. He's about six and he's got a bored expression on his face. I feel a rush of irritation and for a moment I forget how scared I feel. 'Copernicus is amazing because he's one of the greatest astronomers who ever lived. Before he came along, everyone thought Earth – our teeny little planet – was the centre of the universe.'

The boy seems unimpressed. 'I'm Isaac,' he says, then he narrows his eyes suspiciously. 'What's your name?'

I glance at Grandad's notes again, trying to find the name he thought up for me. 'My name is Megernicus,' I say.

'We can't hear you!' shouts an adult voice from the back.

'My name is Megernicus!' This time my voice comes out way too loud, a yell really, and a baby starts to whimper. How has this happened? Grandad promised me that I wouldn't have to say a word and now I'm shouting at people!

Yay-Girl's eyes go wide. 'You're called *Mega Knickers*? Cool!'

'No, *Megernicus*,' I say, but I'm wasting my breath because now all children are shouting out 'Mega Knickers', although some are just yelling 'knickers' and one boy is saying, 'Willy, willy, willy,' again and again.

I look at the entrance to the tent, but there's no sign of Grandad. Now the children are laughing and pushing each other and a couple have even got to their feet. Their parents are looking at me with a mixture of sympathy and irritation.

This is a total disaster. I have to do something!

I force myself to think of the coolest, calmest person I know: Valentina Tereshkova. Not only was she the first woman to go to space, but before that she was a parachutist. She must have felt this fear, when you're standing on the edge of something and you know you have to jump. I picture her strong, steady gaze. If Valentina could throw herself out of a plane repeatedly, then orbit Earth forty-eight times, then I can open my mouth and tell these kids about space.

So I take a deep breath, look at the chattering, squirming children, and I open my mouth. 'That's right,' I say, raising my voice so it cuts across the talking. 'I *am* Mega Knickers, and it's actually a very common medieval name. Now, my grandad thinks that the sun is at the centre of the universe so we're going to prove him wrong.'

'*What?*' Grandad walks back in with Elsa's wriggling in his arms. 'You're talking nonsense! I tell you, the sun is smack bang in the middle of things.'

'Not true,' I say, smiling with relief. I wait for Grandad to join me at the front, but he just holds up Elsa and shrugs. Suddenly, I don't want him to come and take over. I want to finish what I've started. I look back at the notes then hold up a roll of toilet paper. 'Who knows how to use this?' All around me hands shoot up, and children laugh, and that laughter helps me stand a little taller and clear my throat.

'Good,' I say, 'because we're going to use this toilet paper to learn how vast our solar system is, and this should help us understand the immense size of the universe.' I turn to Grandad. 'The sun *is* huge, Grandad Copernicus, but it's just one of over one billion trillion stars in our universe and not nearly as special as you think.'

Soon we've unravelled the toilet roll and it's snaking out of the tent and into the courtyard; children are running around with melons, apples and grapes, trying to work out where the 'planets' should go. I'm so busy answering their questions and trying to stop them from eating the fruit that I haven't got time to think about what I'm doing. 'Everyone go and stand near Earth,' I say, 'but don't tread on it!'

The children rush towards Earth, a cherry tomato. 'Jupiter's the biggest planet in the solar system,' I say, 'which is why it's a watermelon, but we still don't have a sun. If earth is this big,' I hold the tomato between my fingers, 'then what fruit or vegetable could we use for the sun?'

'A pumpkin!' shouts out a dad, getting a bit too into it.

'Not big enough,' I say. I can't quite talk to the adults in the way I can talk to the children, but at least they can hear me now.

'A dinosaur?' suggests a girl.

'Good guess, but that isn't a fruit or vegetable ... Amazingly, if you took all the fruit in the entire world and mashed it together to make one giant, monster fruit, it still wouldn't be as big as our sun!'

Gasps of genuine amazement break out, and not just from the children. I look at Grandad and he grins. This was just what I had hoped would happen. I tear off one piece of toilet paper. 'Can anyone guess how many kilometres this represents?'

Answers are shouted back at me: 'a hundred', 'a zillion', 'seventy-three!'

'One piece of toilet paper represents ten *million* kilometres,' I say. 'Now, who wants to see an egg sucked into a bottle?'

TWENTY-FIVE

'**E**very single object in the universe is made of atoms,' I say, 'including you and me.' I'm up to the last experiment. By my feet, one of the children yawns and another starts nibbling something off the end of her finger. 'To show how *alive* atoms are, we're going to play with balloons.' I pick up the bin bags stuffed full of balloons and tip them out. The balloons float across the tent and the children jump to their feet and start hitting them into the air.

'We're going to see how many balloons we can stick to a person's head using static electricity. I need a volunteer, but I should warn you, it's going to do bad things to their hair!'

'My brother!' shouts a voice from the back of the room. 'Pick my brother!' Through the balloons and jumping children, I see a boy with messy blond hair stretching his arm high into the air. 'Please, pick my brother!' Sitting next to him is another little boy wearing a Minions T-shirt.

Over by the exit, Maggie taps her watch. I need to hurry up.

'OK. You come up here with your brother. We're going to have to rub these balloons really hard if we're going to get them to stick to him.' I get the other children to sit back down and when I look up, the boy is pulling his brother towards me ... only he's not wearing a Minions T-shirt. His brother is tall and dark, and a gold watch is flashing on his wrist. I'd know that watch anywhere. My stomach drops as I stare at Ed King.

He stops in front of me and folds his arms. 'Hello, Meg,' he says.

'What are you doing here?' my voice is a whisper.

He shrugs, looking amused. 'Learning about the Cool Cosmos.'

'And you've been here ...?'

'The whole time,' he says with a smile.

He saw that boy throw the tomato in my eye ... He watched me bounce an egg ... He heard me say that the cosmos 'blew me away on a daily basis'!

And then my mind charges through what I'm about to do to my volunteer: rub balloons on their hair and

135

body, then see if an electric shock will pass between our fingers.

With someone who was seven, this would have been funny. But with Ed, it would be ... so *weird*!

Down by my feet, a boy is fiddling with his balloon. He must somehow undo it, because suddenly there's a hiss of air and the balloon shoots out of his hands and flies round the tent. It flops on the floor by my feet, looking empty and a bit silly.

Wow. I know exactly how that balloon feels.

'Sorry,' I say to Ed, 'but you can't be the volunteer.'

'Why not?' asks his brother.

Suddenly I see a way out. 'Because I need someone a bit smaller. Someone like you!'

'No,' he says, clenching his fists. 'You said my brother could do it. You *promised*!'

'I didn't promise.'

'It doesn't matter, George,' says Ed, patting his shoulder. 'If Mega Knickers doesn't want me to do it, you can take my place.'

'No way. She said you could do it!' In slow motion, George's bottom lip sticks out and it starts to tremble.

'Bless,' says a mum on the front row. 'Let his brother do it, love.'

Are his eyes welling up? I glance at the back of the

tent where Maggie is watching me closely. I'm fairly certain she doesn't want me to make any children cry. 'Fine,' I say, nodding. 'He can do it.'

There's a scattering of applause and George shouts, 'Yes!' and punches the air.

To get through this I'm going to have to stick to the plan and totally ignore who my volunteer is. 'You're going to remove some of the electrons from your balloons like this,' I say, rubbing a balloon on my lab coat, 'leaving them positively charged. Then when you put the balloon on to Ed's hair,' I reach up and balance it on his perfect hair, 'the balloon will cling to the negatively charged electrons, proving that opposites attract!'

'So cute!' says a woman at the back.

'Ignore her,' whispers Ed. 'That's my mum.'

In a panic, I let go of the balloon and it floats to the ground.

George tugs on my lab coat. 'You need to rub it on his hair.'

'Why don't you do it?' I say.

'I'm too small,' he says with a smile. What's happened to his wobbling lip?

'Fine,' I say. 'I'll rub his hair.' I reach up and start rubbing the balloon all over Ed's hair, flattening his sticky-up bit at the front. To cover my embarrassment at being chest to chest with Ed King, I rub extra hard. In the four years we've been sitting next to each other, we've never touched, not even an accidental blazer-brush, and yet here I am giving him a head massage … with a balloon.

I mustn't think about massages.

I must think about Science and Electricity and Atoms.

'Let's get those electrons agitated!' I say in a brisk voice, whipping the balloon backwards and forward then round and round. When his hair is a bushy cloud, I let go of the balloon and this time it sticks.

I smile down at the children who are creeping closer. 'Your turn,' I say, 'and make sure you all get a go.' For the next few minutes, Ed is attacked by children with balloons. Some of their parents join in, and even Maggie has a go.

Eventually, I tell them to sit down. Ed and George stay standing next to me. Ed's looking slightly dazed, a single yellow balloon still clinging to his hair.

'So that's the end of the show,' I say, and I can't help smiling, because I've actually *done* it – I've stood up and spoken to a group of strangers for a long time. In my head, Valentina gives me a high five. 'But there's lots more to see and the telescope tour is about to start in Dome B –'

'Hang on!' shouts Grandad. 'What about the electric shock?'

'We've not got time for that.'

'The tour can start a few minutes late,' says Maggie.

Ed turns to me and whispers, 'What're we supposed to do?'

Everyone is staring up at us, waiting to see what we'll do next. I shake my head. 'It's nothing,' I say. 'I was going to touch fingers with the volunteer to see if I would get an electric shock. But we don't need to do it.'

Our whispered conversation has gone on for too long, but this doesn't bother Ed. 'Why not?'

I try to think of a good reason. The electric shock was supposed to impress a load of children, and make them love what I love, not provide the perfect punchline when Ed tells Bella everything that happened today. I can just hear her shrieking out in science, 'Oh my God, she made you *touch her*?!'

'Come on,' says Ed, sticking his index finger out, 'it won't kill you.'

'Fine,' I say and I move my finger towards his. By our feet, the children lean closer. Ed smiles and raises one eyebrow, and the situation is so funny that I can't help smiling too as I bring my finger closer to his. And then, the moment our fingers touch, there's this tiny flash of white light and a jolt of electricity jumps from Ed to me, tingling through my hand.

'Ow!' he says, pulling his hand back and laughing.

I stare at my buzzing fingertip. 'I didn't think it would work,' I whisper.

'Shock me!' says George, jumping up and down. 'Shock me!'

TWENTY-SIX

After everyone's given me a clap and Maggie's thanked me for my 'highly original and messy show', the audience files out of the tent.

I watch them go, slightly dazed, slightly amazed and totally happy. I bend down and pick up a blueberry that's rolled between my feet. When we were arranging fruit into the solar system, this was my moon. I hold the slightly squished berry between my fingers.

If I can do this, with children, their parents and even Ed King watching me, then maybe I can stand up and do my speech at the NASA competition. And if I can do my speech, then maybe Houston isn't totally out of my reach ...

'So –' Ed says, turning to me.

'Come *on*!' says George, pulling at his arm. 'Don't talk to her. I want to see the telescope.'

'Go with Mum,' Ed says, pushing him away. 'I'll be there in a bit.'

I start packing the rest of the fruit away while Grandad gathers up the toilet roll.

'You're keeping this?' asks Ed, holding up the grapefruit.

'If it's not bashed,' I say, not quite able to meet his eye. The science centre has paid for the props, but I don't think they'll mind if I take them home to make smoothies for me and Elsa.

For a few minutes, we pack up in silence. Even though I've been talking non-stop for an hour, I don't know what to say now it's just me and Ed. This is starting to feel like school.

'Sorry about suddenly appearing like that.' Ed breaks the silence. 'George wanted me to volunteer and it's easier to go along with what he wants. You didn't look very pleased to see me.'

'I was surprised. That's all.'

He helps me arrange the watermelon so it doesn't squash the other fruit. 'Right at the start I didn't realise it was you,' he says. 'At school, you're so quiet and serious ... plus you don't wear a wig.'

I snatch the wig off my head – I'd actually forgotten I was wearing it. For a moment, I try to imagine being like that at school, just going to French on Monday morning and chatting to whoever is waiting outside the room, telling them what I did at the weekend ... It just seems impossible.

Harriet seemed so much better at talking to people that I let her get on with it. She was a science geek like me, but she knew about other things too, about music, TV and clothes. She could talk to me about moon phases, then turn around and talk to someone else about Ed Sheeran, just like that ... But it's not just because I'm out of practice that I don't talk. Honestly, I don't think people want to hear what I've got to say. That's why what I've just done has given me such a massive buzz. A buzz that I don't want to go away.

I make myself look at Ed. 'Maybe I should try to be less serious at school,' I say. 'Do you think I should roll toilet paper down the corridor and arrange fruit on it?'

He laughs. 'Maybe.'

'Do you want a grape?' I hold out the bag to him.

'OK,' he says.

We stand there eating grapes until I realise that it's my turn to speak. 'So ... Why did you come today?'

Ed shrugs. 'It's my brother's birthday so Mum said I had to come as a treat for him ...' He trails off and stares into the corner of the tent. 'Sorry,' he says, 'but I think someone's left a baby behind. It's playing with plums.'

I look over and see Elsa mushing two plums together. 'Don't worry,' I say. 'I washed them.'

'Yeah, but –'

'And she's my baby.'

Ed's eyes widen. 'She's *your* baby?'

My cheeks flush. 'I mean, not mine, obviously, but related to me. We share DNA. Fifty per cent from the mother, *our* mother. We've got different dads.'

Ed looks at me. 'You mean she's your sister.'

'Yes.'

We watch as Elsa abandons the plums and grabs the edge of a table. It tips forward and one of the bags of flour lands next to her, spilling over the grass. Elsa shrieks and plunges both hands into it.

'Oh!' I run over and start scooping the flour back into the bag.

Ed helps me. 'Is she all right with that?' I look up and see that Elsa's turned her attention to one of the eggs we were using earlier. She's trying to put the whole thing in her mouth.

'Yeah … Or do you think she could choke on it?'

He shakes his head. 'Too big.'

'I think it's one of the hard-boiled ones.'

I put the flour back on the table and try to wipe myself down.

'So what's good here?' Ed asks, looking out of the tent.

'Everything,' I say. 'The Thompson telescope is one of the largest in the world and the floor rises up when you press a button. Oh, and I love the spark disc where you can move electricity with your fingertips.' I spread my fingers wide to show him what I mean, then cross my arms. I was getting carried away. I need to remember exactly who I'm talking to.

'Can you show me?' he asks.

I stare at him, trying to work out if he's joking, but he just stands there, a blank look on his face, waiting for me to answer.

'OK,' I say. 'I suppose I can tidy up later.' I walk towards the exit. 'We can start in the light and colour room.'

'Aren't you forgetting something?' Ed says.

'Oh, oops!' I run back and pick Elsa up and she starts slamming the boiled egg into the side of my head. 'See,' I say. 'Definitely hard-boiled.'

That evening an amazing thing happens: I put Elsa in her cot and she falls asleep. No screaming, no tramping over the Downs, no astronomy lessons delivered with a gentle sway. She simply closes her eyes and sleeps.

She must be exhausted from being dragged around the science centre. I showed Ed nearly everything. I thought he'd just look around, but straight away he started freezing crystals and spinning planets. I know he said I was different to how I was at school, but he was different too. It was just small things, like his smile. At school, he does this half-smile, with one eyebrow raised, but when he twisted the dial and heard the squeak of the hidden sound wave he did a proper smile and both sides of his mouth shot up. And I noticed that he bites his nails … I've been sitting next to him for years, but I've never noticed that before.

I hover outside Mum's door until I'm sure Elsa's asleep, then I drift round the flat, doing all the things I've not been able to do during the week. I get some washing-up done, start the washing machine and finally get the paddling pool out from behind the sofa and put it away. As I'm trying to force it back into its box, I think about what Ed said when he realised he had to go and find his mum: 'Thanks for the science lesson, Meg, it was electrifying.'

I shove the paddling pool box to the back of the cupboard.

Electrifying? What does that even mean?

I go into my room, open the window, and flop down

on my bed. I don't turn on the light. Instead, I lie in the dark and stare up at the perfect semicircle of the moon. Was Ed saying hanging out with me was good? Or was he talking about the electric shock? Maybe he was just being sarcastic … Who knows.

A sudden breeze from the window makes the planets on my mobile spin. I raise my finger – the one Ed touched – and with it, I trace the outline of the moon. What I do know is that, right now, I can still hear the laughter from the children when the melon landed in the flour and I can still feel the tingle from when my finger touched Ed's.

What I do know is that right now, I feel alive.

TWENTY-SEVEN

Grandad decides to cook us Sunday lunch, or rather he shoves a couple of jacket potatoes in the microwave and opens a tin of beans. This suits me. I much prefer eating canned food when I'm at Grandad's. He has too much furry stuff growing in his fridge.

After we've eaten, Elsa lies on the floor scrunching up the newspaper while I try out my presentation on Grandad. I'm still filled with confidence from the Cool Cosmos workshop and I want to make the most of it before it slips away from me again.

Grandad sits on the sofa, arms folded, and I stand in front of him holding my speech cards. I read each one in turn and Grandad listens intently as I describe in detail the biomolecules required to start life on a planet, the pros and cons of G- and K-type stars, and how it's possible to photograph exoplanets. Every now and then, he calls out, 'Eye contact, Meg, eye contact!' and I force my eyes to shoot up to meet his for a moment before going back to the cards.

By the time I get to the end, I'm hot and flustered, but I did it and I feel a surge of triumph as I look at Grandad. 'What do you think?'

'Hmmm,' he says, tapping his lip with his finger.

'*Hmmm?*' I say, and all my triumph trickles away from me. It took *weeks* to write the speech and it's complex and detailed and basically as good as I can get it. I know the delivery wasn't perfect but that's the best I've read it yet, and anyhow, I thought Grandad would see through *how* I was speaking and still love what I was actually saying. 'What's wrong with it?'

'Well, you're reading it too fast. It's supposed to take five minutes but you galloped through it in three.'

I nod. 'So I just need to go slower?'

'And speak up; put a bit more emotion into your voice.' He smiles encouragingly. 'Why don't you try it again?'

I go back to my first card. This time, as I read I force myself to slow down and leave proper gaps between each sentence. I try to make my voice animated and I even manage to maintain eye contact for a few seconds. 'Better?' I say after I've read the last card.

'Definitely,' he says, nodding, but then he frowns and drums his fingers on his mug of coffee. 'I still think you need to add something. A bit of passion and pizazz!'

I groan and flop down on the sofa next to him. '*Passion* and *pizazz*? Grandad, I can't do that!'

'Well, you managed it yesterday when you were Mega Knickers. You were on fire. Nothing could stop you!'

I shake my head. 'Yesterday was different.'

'Why?'

'I don't know. I had a costume on ... I was talking to children.'

'Hey, I've still got the costume!'

I laugh. 'No way am I doing this in a wig.'

Grandad thinks for a moment. 'So why was it so much easier talking to the children?'

I shrug. 'I don't know.' I think back to how I felt yesterday when all the little kids were staring up at me. 'I suppose I didn't feel like they were judging me, and if they did think I was weird, that was OK because to kids weird is good.'

'Meg, you are *not* weird.' He says each word clearly, like he's talking to a child.

I turn and look at him. 'Grandad, experience has shown me that when I speak, people at school think I'm weird.'

'And that is *exactly* the problem with your speech!' He slaps his hand down on the sofa to emphasise his point. 'What you see as "weird" – your passion and curiosity – I see as wonderful. Any brainy teenager who wants to win a holiday could have said what you just said … Meg, when you were five, you spilt water on a picture you were drawing. You noticed that all the colours in the paints separated so you abandoned your drawing and spent the next hour dripping water on every colour you had, working out what inks made up each colour.'

'Totally. Weird.'

He shakes his head. 'No, *curious*. You had just discovered chromatography. It was a big moment for you.' I can't look convinced, because he carries on. 'For your tenth birthday you asked me for a subscription to *New Scientist* magazine. Meg, you called your first hamster *Heisenberg* …' He frowns. 'Why did you call it Heisenberg?'

'I couldn't decide what to call him and Heisenberg developed the uncertainty principle in quantum mechanics.'

He throws his hands in the air. 'Exactly!'

'You let Heisenberg escape when you were looking after him and he crawled up the back of the dishwasher and got electrocuted.'

'I know, and I'm sorry I did that, but my point is, Meg, your speech is supposed to be about what space means to you, and *you*,' he pauses here to point at me, 'are currently missing from your speech.'

I feel a lump form in my throat. I knew my speech wasn't perfect, but I thought it was just a matter of practising it. Now Grandad's suggesting the whole thing is wrong. Down by my feet, Elsa starts to pull herself up on my legs. I hold on to her to keep her steady. 'Just say my speech is rubbish,' I say with a laugh.

'It's not rubbish,' he says. 'It's ... safe.'

'Safe rubbish.'

'You've got plenty of time to work on it.'

For a moment, I feel like dropping the cards on the floor (Grandad doesn't have a bin; the floor is his bin) and forgetting about the competition. But I know I can't do that. Yes, I want to go to Houston, but this competition means so much more to me than a free holiday. I've read enough autobiographies to know that people who become astronauts have pushed themselves beyond what they believed they were capable of doing, and they *never* gave up. If I give up on doing this speech, then I'm basically giving up on my dream.

'Maybe I could tweak it,' I say, scooping Elsa on to my lap. 'Explain why I'm so fascinated by Alpha Centauri B.'

'That would be brilliant!' he says, then he drains his cup of coffee. 'Now, I'm going to fire up the hot tub.'

Grandad's 'hot tub' is a rusty old bathtub in the garden that he heats with a bonfire. I don't want Elsa going anywhere near it. I don't really want Grandad going anywhere near it, either.

'I'll take Elsa home,' I say. 'If she goes to sleep I'll take another look at my speech.'

Grandad waves us off at the door, a box of matches and some lighter fluid under his arm. 'Hey,' he calls after me, 'why not add a flour mountain?'

'Not really relevant, Grandad.'

He looks disappointed. 'Egg in a bottle?'

Back at the flat, I take a look at the laminated mission plan I made with Grandad. 'Just over a week until Mummy's home,' I tell Elsa, as I cross off this morning.

'Mamama,' she says, banging her hands on Pongo's belly like he's a drum.

I stare at today's square: Sunday 15th March. Suddenly, I get the feeling I've forgotten something … Something important … And then I remember: I'm supposed to be at Fusciardi's!

It's nearly three. Is Rose already sitting there, looking up expectantly each time someone walks past?

I shake some bricks out in front of Elsa and start to build her a tower. Rose isn't my problem. Elsa's my problem. My speech is my problem. Grandad sitting on top of a bonfire in his Speedos is my problem!

Elsa's so excited by the pig I've popped up at the top of her tower that her eyes light up and her fingers spread out like starfish.

Oh, God … I bet that's exactly what Rose is doing right now! I've seen her do it when the biscuits come out.

The image is too much for me, and with a sigh I get to my feet. 'Come on, Elsa,' I say, picking her up. 'Let's go to Fusciardi's.'

TWENTY-EIGHT

'**M**eg,' calls Rose, 'over here!' Just like she promised, she's saved us a table outside and she's even arranged four chairs in a semicircle facing the sea. 'Hey, you've brought a baby!'

'This is my sister, Elsa,' I say, then I stand there awkwardly, Pongo tugging at the lead and trying to get at a seagull. Now that I'm here, I'm not sure what to do next. Hanging out with friends in cafes isn't something I get up to on a regular basis.

'You sit here,' says Rose, pulling out a chair next to her, 'and then you can squeeze the pushchair in between us.'

While I tie Pongo's lead to a chair, Elsa and Rose gaze at each other, wide-eyed, like two bush babies having a stare off. Then Rose sighs deeply. 'I can't *wait* to have a baby.'

'Seriously?' I look at Elsa. 'Are you sure?'

'And a dog. I'd love to have a dog and a baby.'

I'm tempted to walk off and make her dreams come true, just for a few hours, but that would be too cruel. 'They're both pretty annoying,' I say. 'Especially this one.' I point at Elsa. 'She bites.'

'I think she's absolutely beautiful.'

'Rose, she has *scabs* in her hair!' I bend over the pushchair and part Elsa's fluffy hair so she can get a good look at her cradle cap. 'And have you noticed all the dried snot round her nose? I don't know how she got the glitter stuck in it.'

'It makes her look like a fairy,' says Rose, and her fingers wriggle in Elsa's direction. 'A beautiful little sparkly fairy!'

Then I realise what she's itching to do. 'You can hold her if you want.'

Immediately, Rose whips Elsa out of the pushchair and up on to her lap. She buries her nose in her hair – clearly she isn't bothered by the scabs. 'She smells of babies,' Rose sighs, 'the best smell in the world.'

'If you say so.' I look around. 'So, is it just us?' Part of me sort of hopes it is. I'm getting used to our Biscuit Club now, but meeting up out of school is a whole new level of sociability for me.

'No. Annie's over there on that bench.' I follow her eyes and see Annie sitting with a couple of teenagers. They both look older than her and they're trying to knock a can over with stones.

'I guess those are her real friends,' I say.

Rose nods. 'I don't know where Jackson is.'

Annie sees me watching and waves.

'*Does you want ice cream?*' Rose says in a weird voice. '*Does you?*' I turn round and realise she's talking to Elsa. 'Is she allowed ice cream?' she asks.

'I don't know …' I try to remember if I've seen Mum give her any. 'I guess so.'

'I'll go and get some.' Rose passes Elsa back to me. 'What do you want?'

I scan through the prices on the menu. 'I'll have a glass of milk,' I say, ignoring the Oreo milkshake and caramel hot chocolate.

'Is that all?'

'Yes, thanks.' I hand her the money.

While Rose is inside, Elsa and I take in the view. The sea is calm, barely rippling, and the sky's a hazy blue. It must be the warmest day we've had this year and the sun is almost hot on my face. There are even some children screaming as they run in and out of the sea. Suddenly, I think, *Suncream*, and I take out the bottle that I grabbed

157

before I left the house. I squirt a blob in my hands and try to rub it into Elsa's face. She starts to wriggle and scream and I have to trap her between my legs to keep her still.

'What are you rubbing on her?' I look up to see Annie coming over in her wheelchair. 'Acid?'

'Factor fifty,' I say, holding up the bottle. 'I don't think she likes it.'

'You don't say.' She pulls herself in close to the table, rests her chin in her hands and watches as I attempt to rub the cream into a squealing Elsa. 'I didn't think you'd come,' she says after a moment.

I look up at her. 'I didn't think you'd come either.' I finish with the suntan lotion and drop it back in my bag. My hands are all greasy so I rub them on Elsa's chubby arms.

She shrugs. 'I was down here anyway.' She's wearing black dungarees and a tight purple top. Hanging round her neck is a necklace that says, 'POW!'

'So is this the half-sister?' she says.

'Her name's Elsa.'

'And that revolting object is?'

'Pongo, my dog.'

'He looks evil,' she says, running her hands through his coat. 'I love him.'

At this moment, Rose returns with a heaving tray.

'I got you both ice cream too,' she says shyly, 'and milk-shakes.' Annie and I stare as she places elaborate sundaes in front of us.

Annie takes a cocktail umbrella out of hers and licks chocolate sauce off it. 'God, Rose. This must have cost a bomb!'

Just as I'm wondering how I can possibly afford to pay Rose back, she says, 'It doesn't matter. I used my birthday money.'

'When was your birthday?' I say.

'Oh,' she shrugs, 'today.'

Annie and I glance at each other. I am so glad I decided to come.

'Thanks, Rose.' Annie takes her long spoon and plunges it into the layers of chocolate sauce, ice cream and brownie. 'That was a really kind thing to do.' Then she looks up and smiles at Rose. It's quite a shy smile, and with the sun shining on her dark hair and her pale eyes glittering, she suddenly looks like a beautiful alien.

Elsa decides not to bother with a spoon, or even her fingers. Instead, she just buries her face into her scoop of vanilla ice cream, like Pongo gobbling up his dog food. When she comes up for air, she's got ice cream smeared across her face and hundreds and thousands stuck to her eyelashes.

'Elsa!' I say, pulling out the baby wipes.

'Leave her,' says Annie, grabbing my arm. 'She looks amazing!' Then she dips her finger in Elsa's melty ice cream and daps hundreds and thousands on her own eyelashes, making Elsa scream with delight.

Just then, we hear a rumbling noise, and it's getting louder. A group of teenagers on skateboards are moving towards us along the prom, weaving in and out of pensioners and children. At the head of the pack is Jackson. When they get to our table, Jackson jumps off his skateboard, flips it up with his toe and catches it with one hand. 'Ladies,' he says, 'I'm here!'

'I got you an ice cream!' blurts out Rose.

'Nice.' He turns back to his friends. 'I'll meet you later under the pier,' he says, and their skateboards slam down and they move off like a shoal of fish. He sits down and starts scooping up chunks of ice-cream-soaked brownie.

Jackson seems totally uninterested in the fact that I've turned up with a baby and a dog, or maybe he's just distracted by all the free stuff he's been given. He takes another mouthful of ice cream then wipes his mouth on the back of his hand and looks round at us. 'I just did something amazing,' he says.

Turns out Jackson's amazing thing was skimming a stone six times, but his vivid recreation using sugar cubes helps break the ice. Next, Rose shows us the opal necklace she got for her birthday and then Annie describes a film she watched last night about useless vampires. 'So what have you been up to?' she says, turning to me. 'Except for looking after thingy here.' I'm not sure if she's talking about Elsa or Pongo.

I find myself telling them about yesterday at the science centre, and because they like the bit about Grandad running off at the start, I mention that Ed was my surprise volunteer.

'Ed King was at a kids' science show?' says Jackson, laughing. 'I just saw him in town. He never told me.'

'And did the king of Year Ten deign to speak to you?' asks Annie. 'Was he doing this?' She raises one eyebrow and does an uncanny impression of Ed's wry smile.

I shake my head. 'No. He was being … nice. I think he enjoyed it.'

Annie stares at me.

'What?' I say.

'Bit defensive,' she says, smiling.

Rose leans forward and says in a quiet voice, 'OK, so don't turn round, but I can see Ed and Bella *right now*, and they're walking towards us!'

TWENTY-NINE

'What?' I bang my milkshake glass down, and then, of course, we all turn round and watch as Ed and Bella walk towards the cafe. Bella's arm is looped through Ed's and she's whispering in his ear. I feel my cheeks start to burn. I can't meet Ed here, not in front of everyone! After all the balloon rubbing and finger touching that went on yesterday, I knew it was going to be a bit strange when I saw him again next, but I thought we'd be in school, not sitting outside a cafe with an audience!

'Oh yeah,' says Jackson. 'When I told them I was meeting you in Fusciardi's, Bella said she wanted to come and get an iced coffee.'

'Why didn't you tell us?!' I say.

Jackson shrugs. 'Didn't think it was important.'

Of course Jackson wouldn't think it was important. He's friends with just about everyone in school, from

Year Seven to Year Eleven. Even the teachers high five him in the corridor. Jackson wouldn't understand that for me this is a pretty awkward social situation because, for him, awkward social situations don't exist; his life is simply one long awesome social situation!

For a moment, I consider bunging Elsa back in her pushchair and running off in the opposite direction, but Bella and Ed are approaching so quickly there's just no time. Instead I stare at my ice cream until they are standing right in front of us and I have no choice but to look up. Ed's carrying a load of shopping bags and from the names on the sides I'm guessing they're Bella's.

'Hello,' Bella says. 'What are you lot up to?'

'Eating ice cream,' says Rose.

'I can see that.' Bella's eyes flick from the sundae glasses spread across the table to Annie's speckled eyelashes.

Jackson and Ed share a quick, 'All right,' then we all fall silent. Elsa wriggles on my lap and makes a grab for the sugar lumps. Annie smiles and shakes her head. This is so embarrassing. Why did I have to share all that stuff about the Cool Cosmos workshop? Moments ago I was talking about how 'nice' Ed was and boasting about our fun afternoon, and now here we are, face to face … ignoring each other!

163

'Who's that?' says Bella, pointing at Elsa.

'My sister.'

'Really? You two look totally different.' She shrugs, and turns towards the cafe. 'I'm getting a drink. I'll meet you out here, Woody.'

'No, I'm coming with you,' says Ed, then he gives me a lightning-quick wave, says, 'Bye!', and follows Bella into the cafe.

'Well that was *weird*,' says Annie.

Jackson looks at me and laughs. 'I think he's stalking you, mate. I'd get a restraining order taken out.'

'Seriously, is he Bella's slave?' asks Annie. 'He's carrying her bags for her!'

'He's just being kind,' protests Rose, but they don't get to say another word about Ed King because just then Pongo spots a passing cyclist and goes crazy. If there's one thing Pongo hates, it's moving bikes.

'Shut up, Pongo,' I say, but he keeps tugging at his lead and barking, desperate to get at those spinning wheels. 'Sorry,' I say to the people sitting around us. His bark is so loud that everyone's staring, even the people inside the cafe … even, I guess, Ed and Bella.

'He is going *mental*,' says Jackson.

I try to grab Pongo's collar, but he darts out of my reach, and then there's a clatter of metal against concrete as the chair he's tied to flips over. 'Pongo!' I yell, but he's already dashing after the cyclist, dragging the metal chair along behind him.

A waitress bursts out of the cafe. 'That's our chair!'

Jackson grabs his skateboard. 'I'll get it!' he says, pushing himself off.

'I'm so sorry,' I say to the waitress, dumping Elsa on Rose's lap. Then I run after Pongo as well.

Up ahead, I can see him causing mayhem.

The curving prom is packed with people enjoying the sun. It's almost like a perfect scene on a postcard – complete with ice cream, chips and buckets and spades – only there's a dog tearing through the middle of the scene, scattering holidaymakers in all directions.

'Pongo!' I shout, as an old lady screams and her husband makes a grab for the chair. 'Pongo, *stop*!' But he totally ignores me and I watch as he bounds along, head held high, clearly loving his run along the seafront … even if he is being slightly held back by the chair tied to his neck.

'Stop that dog!' Jackson calls, shooting along on his skateboard and making full use of the path Pongo's cleared for him. 'He's a thief!'

Suddenly, Pongo swerves up some stairs – he seems to have forgotten about chasing the cyclist – and the chair gets wedged between a bin and the wall. I hear a yelp, and by the time Jackson and I get there, Pongo's lying in the sun with his tongue hanging out.

Jackson leans on his skateboard, laughing and trying to get his breath back.

'You are a bad dog!' I say, as I untie his lead from the chair. 'A *very* bad dog!'

Rose appears next to us. 'No he's not,' she says ruffling his coat. 'He's a little cutie!'

'Rose,' I say, 'he's not a cutie, he's a *baddie* … And what have you done with Elsa?'

'Annie's got her,' she says, throwing her arms round Pongo's neck like he's some sort of hero.

We make our way back to Fusciardi's, Jackson carrying the chair and Rose holding Jackson's skateboard. 'Sorry,' I mutter, each time anyone gives me or Pongo a dirty look.

As we get near to the cafe, Rose nudges me and says, 'Look.' Sitting on a bench, their hands wrapped round their drinks, are Ed and Bella. It's almost like they're lying in wait for us.

'We got him!' Jackson says, holding the chair triumphantly above his head.

'Congratulations,' says Bella, then she turns and whispers something in Ed's ear.

He frowns and shakes his head, but after another look from her, he calls out, 'Glad you got your dog!'

For some reason, this makes Bella collapse with laughter. There's something about her laugh, how helpless it is, and how she's looking at me at the same time, that makes me wonder if Ed's told her about yesterday.

I feel my cheeks burn and I start to walk faster, tugging Pongo along behind me, and then I hear Bella's voice, rising loud and clear above the seagulls and the waves, saying, '*Sooo* embarrassing!'

I'm not quite sure if she's talking about me or Pongo, and I'm not hanging around to find out. She right. That was *sooo embarrassing* and the only thing that can make me feel better right now is a huge glass packed full of ice cream, cake and cream.

We find Elsa slumped on Annie's lap, chewing a wafer and staring at the sea. Annie's arms are wrapped round her waist. 'I like her,' she says. 'She doesn't talk and she smells kind of milky.'

'Doesn't she!' says Rose.

Elsa looks sleepy so I leave her with Annie and sit down, only this time I twist Pongo's lead several times round my wrist. We all go back to our melting sundaes.

After a moment, Rose says, 'Did you see that lady's face? She went purple!'

'Pongo made her drop her chips,' I say.

'She shouted, "Yobbo!" after you,' says Rose.

'I've never been called a yobbo before,' I say.

'I have,' says Jackson, 'loads of times,' and for some reason this makes us burst out laughing. Elsa jiggles up and down on Annie's lap and then she starts laughing too.

'Oh no,' says Annie, 'I just realised something.'

'What?' says Jackson.

'Look at us.' She shakes her head. 'We've only gone and *socially connected*. Mr Curtis is going to be unbearable.'

'To Biscuit Club!' says Jackson, raising his milkshake glass. Rose and I join him and we chink glasses in the middle of the table.

'No way,' says Annie, shaking her head again. 'Absolutely no way.'

When Elsa and I get home, I do my usual checks and look at my texts, emails and Facebook. There's nothing from Mum, but I do have a friend request, from Annie.

I'm not Facebook friends with anyone from school. If I accept, then Annie will see that most of my 'friends' are telescopes or space agencies, and she'll see the hundreds of moon photos I've shared. But then I realise that I'll see what she loves too and I think I'd like to know that. Before I can change my mind, I click accept.

So now Annie and I are friends. It's official.

She sends me my first message while I'm feeding Elsa

pasta shapes. She posts a photo on my timeline of a man's hairy bum. Below it she's written: *Thought you'd like to add this to your moon collection.* I stare at the picture wondering what the Sussex Stargazers will make of it. Suddenly I get another message: *Let me know if you want to see a black hole, you space freak. X Annie*

I'm smiling when I look up to see Elsa casually flip her bowl of pasta on to the floor. She hangs her head over the side of her high chair and watches as Pongo bounces around, gobbling it up.

'That's annoying,' I say. 'I haven't got any more left so now you're going to have to sit there while I make you some toast.'

'Da?' says Elsa, holding out a single pasta spiral to me. I reach out for it, but just before I can take it, she lets it drop to the floor then laughs like mad. I feel the usual prickle of annoyance, but then something new happens. I pick up the piece of pasta and hold it out to her. As her hand is reaching for it, I let it slip through my fingers.

'Whoops!' I say.

Elsa's head falls back and she laughs so hard that it's impossible not to join in. Then I realise that the prickle has faded away to nothing.

It's amazing what a positive effect a hairy bum can have on your mood.

THIRTY

Back at school, Ed and I don't talk about Saturday, and we certainly don't share any lightning-quick waves. The first time I see him is in maths and he arrives after the lesson has started. A paranoid part of me wonders if he's done this on purpose, but he doesn't do anything else to suggest he's avoiding me. In fact, it's like the hair rubbing and electric shock never happened. Two minutes into the lesson, he leans towards me and whispers, 'Got a pen?' and that's it. Everything's back to normal, with Ed checking his score against mine in an equations test and casually asking if I'm ready to be 'totally destroyed' in the NASA competition as we leave the room.

I'm actually more nervous about going to science and seeing Bella, and discovering if Ed's told her about the Cool Cosmos show. But it's business as usual and as the lesson goes on, and Bella squabbles with Raj about a calculator and calls me a 'nerdasaurus' for owning a pen with a spirit level, I realise Ed *can't* have told her about Saturday.

And I'm relieved, of course I am – if Ed had told her everything I'd done, Bella would have destroyed me – but I'm also left feeling a bit flat. I thought that something changed on Saturday, and that the way Ed and I had laughed and talked as we went round the science centre would transfer to school in some way. But it looks like I got that wrong: Bella and Raj are arguing, Ed's rolling his eyes and joining in occasionally, and I'm just sitting here in silence, like I'm invisible.

Nothing's changed at all.

THIRTY-ONE

'**D**on't talk to me, Meg,' says Ms Edgecombe. 'I need to concentrate on not killing anyone.'

It's the next day and I'm sitting at the front of the minibus beside Ms Edgecombe as she drives us to Sussex University. Not talking suits me as it gives me time to text Grandad to remind him to pick up Elsa. It also means I get to stare out of the window, watch the countryside fly past, and think about Little Acorns, or, more precisely, Dawn.

I'm not sure if I'm being paranoid, but this morning Dawn started asking me questions about Mum. It felt like she was trying to catch me out. 'Did you get Elsa's bag ready today?' she asked. When I told her that I put everything in and then Mum checked it, she narrowed her eyes and said, '*Riiight*,' really slowly. Then she asked why Mum had stopped putting in organic baby wipes. 'Too expensive,' I said, deciding to stick to the truth.

I'm glad Grandad's picking Elsa up this afternoon. He's a much better liar than me.

Soon we're turning off the dual carriageway and I see a jumble of buildings squeezed into a gap in the hills. 'Here we are,' says Ms Edgecombe.

'It's huge,' I say. The university looks like a small town. It even has road signs directing traffic to the different departments.

'First time you've ever been here?'

I nod, staring at the looming concrete buildings. 'First time I've been to any university.'

She smiles. 'I think you'll like it, Meg.'

Once we've parked, Miss leads us across the campus and I try to take in every detail: the sweeping lawns, the groups of students, the church that's shaped like a circus tent. We pass a girl sitting on a wall, totally absorbed in a book. She's all alone, but she doesn't stand out or seem at all bothered. In fact, as I look around I see there are loads of students on their own.

I feel more at home at this huge university than I do at school.

A PhD student called Jolina meets us in the reception area and takes us to a door secured with a keypad and plastered with *WARNING* and *DANGER* signs. She explains that she's going to give us a tour of a research lab. 'Is anyone here interested in quantum mechanics?' she asks. 'Because that's my passion.'

Jolina is young, she's wearing skinny jeans, she's got a tattoo of a flying swan on the inside of her wrist … and her passion is quantum mechanics. I put my hand up, suddenly not caring that everyone has turned to stare at me. 'I love quantum mechanics,' I say.

Jolina smiles. 'Good,' she says, 'then you'll like it in here, because we're trying to build the world's first quantum computer.'

The lab is quite simply the most amazing place I've ever been in my life.

It's dark and crammed with lasers, computers and a mass of wires that twist across the ceiling and walls. Heavy plastic curtains divide the room into sections and a deep sucking noise echoes constantly throughout the lab.

'That's cooling the ions to minus two hundred and sixty degrees,' says Jolina, raising her voice to be heard over the machine. 'I don't really notice the sound now.'

She stops by a computer and points at the screen. 'This is an atom I isolated this morning.' She says this casually, like she's talking about a cup of tea she made.

We lean forward and stare at the single fuzzy dot. Ms Edgecombe laughs. 'I never thought I'd *see* an atom!'

'Does anyone know how small this little thing actually is?' asks Jolina. No one speaks so she looks straight at me, the girl who 'loves' quantum mechanics. 'Do you know?'

I do, sort of. And because I feel like we're in my world now, where being fascinated by quantum mechanics is normal, I clear my throat and start to talk. 'There are three thousand million, million, million molecules in a drop of water,' I say, 'and each one of those molecules contains three atoms.' Jolina nods so I carry on. 'If you know there are around five sextillion atoms in a drop of water, you can almost understand how tiny that atom is.'

Jolina says, 'Beautifully put,' and her smile gives me the confidence to carry on.

'It's amazing,' I say, nodding at the miraculous dot, 'because *that* is basically what every single thing in the universe is made of.'

Someone leans close to me. I smell lemon and vanilla. 'Calm down, *Mega Knickers*,' Bella whispers in my ear.

An icy feeling sweeps through me and all my excitement vanishes. Ed tuts, which only makes Bella laugh and say, '*What?*'

Jolina's started to talk about lasers, but I can't concentrate on what she's saying, and it's not just because Bella made me feel stupid. Knowing that Ed has told Bella all about the workshop, and that they must have been laughing about me behind my back, makes me feel as alone as that buzzing atom on the screen.

I fall to the back of the group, and watch the rest of the tour in silence. At the end, when Jolina says, 'Does anyone know how many quantum numbers are needed to describe the properties of an electron in an atom?' I look away.

'Two?' says Ed.

Four, I think. *It's four.*

'No,' says Jolina. 'There are four.'

THIRTY-TWO

When the tour is over, we're taken to a lab where we start defusing alien bombs and illuminating streams of water drops with a strobe. The teacher tells me I'm 'a natural' and even hands me a prospectus for the university. I hold the brochure on my lap as Ms Edgecombe dismisses everyone for lunch. 'Make sure you're back here in an hour,' she says.

Once everyone else has gone, I go out into the corridor. I find Ed leaning on the wall opposite, waiting for me. He stands up. 'Ready to work on our presentations?' he asks.

I look at him. I'd forgotten all about that. Right now, Ed doesn't look like someone who would ever allow a balloon to be stuck to his hair. He just looks like the tall, good-looking boy who for years has either ignored me or tried to beat me, depending on what's suited him best.

I shrug. 'OK.'

'So where shall we go?'

'Wherever.' I know I sound rude, but I don't care. 'Here?' I say.

'Here? In this corridor?' He laughs. 'Let's go to that cafe we walked past.'

'Fine,' I say, and I follow him outside, across the lawn and up a flight of stairs.

We stand outside the crowded cafe and students pass us, looking curiously at our uniforms. 'Do you think this is OK?' he says, hanging back.

I look at the prices on the menu. 'It's fine,' I say, pushing open the door. 'Come on.'

After Ed's bought sandwiches and crisps, and I've got a hot chocolate, we find a free table. Even though the cafe's busy, it's strangely quiet because so many of the students are working. I get out the roll I brought from home, my phone and a pad of paper. 'So,' I say, 'do you want to go first? Read through your notes?' I write 'Ed's Presentation' at the top of a piece of paper.

'Was your dog OK?' asks Ed.

I look up. For a moment I don't know what he's talking about. Then I realise he's talking about Pongo's dash along the sea front. 'Oh, yes, he's fine. Have you brought your stuff with you?'

'You had to look after your sister again, didn't you?' I

nod and Ed plays with the wrapper on his sandwich. 'I didn't realise you were friends with Jackson and Annie.'

I look at him. 'We've not got long. We should get on with this.'

He starts to open his sandwiches, then puts the packet down. 'Look, Meg, are you angry with me, or something?'

I feel my cheeks start to go red so I stare out of the window. The whole of the university is stretched out in front of me. I watch a girl and boy kick a football backwards and forward across a road. When I can be sure that I can speak in a normal voice, I say, 'I suppose I didn't like what Bella said.'

'Oh,' he says, 'the Mega Knickers thing.'

'Right. Mega Knickers.' I look back at him. 'I mean, did you tell her everything?'

'About Saturday? Um ...' Now it's his turn to look embarrassed. 'Quite a bit, but I didn't know it was some kind of secret.'

'You didn't think she might *go on* about it?'

He opens his crisps. 'Well, I know she's got a big mouth and she likes making people laugh, but –' he shrugs '– she usually knows when to stop.'

'She *never* stops. She's been saying stuff like that for years and you laugh along with her.'

He sits back in his seat. 'If it bothers you so much, why do you never tell us to shut up?'

'That's easy for *you* to say!'

Something about the way I say this makes him put down his crisps and look up at me. 'What do you mean?'

'Well, you go around school with your friends, laughing at people, and –'

'No we don't!'

I can tell he's getting angry, but I'm angry too. He didn't call me 'Mega Knickers' back in the lab, but he might as well have. 'You laugh at me in science all the time!'

'That's called trying to be nice, Meg. You never speak to us so what are we supposed to do? Just ignore your silent, lurking presence?'

'My *what?*'

A man at the next table turns round to stare at me; Ed leans back and does this smug smile. 'Bella's right about you.'

'Why? What does she say?'

'That you're *uptight*. I told her you're not – or at least you weren't when you were running around that tent throwing things in flour – but at school you never even crack a smile. You need to lighten up, Meg, and ...'

'And do *what?*' I say loudly.

180

'Let your hair down!'

A rush of irritation sweeps through me. 'Yeah? Well, Annie's right about you!'

He raises one eyebrow. 'Go on.'

'She says you look down your nose at everyone and do this all the time –' I raise one eyebrow and attempt to do his one-sided smile. Ed bursts out laughing. '*See?*' I say. 'You're doing it right now!'

'Well, it looks like we're both friends with someone who doesn't know when to be quiet!'

We stare at each other across the table. Ed's chin is slightly raised and I don't think I've ever seen him look this arrogant. I feel so angry with him right now that I don't think I can eat my roll.

I turn away and sip my hot chocolate even though it burns my throat. I hear Ed tear open his crisps.

Then I notice that my phone is vibrating on the table. I snatch it up and see that it's an unknown number. Immediately I think it's someone at the nursery. 'I've got to take this,' I mutter, pushing back my chair and walking out of the cafe.

'Hello?' I say as the door bangs shut behind me.

'Meg?' Mum's familiar voice rings out. 'Is that you, baby?'

THIRTY-THREE

As Mum describes the village she's staying in, I walk away from the cafe. I take a left, then a right, then I keep on going until I'm halfway up a grassy slope.

'The medical centre is very basic, Meg, but the people are wonderful. There are no street lights so you can see thousands of stars at night. You'd love it!'

I sit down with my back against a wall and wait for her to stop.

'They need help so much, sweetheart. I know that I'm making a real difference ...' She pauses for a moment, then says, 'How's Elsa?'

'She's fine.'

'What did she have for breakfast today?' The line is starting to sound crackly. 'Is Dad remembering to put on her eczema cream?'

I think back to this morning. 'She had Weetabix and banana … Hang on. Elsa's got *eczema*?'

'Weetabix and what? I can't hear you, Meg.'

'Banana!' I shout. 'Banana!'

'Did Dad warm the milk?'

I stare at the distant hills. 'Mum, we're not at Grandad's. I decided to look after her at the flat. Grandad's house is such a state and I knew I'd end up looking after him too.'

'So, what, the two of you are on your own each night?' For the first time, I can hear worry in her voice.

'Yes, and we're doing just fine.' I stop talking. My throat hurts. I'm not sure if I can speak without crying. 'I just thought it would be easier this way.'

'You should be staying with Dad.' Mum says this as though somehow this whole situation is my fault.

'No, we shouldn't,' I snap back. 'He falls asleep smoking, Mum. The other day I found his chickens in the street – he'd just gone out on his bike and left everything unlocked.' I've got a hard, angry ache in my chest. 'You should have known Elsa and I couldn't stay with him.'

After a moment, Mum says. 'Well, I bet you're doing brilliantly, Meg. Elsa probably hasn't even noticed I've gone.'

'She has!' My voice comes out loud, like I need her to hear this wherever she is in Myanmar. 'She misses you.'

'Meg, I'll be home in a week. If you could see the work we're doing here, you'd understand why I had to come. They need me.'

We need you, I think, but I don't say it. It's like I don't think she deserves to know. Instead, I say, 'You know I've got the NASA competition next Saturday?'

'I said I'll be back in a week. Look, I'm going to have to go. I'm on someone else's phone.' I can sense her pulling back from me, trying to get further away than she already is. I imagine the sun shining down on her, glittering on her bracelets and I feel so angry that I don't trust myself to speak. 'Thank you for looking after Elsa, but remember your grandad's probably not as hopeless as you think. You can always take her round there if it gets too much for you. Big hugs, my love!'

The line crackles then goes dead.

I thought speaking to Mum would make me feel better, that I might understand why she thought it was OK to just leave us like she did, but I feel even worse than I did before. I shut my eyes and rest my head back against the wall. Somewhere a bird is singing. It's so peaceful here, but my mind is all tangled up. I get that Mum is helping people – when she puts her mind to something she can do amazing things. I should probably feel proud that she's just dropped everything to go and help them.

But I don't feel proud. I feel jealous. Jealous that they've got her and that I haven't. And angry because she found it so easy to leave us.

I've spent so much time wanting to be free from Mum and the chaos she brings into my life, but now it's happened, I feel more tied to her than ever before.

THIRTY-FOUR

'**O**i, Meg!' I open my eyes. At the bottom of the slope, Ed is shading his eyes and looking up at me. 'I've been looking for you everywhere.'

I get up and brush grass off my trousers. I've been sitting here so long my legs have gone dead. 'No one asked you to.'

He gives me an uncertain smile. 'You all right?'

I join him on the path. 'Yep. Just … thinking.'

'About quantum mechanics?'

'Something like that.'

'I've got your bag,' he holds it up, 'and I'm lost. Can you use your superior skills to get us back to the physics department?'

'OK.'

We start walking along a covered walkway. 'So who was that?' says Ed.

'My mum.'

He looks at me curiously. 'You ran off fast.'

'The reception was bad.'

'My mum's always ringing me, but I let it go to voice-mail.' He starts telling me about how his mum gets in touch if he's one minute late from school and that once she got him pulled out of football practice to check he was OK. I let him talk, saying the occasional 'mmm', and at the same time leading us back to the physics department.

'Hang on,' he says as we walk towards the class-room. 'Are you still angry with me? Are you not speaking to me?'

'I'm speaking.'

'Only just. You do realise that we still haven't heard each other do our presentations and the competition is just under two weeks away?'

I stop outside the door to the classroom and shrug. I can't even begin to explain how little I care about the competition right now. 'Stop being so uptight, Ed,' I say. 'You need to let your hair down.'

'God, you're annoying,' he says. 'I think I might have preferred it when you were being all silent and lurking.' Then he turns away from me and walks into the room.

Ms Edgecombe looks up. 'You two are late.'

'Ah, leave them alone, Miss,' says Bella. 'Ed was asking Meg to the dance!'

I freeze in the doorway and all the conversations taking place in the room stop too. Bella's hand flies up to her mouth. 'Sorry!' she says.

As I feel a blush creeping up my cheeks, Ed shakes his head and smiles. 'Seriously, shut up, Bella.'

She bursts out laughing. 'What happened? Did she say no?'

He goes to his seat and throws his bag under the bench. 'Very funny,' he says. 'Finished yet?'

I go over to my desk. Once again, I'm stuck in the middle of one of their jokes: the one about how hilarious it would be if Meg Clark went to the dance with Ed King. Ever since Bella turned up in science with her pink ticket, I've been waiting for her to say something like this. It looks like Ed and I meeting up at lunchtime has given her all the inspiration she needs.

'Meg,' Bella says, 'why don't you want to go out with Ed? Is it because he's not as interesting as that dot in the sky?'

I unzip my pencil case and get out a pen as Ms Edgecombe says, 'Let's get back to work.'

'But Ed's lovely, Miss!'

Across the room, there are giggles and whispers, and I

can feel people staring at my back. Suddenly all the anger I've been feeling towards Mum, and towards Bella and Ed boils up inside me.

I bang down my pen and turn to face them.

Bella looks delighted.

'I would *never* go out with Ed,' I say, jabbing my finger in his direction. 'And even if that "dot" – otherwise known as asteroid TR7768 – hit Earth and wiped out every single human being except Ed, I *still* wouldn't go out with him!'

Bella grins. 'What if the survival of the human race depended on it?'

Behind her, Ed sighs and shakes his head.

'Well, goodbye human race!' I say, and I actually *wave* at her before spinning back round.

There's this moment of silence before everyone collapses with laughter. I stare at my pencil case. It's got the periodic table printed on it so it's a good pencil case to stare at. *Co: cobalt, Ni: nickel, Cu: copper,* I read, but my stupid words are still ringing painfully in my ears. *Otherwise known as asteroid TR7768 ... Goodbye human race?* What was I thinking? Why didn't I just ignore her? This is why I avoid talking: bad things happen when I open my mouth!

Ms Edgecombe puts a worksheet in front of me and

gives my shoulder a squeeze. 'Ed's better than extinction,' she says quietly.

When we get back to school, I'm the first person off the minibus. The last workshop was terrible. Everyone on my table kept asking me if I'd go out with them in the event of an apocalypse and then they moved on to celebrities and then animals – *Meg, what about a really hot woodlouse?* The fact that I was ignoring them didn't put them off. In fact, I'd say it only encouraged them. Bella and Ed were strangely quiet, though, and now I'm worried that they've realised the joke went too far and one of them will try to apologise. I put my head down and walk straight out of the school gates. I just want to forget that this afternoon ever happened.

I find Grandad in the flat giving Elsa the bubbliest bath I've ever seen. 'I've been experimenting,' he says, tipping something pink into the water, 'and you'd be amazed, and possibly horrified, by what makes the best bubbles.'

Elsa smiles at me through a bubble beard. 'Beb … beb!' she says.

'Great,' I say, flopping down on the toilet seat. I'm guessing Grandad doesn't know about Elsa's eczema either.

Grandad looks at me. 'You all right? Did the trip go well?'

'Mum rang.'

Grandad's face lights up. 'How is she?'

'Great. She's having an amazing time.'

'Beb!' shouts Elsa. She's standing up now and reaching for me. 'Beb!'

We look at her. 'I think she's saying your name,' says Grandad.

'Beb,' says Elsa, and I pick her up out of the water. She throws her arms round my neck, soaking my school uniform.

Whatever Grandad put in the bath, it's made her very slippery. 'That's right,' I say, resting my head against her soapy hair. 'I'm Meg.' Then I hold on tight to her, even though she's wriggling to get away.

THIRTY-FIVE

I force myself to go to school the next day. I haven't had a day off school since Year Eight and I'm not going to start now just because I freaked out at some stupid joke. I get a lot of amused looks from people who were on the trip, but I ignore them, hold my head high and walk straight to my first lesson – maths. As soon as I'm seated, I put my head down and start working so I can be totally distracted when Ed turns up.

A few minutes after the lesson has begun, I hear him sit next to me. I keep scribbling numbers as if my life depends on it. Luckily, we're doing a practice exam paper so we're not allowed to talk and at the end of the lesson, Ed's up and out of his seat before I've even put my books away.

I guess he wants to ignore me just as much as I want to ignore him.

It's a relief to get to Biscuit Club – a place where I can be certain I won't run into Bella or Ed. While Mr Curtis is off making our cups of tea, Jackson tells us about some gruesome accident at the skate park. Suddenly, Annie interrupts him and says, 'I want to hear about Meg's trip.' She smiles at me and there's something about her smile, something that makes me wonder what she's heard.

I start to tell them about the research lab and all the amazing things I saw. Then, because they're all watching me and listening, and because somehow just talking about yesterday is making me feel better, I find myself telling them how Bella called me Mega Knickers and about going to the cafe with Ed. 'And then,' I say, 'Ed told me I should let my hair down.'

Annie is outraged on my behalf, just like I want her to be. 'He's so smug,' she says. 'I hate the way he and his mates sort of *roll* round the school with their hands in their pockets, looking for someone to mock.'

'Eurch!' says Jackson, from his beanbag. 'They put their hands in their pockets? What scum! People like that don't deserve to live.'

'Shut up,' snaps Annie. 'You don't get it because you're a hands-in-the-pockets person yourself. In fact, why are you even here? You should be out in the corridors with them right now, *mocking*!'

Jackson laughs. 'Oh, like you don't mock, Annie?'

She doesn't use her words to answer him. She uses a single finger.

'Ed didn't laugh at me,' says Rose. Sometimes, until she speaks, you can almost forget she's sitting there.

'Explain,' says Annie.

'Well, once I was taking a photo of an oily puddle because it had a rainbow in it and Raj said, "Do you think it's unicorn wee?" You know, laughing at me because –'

'You believe in unicorns?' says Annie.

'Exactly. Then Ed said, "I think it's a cool puddle"!' She smiles round at us as if she's just proved Ed's some sort of saint.

'Can I see the photo?' says Jackson, totally missing the point, and Rose pulls out her phone.

Annie turns to me. 'So was that it? Did anything else happen?'

'Just some mind-blowing physics.'

'Right …' she says, narrowing her eyes. 'You sure that was all?'

I pause. I haven't mentioned the whole Ed-date thing. It's just too humiliating to share. But what Bella said about Ed asking me to that dance has been driving me crazy – even for Bella, it was a strange thing to say and kind of came out of nowhere – and I'd love to talk to someone about it. Plus Annie's still got that knowing look on her face. What's the point of keeping quiet if she's already heard about it?

I glance over at Jackson and Rose, to check they're still engrossed in unicorn wee. 'There was one other thing.'

'I knew it!' she says, sitting back and smiling. 'You've got this frown on your face … I mean, a bigger one than usual. So what happened?'

Quickly, I tell her about the whole Ed-dance conversation, describing exactly what Bella said and how Ed just sat there, shaking his head and laughing. And then I tell her what I said about the asteroid wiping out everyone on Earth. I even tell her about my wave.

Annie stares at me. 'Meg, you have *got* to work on your put-downs.'

'I was embarrassed. I said the first thing that came into my head!'

'Obviously.'

'And today has been so bad: Ed won't look at me, people who were on the trip won't stop looking at me, and Bella's just had this smile on her face …' I trail off because Annie's eyes have gone wide.

'You don't think …' she says.

'What?'

'You don't think that Bella could have been serious? Maybe Ed really *was* going to ask you to the dance. Maybe your whole nerd-look gives Ed the hots!'

'What? No!' I shake my head.

'Go to the dance with him! I'm going. We could hang out together and embarrass boys by asking them to dance.'

'*Annie*, Ed didn't ask me to the dance: it was just a joke of Bella's! I've been sitting next to Ed King in lessons for nearly four years and he only speaks to me if he's got something sarcastic or competitive to say.'

'Boys are weird, Meg. One way you know for certain that they like you is if they throw something at you. Has he ever done that?'

I think for a moment. 'Never.'

'Well, does he look at you? You know, like this ...' Annie opens her eyes wide, tilts her head to one side and gazes at me.

I can't help laughing. 'Ed only ever looks at me if he has to, like if he needs to borrow a pen.'

She narrows her eyes. 'How often does he do that?'

'I don't know, a few times a week?'

'Oh my God!' Annie grabs my arm and squeezes her green nails into my flesh. 'Ed doesn't need *pens*. He's like you, a stationery perv.'

'What? How do you know that?'

'Because I watch people, Meg, and I see *everything*.' She lowers her voice. 'Rose, for example, only wears make-up on the days that we have Biscuit Club – read into that what you will – and Ed King has two pencil cases: the typical scuzzy boy one he gets out in lessons, with a ruler and a broken pen in it, and a backup that he keeps in his bag that is literally *bulging* with writing implements!'

'So you're saying that every time Ed asks me if he can borrow a pen ...'

'He's using it as an excuse to melt into your super-clever eyes and check out your geek-rack!'

I cross my arms. 'No way. I don't have a geek-rack. I don't have any type of rack!'

'We've all got racks, Meg.'

Just as I'm about to tell her to shut up, my phone starts to vibrate. Mr Curtis is still out of the room so I take it out of my pocket. It's a message from Little Acorns: *Elsa is running a temperature and her nappies are nasty. I've tried to ring home, but your mum's not answering and her mobile's switched off. Please can you or your grandad come and collect Elsa asap. Thanks!*

'What's the matter?' says Annie.

I look up. 'It's my sister. She's ill and the nursery wants me to take her home.'

'Can't your mum do it?'

'No. She's busy. I'll try my grandad.' I ring his house but he doesn't pick up and his mobile goes straight to voicemail. 'No answer,' I say.

'OK, so just tell Mr Curtis when he gets back. He'll let you go if it's an emergency.'

I think about the questions Mr Curtis will ask, how he'll want to speak to my mum to check I'm allowed out of school. The panic that I'm becoming so used to bubbles up inside me, making me feel hot all over. 'No. I can't do that.'

Annie stares at me. 'That frown's come back and it's bigger than ever.'

'Yeah, well … I'm worried.' For a moment, I think about telling Annie everything. Maybe she could make me feel better about Mum, just like she's made me feel better about Bella and Ed … No. I don't really know her and if I tell her; things will only get more complicated than they already are.

Annie's hand lands on my arm again, only this time her fingers don't dig in. 'Relax, Meg. I can get you out of school. It's so easy.'

Five minutes later, Annie's forged note about my ortho-dontist's appointment (*investigative wisdom tooth work*) has been signed off by Mr Curtis and the receptionist.

'Wisdom teeth?' she says. 'Nasty. I imagine you'll be needing tomorrow off as well.'

'Maybe …'

'Off you go then!'

And that's it. I'm walking out of school, a free woman. Well, as free as a fifteen-year-old can feel when she's going to pick up her baby sister with her 'nasty nappies', whatever that means. I walk quickly down the high street, trying not to think about all the work I'm going to miss at school and reminding myself that Mum's back in just five days.

Even though five days feels like six years away right now, I can't help smiling.

Geek-rack. Annie doesn't know what she's talking about …

THIRTY-SIX

'**H**ere she is,' says Dawn, dumping Elsa in my arms.

Usually when I pick Elsa up, she gives me some sort of violent affection like scratching my face or grabbing at my nose, but today she just slumps in my arms and sucks her thumb. I put my hand on her red cheek. It feels dry and far too hot. 'What's wrong with her?'

'She's running a temperature. Your mum will know what to do.' Dawn passes me her bag. 'I'm surprised your mum sent her in because she obviously wasn't right this morning.'

'She ate all her breakfast.'

'She had a temperature,' says Dawn, folding her arms.

'Sorry,' I say, because I think it's what she's waiting for. Then I turn and walk down the path.

'Tell your mum not to send her back until she's totally better.'

'I will!' I call back.

I take Elsa straight home then ring Grandad. This time he answers.

'She's boiling hot,' I say, tucking the phone under my ear and unbuttoning Elsa's cardigan. 'What should I do?'

'When I've got a temperature I have a nip of whisky then go for a dip in the sea,' he says. 'Works every time.' After I point out how spectacularly unhelpful this advice is, he tells me to give her Calpol, adding, 'Babies love the stuff.'

'Yep, we've got some,' I say once I've checked the medicine cupboard.

'Give her a bit of that and she'll be back to normal in an hour. I'll pop round and see how she's doing.'

My first instinct is to put him off, tell him she's fine with me, but Elsa's behaving so strangely that I would quite like to see him, no matter what madness he might bring with him.

Elsa slurps the medicine straight down then I put her in her cot and she curls up on her side and watches me through the bars.

'I'm going to sit on the bed and work, OK?'

She rubs her face on one of her muslin cloths and

201

carries on staring at me so I get out my speech cards and start reading through them, looking for places where I can 'add pizazz' or a bit more Meg ... whatever that means. Every now and then I glance up at Elsa because it's slightly unnerving how quiet she's being.

After an hour, I hear the front door click open and Grandad walks in. He's wearing Lycra shorts and his anorak, which tells me he's taking his bike on the Downs.

'Where's the patient?' he says, going over to Elsa. 'Hello, there!' Elsa flops on her back and smiles up at him. Grandad sits on the end of the bed and puts his hand through the bars so he can stroke her forehead.

'Cup of tea?' I say.

'Go on then. I brought round some cakes.' He passes me a Tupperware box. 'They taste better than they look.'

I open the box and see a crumbly green mess. 'I hope so.'

'They're made from foraged seaweed. Loads of vitamin C in them.'

Grandad's right. They do taste better than they look and while we drink our tea and eat green sludge cake, Grandad suggests various ways I can improve my speech. Basically his suggestions are ideas for costumes, because he thinks every situation in life is improved with fancy dress. I tell him that there's no way I'm dressing up as a star, a planet or an alien, but that I will wear the necklace Mum gave me with the letter 'M' written as binary code.

'It's relevant, but it won't make me look stupid,' I say.

'It won't make you look anything,' he says with a shake of his head. 'No one will even see it.'

We carry on talking about the competition and at some point Elsa falls asleep and starts snoring. It's strange hanging out in Mum's bedroom when she's not here. It feels like she's just in the kitchen or something. Her grey jumper is still draped across the corner of Elsa's cot and her Tinker Bell nightie is poking out from under her pillow. Also, every now and then I get this faint Mum smell – a cross between mint tea and incense.

We've moved on to exciting facts I could add when Grandad suddenly pulls a postcard out of his pocket. 'I got this today,' he says, passing it over. 'It's from Alice. Sounds like she's enjoying herself.'

On the front is a photo of temples rising majestically through the mist. I turn it over. All that is written on the back are the words, *I don't know where I'm going, but I'm on my way! X Alice*

I stare at the words. 'Well, she did know where she was going,' I say. 'She bought a plane ticket, got on a plane and flew to Myanmar.'

Grandad laughs. 'True, but I think she's referring to

her emotional journey rather than the physical one. She's been wanting to get back into nursing for some time. Maybe that's what she means.'

I drop the postcard among the clutter on Mum's bedside table. Grandad sees the look on my face. 'What's the matter?'

I start collecting up all my speech cards and arranging them in order. 'Mum knew how much I wanted to go to Houston. How come we didn't have the money for that, but she could pay the airfare to go to Myanmar?'

'I doubt she's got the money to pay for that either. There'll be a big credit card bill on its way soon. Alice doesn't always think before she acts.'

'Well, maybe she should.'

Grandad looks up at me and frowns. 'Don't be like that, love. I know she's doing her best.'

'If she was doing her best she'd be here, right now, looking after Elsa, and I'd be at school!'

'Meg, when Alice's mum died, I was living –'

'In a tree. I know, Grandad, you've told me loads of times.'

'So Alice came to live with me and we hardly knew each other. I'd been abroad most of her life, popping back to see her every now and then. I did my *best*, but my best was *rubbish*.'

I shake my head. 'You're always making excuses for her.'

'No,' says Grandad. 'I'm just telling you what happened. I'd be the biggest hypocrite in the world if I criticised her for going away for two weeks – I used to go away for months, years!'

'Well … you're here now,' I say quickly, 'and just because you weren't around when she was little, doesn't mean she has to do the same to us. She could try.'

'I think she is trying.'

'Well, maybe she needs to try harder!'

My voice comes out so loud that we both automatically look towards Elsa in her cot to check she hasn't woken up. Grandad reaches out and pats my foot. 'I know,' he says. 'And now you're having to miss school, which you hate. Why don't you go back in now I'm here?'

I shake my head. 'I can't. They think I'm having some sort of tooth operation.'

'Well, Elsa's asleep, so how about I take Pongo for a walk, leave you to catch up with some work?'

And get out of an awkward conversation, I think, but still I nod and say, 'OK, thanks, Grandad.'

Just as he's leaving the room, he stops and drums his fingers on the doorframe. 'I know Alice drives you up the wall, but have you ever wondered what life would be like if she was different?' He raises one finger up in the air and says dramatically, 'One must still have chaos in oneself to be able to give birth to a dancing star!'

Whenever Grandad speaks like this, I know he's quoting someone and he's expecting me to say who it is. I haven't a clue about this one so I take a guess. 'Was that Nietzsche?' If in doubt, I always go with Nietzsche or Galileo.

'Well done!'

'And what you're saying is …'

'The greatest ideas and innovations are often the result of chaos.'

'Yeah, and they're also often the result of going to school and getting good GCSE results instead of sitting around in your mum's bedroom looking after your sister!' I flop back on the bed.

He laughs. 'Well, maybe,' then he shouts for Pongo. 'I hope he's in a hunting mood. I fancy rabbit pie for dinner.'

'He catches more squirrels than rabbits.'

'That'll do,' he says, then he gives Elsa a last stroke on the head and clips on Pongo's lead. 'We'll be back in an hour or so.' Just before he goes, he turns and raises his fist in the air. '*Poyekhali*, Meg!'

Poyekhali. It means 'Let's go' in Russian and it's what Yuri Gagarin said the moment his rocket blasted off from

206

Earth and he became the first human being to visit space. Basically it's Grandad's motto for life; he's got it tattooed on his arm, and so has Mum. I bet she took a look at it when she got on that plane to Myanmar.

Usually I'd shout, '*Poyekhali!*' back, but right now I'm feeling that my family could do with a bit less adventurous spirit. Instead, I say, 'Watch out for badger holes,' and Grandad's punched fist dissolves into a wave.

THIRTY-SEVEN

With Elsa asleep and Pongo out with Grandad, the flat is unusually quiet.

I take advantage of the unexpected free time and have a long bath, then I sit on the floor next to Elsa's cot and start writing an English essay. Every now and then I stick my hand through the bars to feel her forehead. At some point, I get distracted by Facebook. Annie's sent me a picture of a skull-shaped asteroid and her message reads: *I've found something we can both appreciate.*

I go on her page and lose myself looking at her life, or at least the life she wants to share. She's got a lot of friends and I recognise some of them from Sixth Form, and she seems to be into animals, living or dead. She reposts pictures of badly stuffed animals, and there are also films of donkeys wagging their tails and puppies wearing clothes. Oh, and her rats. She might have as many pictures of her rats as I have of moons.

I send her a picture of Kleopatra, an asteroid shaped like a dog's bone. A few minutes later she replies: *OMG! We have so much in common!!!*

That's when I remember Elsa. This time when I rest my hand on her forehead it feels far hotter than before and her cheeks are bright red. I take her temperature and the thermometer reads thirty-nine degrees.

That can't be good. I check a few websites and they all seem to agree that you need to contact a health professional if a baby's temperature goes over forty, but I can't do that. What would a doctor say if they came round here and found us on our own? Before, when Elsa's been ill, Mum's taken her to the out-of-hours surgery at the hospital, but a fifteen-year-old can't turn up with her baby sister with some lame story about her mum's slipped disc.

I try Grandad's mobile but it goes straight to voicemail, and there's no answer at his flat. He said he'd be back 'in an hour or so', but he's already been gone for over two. I stare down at Elsa as I try to decide what to do. She's started making these whimpery noises like she's halfway between being asleep and awake. I put the thermometer on her forehead and this time it reads forty. I can't wait for Grandad – who knows what's distracting him. I'm just going to have to get Elsa's temperature down myself.

I lift Elsa out of her cot and lie her on Mum's bed. Her head flops to one side, but she still doesn't wake up. I take her out of her sleep bag and pull open the poppers on her Babygro. Without touching her, I can feel the heat radiating off her chest.

'Elsa?' I give her shoulder a shake. 'Wake up. I've got some yummy medicine for you.'

Her eyes flutter open, but when she sees me, her face crumples and she starts crying. It's not her usual scream, but something much weaker. I try to squeeze the medicine into her mouth, but she shakes her head and half of it ends up dribbling down her chin.

'Now you're going to be sticky *and* hot,' I say, trying to hide the panic that's building up inside me. I get her to drink some water from a sucky mug, but then she pushes it away, and carries on crying.

'Elsa.' I lie next to her and hold her foot. I don't want to get any closer in case I make her even hotter. 'I know you feel horrible but it's really a brilliant thing that you feel this ill.' Still whimpering, she sticks her thumb in her mouth. 'Really!' I say. 'You have an infection and your amazing body is fighting it. Right now, your inner core,' I draw a circle on her chest, 'is getting hotter. Your body is killing the bacteria and viruses inside you.' She grabs hold of my finger. 'See, you're already getting stronger!'

For the next hour, I lie next to her, obsessively touching her forehead and checking her body to make sure she's not got any rashes and slowly, slowly, her temperature drops. Eventually she drifts off to sleep. As I listen to her ragged breathing, I find myself thinking about what Grandad said. What if he's right? What if Mum can't help putting herself first and going off and leaving us because that's what happened to her when she was little? If that's true, then does that mean that I'll be like that when I grow up? *No*, I think, *because I'll never have children and that way I'll never make anyone feel as scared as I feel right now.*

I look at Elsa. Her arms are flopped above her head and she's stretched out like a starfish.

A horrible thought creeps into my mind. What if it's too late to stop the pattern? What if I've already become that person who turns away from people? I remember what Ed said, about how I 'never even crack a smile', and how I refused to let Grandad come and stay round here. I feel a tightness in my chest and I stroke Elsa's damp hair off her forehead. I thought my loneliness was temporary, but what if I've got it for life?

I put my finger back in Elsa's hand. Even though she's

211

fast asleep, her fingers curl around it and hold on tight. It feels like she's never going to let go.

We must fall asleep like that because when I wake up a bit later, we're still holding hands. I ease my finger out of her grasp then put her back in her cot. The thermometer says her temperature's down to thirty-eight, so I put a blanket over her and stand there looking down at her.

Suddenly, there's a bang and a clatter as Pongo and Grandad come into the flat.

'Sorry I'm late, love,' Grandad says as he bursts into the room. His cheeks are rosy red and he brings a bit of the cold night air in with him. 'I was out for longer than I realised, then I discovered one of the chickens had escaped –'

'*Shhh!*' I say, nodding towards Elsa.

'Ah, been sleeping the whole time, has she?'

I think back over the trauma of the past few hours. 'Kind of,' I say.

'I thought I'd make us fried egg sandwiches – Pongo didn't catch a rabbit or a squirrel – and that I might stay here tonight, help you keep an eye on Elsa. What do you think?'

I pull Elsa's blanket up so that it's covering her hands. Then I turn and look at Grandad. 'I think that's a really good idea.'

THIRTY-EIGHT

I wake up the next day to find the electricity turned off and Grandad trying to mend a broken light in the living room. Once I've helped him fix the light, and Elsa's woken up happy and cool, Grandad goes home to look after his chickens, leaving a trail of destruction behind him – newspapers are scattered across the kitchen floor (he went through the recycling searching for a cross-word), my toolbox is tipped over in the front room, and mud and leaves are scattered over the carpet from his walk with Pongo.

It doesn't matter. I've decided to take the day off to look after Elsa and it won't take me long to tidy up. It was nice having him here this morning. Messy, but nice.

'Are you sure you don't want me to take her?' Grandad asks as he leaves the flat.

Elsa's hands tighten round my neck.

'A day off school won't kill me,' I say. I know that what Elsa needs is a calm, quiet day at home, and Grandad's incapable of doing either calm or quiet.

Even though Elsa hasn't got a temperature any more, she's sleepier than usual so in between watching *Peppa Pig* and building towers, I have a lot of time to think. I think about Mum being my age and going to live with her dad, a man she hardly knew, and I think about Elsa. When she's fifteen, I'll be over thirty! That's so old …

I realise I've never included Elsa in any of my big plans for the future. I try putting her in a few of them, just to see how it feels, but it's hard because I don't know what she's going to be like. As the day goes on, though, I realise that there are some clues about who grown-up Elsa will be. Stubborn, I think, as she refuses to put on the red socks I've chosen. When I watch her study a jigsaw piece, then turn it and slot it into place, I see that she's already clever. And when I'm lying on the sofa and she's playing, she tries to feed me increasingly bizarre things – my phone, a fairy, her shoe – and the more surprised I am by what she produces, the more she laughs.

Stubborn, clever and funny.

I decide I'm looking forward to meeting future Elsa. And just like that, I realise I *can* see Elsa and I together in the future. Mum might bring her to visit me at university

and I could show her the experiments I'm working on …
Or we could go to Chile together to see the Giant
Magellan Telescope. It's supposed to be finished in 2025
and will be ten times more powerful than the Hubble
telescope. Elsa will be eleven and I'll be twenty-five. I
know Mum will let me take her.

Suddenly, I'm flooded with ideas for things we can do
together, and I realise I don't even have to wait until she's
older. I know she already loves it at the science centre –
we can go back when she's better. And in a few years
she'll be riding a bike and we can go up on the Downs
together. 'Elsa,' I say, and she looks up from her puzzle.
'Do you want to go to Chile with me to look into space?'

She gives me a big smile and says, 'Da!', then just to
prove she's really up for it, she throws a piece of jigsaw
puzzle at my face.

THIRTY-NINE

Back in school the next day, I get to science early only to discover Ed is already sitting at our table. There's no sign of Bella or Raj. When our eyes meet I want to turn round and walk straight out, but instead I check my blazer is tightly buttoned over my geek-rack and take a deep breath. I'd better get this over with.

I go over to our table, sit down and take out my pencil case. I put it at the front of the desk next to his virtually empty pencil case. Then I stare straight ahead at the whiteboard and pretend to be fascinated by Ms Edgecombe's $E=MC^2$ screen saver. Ed does the same. A few seconds pass. I shift on my stool. Ed leans forward and clears his throat.

Then, out of the corner of my eye, I see him turn to face me and the blush that has been creeping over my face since I walked into the room reaches epic proportions. 'Meg,' he says. I swallow and nod, but I can't bring myself to look at him so instead I rummage through my pencil case. 'I've been thinking about what you said in the cafe … About me laughing at you.'

OK, that is not what I thought he was going to say.

In a rush, he says, 'I did it on the science trip, and you're right, I've done it other times too. I thought it was funny, that we were having a laugh together, but I obviously got that wrong … What I'm trying to say is *sorry*.' He laughs. 'My mum says that sometimes I can be an arrogant little … twit … Only she doesn't say "twit".'

This makes me smile and I look up at him. 'My mum says I can be cold.'

He shakes his head. 'If your mum had seen you with those kids being Mega Knickers, she wouldn't have said that … Meg, there's something else.' He glances at the door. 'You know what Bella said on the science trip, about me asking you to the dance?'

My blush creeps back and my eyes shoot back to my pencil case. 'Oh, that.' I shrug as if I've barely thought about it. 'It doesn't matter.'

'Well, it does because we sit next to each other in all these lessons and it's going to get a bit awkward if I don't –'

I interrupt him. 'Honestly, Ed, it's fine. Just don't mention it. Please.'

'Don't mention what?'

'The dance.' I line up two pens and a pencil.

'What, never?'

'Never, ever,' I say. I couldn't bear listening to him apologise about that. It would be too humiliating.

The door to the classroom opens and we look up to see Bella standing there with Chiara.

'Just to clarify,' says Ed, 'if I never mention the dance in your presence again, then we're fine?'

'That's right,' I whisper. We really need to stop talking about this. Bella is coming over.

'Great,' says Ed. 'So when can we work on our presentations, because we really need to meet up. Saturday – tomorrow?'

What? Is he insane? I shake my head. 'No, I'm baby-sitting all day.'

'That's OK, I'll come round to your place. Two o'clock?' Across the table, Bella drops her bag on the floor. She's giving her full attention to her phone. 'Or I could mention a certain D.A.N.C.E. –'

'Fine, my place!'

'All right, losers?' Bella sits down on her stool. 'What're you two talking about?'

'Kepler's laws of planetary motion,' says Ed without missing a beat.

Bella makes a face and starts to put up her hair and I sharpen my pencil as if my life depends on it. What just happened? Did Ed blackmail me into inviting him round to the flat? And why did I agree?

'You all right, Meg?' says Bella, pausing mid-hair-twist to look at me. 'You're all red. Like a tomato.'

I'm too flustered to say a word, but I see Ed give Bella a meaningful look. 'OK, OK,' she says, laughing. 'Sorry, Meg, I take it back. You definitely *don't* look like a bright red glowing tomato, you look totally normal.'

Ms Edgecome saves me from this utterly strange situation by flicking off the lights and starting a film about bubbles. I sit in the dark and try to take in all the interesting points that are being made about water molecules. Just as a cartoon bubble is floating across the screen, I feel a tap on my arm. Ed slides his planner across the desk. There's one word written on it: *Address?*

How is this happening? I think, staring determinedly at the screen. I watch as the cartoon bubble bursts in slow motion.

Actually, I know why this is happening.

I said Ed could come round because I want him to. I could try telling myself it's because of our homework, or because he was about to talk about the dance in front of Bella, but that wouldn't be true.

When our fingers touched at the science centre, something connected us. It was just something tiny, but each time I see him, or we speak, it seems to grow and become more solid. I can feel it right now, a connection that's pulling us together, even though there are at least five centimetres of space separating our blue blazers.

It would be easiest to run away from this *thing* that's building up between us, because I don't know if Ed's feeling it too, and to be honest, it's scary. My pen hovers over Ed's planner. Before Mum left, I was just this satellite orbiting home and school, watching the mayhem going on around me, but never joining in. My life was safe and quiet ... My life was lonely.

Up on the screen, a mass of rainbow bubbles fills the screen.

I take a deep breath and write my address on the planner. No matter how frightening this is, I'm not going back to watching from a distance. *Poyekhali!* I think, as I slide the planner back to Ed.

FORTY

I'm queuing up outside PE when Annie glides down the corridor. She goes straight up to Mr Badal and hands him a note. He reads it then clicks his fingers in my direction. 'Clark, you're needed in Learning Support. Off you go.'

I follow Annie back down the corridor. 'What's going on?'

She shrugs. 'I was bored. I wanted someone to talk to. The note says that they need to do some tests on you.' She looks up at me and grins. 'Did you notice that Sir didn't even question it?'

Annie's going so fast that I have to trot to keep up with her. 'So where are we going?'

'To the best place in the entire school.' She pushes open the door to Learning Support. 'You'd better be quiet,' she says. 'You're not supposed to be here.'

'I don't want to be here!' I say, but she's already disappeared round a corner so I have no choice but to follow her. I find her waiting outside a door labelled *The Oasis*.

'Ever been in here?' Annie asks.

'No, but I've always wanted to.' The Oasis is the sensory room that our school put in last year. We had an assembly on it, explaining how light and music can help students with autism and other special needs.

'Come on then.' She pushes open the door. 'I told Jan that I was feeling angry so I've got it to myself for the whole hour.'

I step inside. The room is entirely blue. In the corner are three tubes filled with rising pink bubbles and the floor is covered with huge cushions and beanbags. I slip off my shoes and Annie pulls herself out of her wheelchair. Without using her crutches, she walks across the room, lurching from side to side. 'It's OK to look,' she calls over her shoulder. 'Sometimes it's best just to have a really big stare until you get used to me.'

'Sorry,' I say.

'I said it was OK, didn't I?'

'So do you feel angry?' I ask, following her across the room.

'Yeah ... a bit.'

'Why?'

'Oh, all the usual boring teenage stuff: school, spots, arguments with friends … And added to that I've got a serious amount of bum ache at the moment.' Her eyes flick to me. 'But don't even think about trying to talk to me about it.' She picks up a boomerang-shaped control, presses a button and the room is flooded in red light.

'There's a ball pool,' I say to break the silence.

She smiles. 'Get in if you like.'

So I go to the ball pool, climb in and sink down in the white balls. Annie presses another button and the balls glow pink.

'Wow!' I ripple my hands through the balls. 'Hey, I'm almost weightless!'

Annie lifts herself on to the edge of the ball pool, pulls her legs over and slips in next to me. Then she throws a ball at me and it bounces off my head. 'Here, you have a go.' She passes me the controls and I start pressing buttons at random. I change the colour of the bubble tubes then I make a film of the sea appear on the wall. While I'm trying out the different music, we talk a bit about Biscuit Club and Annie puts forward her dubious theory that Mr Curtis is actually working for the government and is planning to recruit us for a teenage superhero unit.

'I'd be the kick-ass leader, who uses her bionic wheelchair-strengthened arms to slap baddies down.'

223

'Who would I be?'

'The one who stays back at the base hacking into the CIA and stuff. Give it here,' says Annie, taking the control off me. 'I've got one you'll like.' She plunges the room into blackness then stars start circling the ceiling. The balls glow white like little moons. 'What music do you want? Heavenly Realms or Ocean Waves?'

'Heavenly Realms, of course.'

Ambient music fills the room and I lie back and stare at the stars. My whole body relaxes. This is so much better than hockey. Suddenly, I realise that the boldness that made me want me want to write my address in Ed's planner hasn't gone away. I turn to Annie. 'Something funny happened in science today.'

'Go on,' she says, and another ball bounces off my head.

'I don't really know *how* it happened, but Ed King is coming round to my place tomorrow.'

Annie sits up and balls spill on to the floor. 'Oh my God. That's a bit *datey*, Meg!'

'I knew you'd say that, but we're going to do our science homework.'

She laughs. 'You keep telling yourself that.'

'What? It's true!' Now it's my turn to throw a ball at her.

'You live in a flat, right? No lift?'

'No, just three flights of wee-smelling stairs ... that Ed King is going to be walking up.' I'm actually blushing at the thought. I can't help thinking about that huge four-wheel drive that's always picking him up.

'Shame. I almost want to be there, but three flights of stairs is a lot of effort. What're you going to wear?'

'Annie, it's not a date!' Then, after a moment, I say, 'I'm going to wear my NASA T-shirt.'

Annie sinks down and her smile is half-hidden by the balls. 'Did you know that there's a word for people like Ed? *Sapiosexual*. It's when someone's attracted to intelligence.'

'We're working on our presentations for the NASA competition. There's nothing *sexual* about it.'

Suddenly the room is flooded in pink light and petals float around on the wall. 'If you say so,' she says, 'but there's a test you can do. When he's round at yours, look deeply into his eyes and say something clever like, "The square root of one thousand is twenty five." If his pupils dilate, then he's definitely a sapiosexual.' She grins. 'Do it for me!'

'I would, but the square root of one thousand is *actually* closer to thirty-one point six.'

'Perfect. Say exactly that!'

Then I throw a handful of balls at her and she calls me a sapiosexual and throws a load back at me and soon we're having a sensory ball fight.

FORTY-ONE

'Elsa, they're not for you.' I lift the bowl of crisps out of her reach and put them on the table. Ed's due any minute now and I've spent all morning sorting out the flat. When Elsa woke up this morning at the crack of dawn, I suddenly saw the flat through Ed's eyes and realised that to him it might look a bit, well, freaky.

I couldn't do much about the saris and scarfs pinned across the ceiling, or the airbrush mural of fairies that Mum painted on the living-room wall, so instead I did some de-cluttering. I reasoned that Ed wouldn't be going in my room, so I piled all the plush Disney toys on to my bed and also put Mum's life-size Kristoff cut-out in there. Then I vacced, washed up and cleaned the bathroom.

I actually cleaned the toilet for Ed King. How surreal.

Elsa and Pongo were predictably unhelpful, but food and *In the Night Garden* kept them both distracted.

I look at the bowl of crisps. Is it a bit datey? I mean, I know crisps aren't datey, but somehow the bowl gives them a bit of a party vibe and this isn't a celebration. This needs to look like serious homework is about to take place. I'm just about to take the bowl back into the kitchen when the doorbell rings and my stomach flips over. In a panic I throw one of Elsa's jumpers over the bowl then follow Elsa, who's already tottering into the hallway.

Through the glass of the front door, I can see the silhouette of a dark, man-shape. Just the sight of that tall shape makes me feel a bit breathless … Oh, God. Why did I agree to this? Then I remind myself Ed's not a man. He's a teenager, just like me. We're just two teenagers who have to talk about space. Nothing scary about that.

I glance in the mirror to check there's nothing strange on my face and that I look OK in my jeans and grey T-shirt. Grandad gave me the T-shirt for my birthday and told me it had actually been into space with Karen Nyberg. It hasn't – the label says Topshop – but I still love it and you can tell how much I've worn it by the faded NASA logo. The doorbell rings again and I take a deep breath and tuck an escaped strand of hair behind my ear. I grab Pongo's collar. *Definitely nothing scary about this*, I tell myself as I open the door.

And there he is, looking as tall and smart as ever. He smiles at me – at least, I think he does – but then there's a flurry of movement as Pongo leaps towards his checked shirt, and I'm holding Pongo back and Ed's passing me at the same time. Suddenly, we're all squeezed into the tiny hallway and I can't get out of the way because Elsa is sitting on my foot.

'This way,' I say, dragging Elsa into the living room.

Ed follows, then stops in the doorway and stares at the mural. 'Wow!'

'I know. Mum likes fairies. It's a bit strange.'

'It's good. Did she do it?'

I nod. 'She loves art.' I look at the mural. I suppose it is good, but I've been living with all those little elves and fairies for so long that I forgot it was Mum who painted every single one of them.

Ed sits on the sofa and starts getting paper and textbooks out of his rucksack. The sight of his AQA physics book sitting on our coffee table manages to be both alarming and reassuring at the same time. 'Where is she?' he asks.

'Who?' I peel Elsa off my foot and sit on the sofa.

'Your mum?'

'Oh … She's at work.'

'You've got everything ready,' he says, looking at the

Post-it notes, highlighters and laptop I've got set up on the table.

'We've got a lot to do … Well, I have,' I say and I start flicking through my cards. 'I thought my speech was fine, but recently I've been having second thoughts … Do you want a drink?'

'Er –' he says.

I shake my head. 'No, I'll do that later. We should work. Do you want me to tell you what my speech is about?' Wow. I am talking *fast*. 'My grandad says my speech is lacking in passion.'

Ed blinks and I instantly regret my choice of words. 'OK,' he says, and I perch on the edge of the sofa, feeling slightly dizzy from all my fast talking. As I start talking about NASA's Ames research centre and radiation and gravity, I feel myself relaxing and when we argue about migrating planets we could almost be sitting in science … I just have to ignore the fact that Pongo is resting his drooling mouth on Ed's knee and that Elsa is ramming her baby walker into his feet.

'Why's it mooing?' Ed asks, as Elsa slams her hand down on a sheep button.

'Because babies like animal noises.'

'But it's a sheep.'

'It was broken when we got it,' I say. I don't bother

telling him that like everything else in our flat, it came from the charity shop where Mum works.

'So why haven't you fixed it?' There's this note of challenge in his voice. If there is one area of science that Ed and I are really competitive in, it's electronics. Ms Edgecombe once got us to build the same circuit in front of the class and I beat Ed by one second. I won a Snickers and I've got the feeling Ed's never forgotten it.

I shrug. 'She doesn't care.'

'Meg, your sister is going to grow up thinking that sheep *moo*. You are wilfully encouraging her ignorance. Have you got a screwdriver?'

'Of course I've got a screwdriver.' I jump up. 'I'll get my toolbox.'

Five minutes later, the back of the walker is off and Ed and I are sitting on the floor surrounded by wires, drills and bolts. We realise we're missing some parts, so I get Elsa's Thomas train and her flashing hammer and we take those apart too. At first we're both quiet, concentrating on the fiddly job we've created for ourselves, then I notice Ed's watching me as I get to work with the soldering iron.

'You really like doing this, don't you?' he says.

His scrutiny makes me look back down at the wires. 'Yes,' I say. 'I love finding out how things work.'

'Me too.' He moves closer so he can hold a wire still for me. 'That's why I like science.'

'Did you used to take stuff apart when you were little?'

'All the time! My toys, my bike ... Mum's coffee machine.'

'Once I noticed the DVD player was sticking so I took the back off it.' I look back up at him. 'I was five.'

'Maybe you'll be an engineer when you're older.'

I shrug. 'I don't think so ...' He passes me a screw and I say, 'What do you think you'll do?'

'I've not thought that far ahead ... Maybe I'll mend toys.'

I press the cow and it quacks. 'You'll have to get better at it.'

He tuts and peers at the circuit board. 'I'm sure you were doing the cow.'

Once we've got all the cows mooing and the ducks quacking we put the toys back together. Ed tells me about how he once stuck a bath toy to his forehead to make his brother laugh, but when he pulled it off he was left with a suction mark. 'It was in Year Eight,' he says. 'I had to walk around school with this big red circle on my forehead! Don't you remember?'

I shake my head. I don't bother telling him that I was

probably too intimidated by Ed and his friends to even look at him in Year Eight.

'Well, I can remember something that happened to you in Year Seven,' he says.

'What?' I feel a flutter of panic inside as I try to remember if I did anything particularly humiliating back then. When I started secondary school, I was so clueless I actually wore a 'This girl loves science' T-shirt on non-school-uniform day – it had two big pink thumbs pointing up at my face – and I read out my 'Day in the Life of an Atom' poem in assembly. But then the eye-rolling began, and the sniggering ... And then Mr Harper said 'photosynthesis' in *that* voice ...

'You and your friend won a prize for making a go-kart,' says Ed.

'Oh, *that*.' My panic slips away. That go-kart was awesome. We were the only girls in the Formula One club and our kart was so fast we were picked to go to the regional finals. 'Yeah, we did win a trophy, but then we got beaten in the finals by a boy from another school.'

'I really wanted a go on that go-kart,' Ed says, then he tests the toy hammer by banging it on the floor. He nods to the corner of the room. 'Does Elsa usually sleep in a dog basket?'

I look over and see that Elsa's crashed out in Pongo's

bed. 'Only sometimes.' I go and tuck a blanket round her. Pongo hardly uses his bed so it isn't too hairy.

Ed's rummaging through my toolbox. 'We need some tape.'

'It's in my room.' I push Pongo's nose away from Elsa. Now someone else is in his bed he wants to get in there too. 'No, Pongo,' I say, and he flops down next to her. I'm just giving his wiry tummy a scratch when I hear a door open … My bedroom door!

FORTY-TWO

I find Ed standing in the doorway, staring wide-eyed at the mountain of Disney on my bed. 'I never had you down as a cuddly toy person, Meg.'

'They all belong to my mum,' I say, 'well, except these two.' I pull two plush microbes out of the pile. 'Meet E. coli and Botulism. My mum gave me these.' I know I'm babbling, but Ed's still staring at all the Tiggers and Olafs. He picks up a pea pod and unzips it. Three little peas tumble out. Then his eyes fall on the life-size Kristoff.

'Mum's,' I say quickly.

'I guess your Mum's into Disney as well as fairies?'

'Haven't you ever wondered why I'm called Megara?' He looks blank so I sift through the toys until I find the only crocheted doll. 'Meet Megara from *Hercules*.'

'I've never seen it.'

'Not many people have, but everyone knows who Elsa's named after.'

'Oh yeah,' he says, pulling out Mum's biggest Elsa doll. 'So what's the fictitious Megara like? How come your mum chose to name you after her?'

I look at the little crocheted doll. Mum actually got someone to make it for her. 'I can't remember,' I say. 'I've not seen the film for years.' I put the mini-Megara on my bedside table. 'Mum says she's feisty.'

Ed starts looking around, taking in my globe and all the space posters. 'Who are they?' he asks, pointing at the laminated pictures I've stuck to the wall.

'They're all the woman who've ever been into space. Fifty-nine, so far.'

I try to read the expression on Ed's face as he studies the pictures of suited-up astronauts. Then he goes to my desk and picks up my Russian phrase book. 'Are you learning Russian?'

'Da,' I say.

'Because …?'

I straighten up the book he's put down. Except for Harriet, Ed is the only person from school ever to set foot in my bedroom. Part of me wants to march him back into the living room and get him working on our speeches again, but he seems genuinely intrigued by everything –

he seems genuinely intrigued by *me* – and I realise that I want to tell him the truth. But that's a big step. I look up at Valentina Tereshkova and she looks calmly back at me. *Just jump*, her eyes say. I turn to face Ed.

'I'm learning Russian because the Soyuz rockets that take astronauts to the International Space Station have control panels and instruction booklets written in Russian.'

He stares at me. 'So you actually want to be ...'

'An astronaut,' I say, and as soon as the words are out of my mouth, I feel like I've just said I want to be a princess or a dinosaur. I laugh. 'I mean, I know it's extremely unlikely to happen ...'

'Why?' He fires this back at me.

'Because hardly anyone gets to do it, but I've got a plan B – becoming a test pilot.'

'Stick to plan A,' he says. 'You'd make a good astronaut.'

His words make the tingle of connection come rushing back. 'Look up,' I say. He tilts his head back and takes in the galaxy Mum painted on the ceiling. 'You need to lie down to see it properly.' I go to the bed and sweep the toys on to the floor. Ed hesitates and too late I realise what a weird thing I've just asked him to do. 'She did the interstellar dust and the Perseus arm really well,' I say quickly, deciding to go full-on technical so he knows I want him to lie on my bed purely in the interests of astrophysics.

'OK,' he says, then he lies down, crosses his feet at the ankles and stares up at the ceiling. 'Which one is the Perseus arm?' He shifts closer to the wall. 'Show me.'

Still in the interests of astrophysics, I lie next to him, making sure I leave a gap between us. 'There.' I point at the middle arm of the spiral that's speckled pink, turquoise and white.

'What's the name of the arm coming right out of the middle?'

'The Scutum–Centaurus.'

He turns to look at me and suddenly all I can think about is what Annie said about sapiosexuals. 'Ed,' I say, trying to casually check out his pupils.

'Yes?'

Too late, I realise that you can't casually check out someone's pupils without staring deep into their eyes. 'Did you know that we're around twenty-six thousand miles from the galactic centre?'

After a moment, he says, 'I didn't know that … but I do know that our galaxy is roughly one hundred and twenty thousand light years in diameter.'

Now he's looking at me and I'm looking at him and I

haven't got a clue what his pupils are doing because I'm so worried that mine are expanding faster than the universe.

'That's big ...'

He nods and then I realise that somehow when I turned to face him, my arm moved over and now *our fingers* are just touching and neither of us have moved our hands away.

'Meg,' says Ed, and his little finger sort of loops round mine. I nod, but I can't speak because there's a chance that we are *holding fingers*. How can such a tiny force create such a powerful counter reaction inside my body? 'I think –'

But I don't get to find out what Ed thinks, because there's a scuffle of paws, a flash of grey fur and Pongo crashes between us on the bed, barking and licking our faces. I jump up as Ed tries to push Pongo away.

'I heard Elsa,' I say, then I shoot out of the room, kicking plush Winnie the Poohs and Olafs out of my way.

FORTY-THREE

'**W**ake up!' I whisper, shaking Elsa's shoulder. I can hear Ed walking down the corridor so I pick her up and rock her up and down until her eyes flutter open. Ed appears in the doorway, smoothing down his hair and straightening his shirt. I grab a book off the table. 'I was thinking I could use this to improve my introduction.'

'*The Very Hungry Caterpillar?*'

I look down at the book. 'Wrong book,' I say.

'So,' he says, not quite able to look at me, 'why don't you read me your whole presentation?'

'OK.' I sit down and put Elsa between us as a barrier against accidental finger touching. 'But I can't look at you when I do it. I'll just read through my introduction.' Ed nods and picks up a pen. I stare at my first card ... I can't take in a single word. Whatever happened just then has rewired my brain. *Solar system*, I read ... Does Ed like me? *G-type stars … radiation …* I mean, I know he likes me – he wouldn't have put so much effort into coming round today if he hated me – but does he *like* me? *The material begins to heat up …* Like my cheeks, right now! What is *wrong* with me? I have to look at him, act normal. I force myself to glance in his direction, but the moment I see his dark eyelashes, his frown of concentration, I know.

I know that I *like* Ed.

He stares back at me. 'What?'

An astronaut must remain focused even when potentially catastrophic events are unfolding. 'I just remembered a YouTube film I can use,' I say. 'It's about Alpha Centauri B, the star hiding behind Alpha Centauri. That's where the Goldilocks planet might be.'

He nods. 'Sounds good. Let's see it.'

And that's how Ed and I end up watching space films. Outside, dark clouds roll in and rain starts to patter against the window, but there's something good about sitting on the sofa with Ed, eating crisps and watching back–to-back Hubblecasts. Usually I watch these on my own, but it's so much better watching them with someone else. And I suppose it might seem a bit datey, if Elsa wasn't constantly trying to force-feed us plastic fruit and eggs.

It's almost dark when Ed checks his phone and says, 'I'd better go. Mum wants me back for dinner. She's making toad in the hole.'

I take in this little bit of information. I've always imagined that Ed would have things like olives and fettucine for dinner … I don't actually know what fettucine is, but it matches his ironed shirts better than toad in the hole.

'I suppose I should feed Elsa,' I say. Right now she's standing up on my lap, trying to suck my face. It's what she does when she's hungry. I hold her hands and she bounces up and down.

Ed starts packing his books away. 'Won't your Mum do that?'

'She's at a festival,' I say, forcing myself to keep bouncing Elsa.

'Beb … Beb!' she says, again and again.

'Like last weekend?' Ed's got a look on his face that I recognise from school, the one where's he's working something out and getting close to the answer. I try to remember if I talked about where Mum was when we were at the science centre.

'That's right.'

He nods and pulls on his jacket. Then he sits back down on the sofa. 'But I thought you said she was working?'

My heart speeds up. 'Did I?' For a moment, I think about inventing some job Mum could do at festivals – Thai massage or reading tarot cards, but I don't think I can get away with lying to Ed. Instead I stop bouncing Elsa and look at him. 'You're going to be late for your toad in the hole,' I say.

He stares straight at me. 'Meg, where is your mum?'

'My mum's in a village in Myanmar,' I say, then I laugh because Ed looks so amazed and it's such a huge relief to tell someone. 'At least, I think she's in a village in Myanmar. To be honest she could be anywhere in the world right now. She's not exactly been keeping in touch.'

After a moment he says, 'When did she go?'

'Nearly two weeks ago. It feels like it's been months.'

'So she's just left the two of you on your own and gone on holiday?'

This sounds so bad, like a headline in a newspaper. 'It's not a holiday,' I say. 'She's working at a clinic for sick children. It was a last-minute thing. She thought we would stay at my grandad's place, but he's got a lot of animals and it's messy so I decided that we'd stay here.' Then I say firmly, 'I've got everything sorted out.'

He does this quick laugh, like he still can't believe it. 'So that's why you've been looking so tired and acting strange at school.' He's got his phone in his hand and I suddenly wonder if I've been stupid trusting him. What if he rings Bella the moment he leaves the flat? What if he tells his parents?

'Ed, you mustn't tell *anyone*.' My voice rises. 'If people knew we were on our own here, Mum would get into trouble. They could take Elsa away from her … from me. We're doing fine.' My hands tighten round her and for a horrible moment I think I might cry.

'Don't worry,' he says. 'I won't tell anyone.'

I rest my cheek on Elsa's smooth head. 'Mum's back on Monday – I've nearly done it.'

Elsa escapes and crawls towards Ed. When she reaches him, she makes a grab for his hair.

'Has it been hard?' he asks, wincing as her little fists tighten.

I laugh. 'The hardest thing I've ever had to do.' I hold up my speech cards. 'I don't know how I'm going to get ready for the competition.'

'I can help you. It's what we're supposed to be doing right now.'

'You're aiming to "totally destroy" me, remember?'

'Oh yeah,' he smiles and shrugs. 'Well, my total destruction will be more satisfying if I've got an equal opponent.'

I'm about to say, 'It's fine,' but instead I say, 'I want to add this bit about atomic absorption – the Beer–Lambert Law – but I'm having problems with an equation.'

'I am *amazing* at the Beer–Lambert Law!' he says.

'You've never heard of it, have you?'

'No,' he admits, 'but by tomorrow I'll be able to write a PhD on it.' Then Elsa kind of ruins his boast by grabbing hold of his nose and squeezing really, really hard.

FORTY-FOUR

It takes a while for Ed to leave. While Elsa plays with Pongo in the hallway, we stand on the balcony and Ed quizzes me a bit about the stars I see when I go up on the Downs. In the end, I get my binoculars and show him Jupiter, which is just starting to appear.

'I'd better go,' he says for the second or third time. He hands me my binoculars and walks towards the stairs. He stops at the last moment and turns. 'Thanks for the crisps,' he says, then he gives me a wave and he's gone.

I go into the flat and pick Elsa up. Then I stand with my back against the door and I smile. Elsa's staring at me, blowing raspberries. She stops and points a finger at my mouth. 'Da?' she says.

'I'm just happy,' I say. 'Really, really happy.'

My happiness lasts all evening and is given a boost on

Sunday when Ed sends me a friend request on Facebook. I accept straight away. He knows about my mum. Who cares what he thinks about my moon pictures? Annie notices this development and sends me a series of direct messages:

> *Annie: Did he bring flowers?*
> *Me: No. Just his AQA physics textbook and a scientific calculator.*
> *Annie: The dirty dog! Did you test him for sapiosexuality?*
> *Me: Your theory is bogus. I refuse to take part in a flawed experiment.*
> *Annie: Ooooh ... I like it! Maybe I'm a sapiosexual ...*

Two minutes later:

> *Annie: OK, I know I sound like the type of revolting girl that I despise, but did you *kiss* him?*

This message is accompanied by a GIF of an elf vomiting a rainbow.

> *Me: NO!*
> *Annie: So what did you do?*

Me: We made a baby walker moo.

Annie: What? Is that code for something disgusting?

Me: No. We literally made a baby walker moo.

Annie: I was not expecting that.

Me: Neither was I.

FORTY-FIVE

When I hand Elsa over to Dawn on Monday, I practically throw her into her arms. My last handover! Right now, Mum is on her way home. I don't know what time she'll get back, but she can definitely drop Elsa off tomorrow.

I'm about to go when Dawn hands me a letter and says, 'It's from Christine, the manager. It's for your mum.'

I slip the official-looking envelope in my bag. 'I'll make sure she gets it.'

'It's a bill,' Dawn says, and although she doesn't actually smile, I get the feeling she's enjoying herself.

'I thought Mum was up to date with the fees?' This was one of the first things I checked when Mum left.

'She is, but we've had to charge for Elsa's lunches. Your mum usually provides a packed lunch – she was very particular about organic food – but when she hurt her back she stopped putting them in.'

I nod as if this isn't news to me at all. 'It all got a bit much,' I say. 'How much do lunches cost?'

'Two pounds, so that's twenty pounds your mum owes us. Really, we need it today. We have tried ringing, several times.'

I try to remember exactly how much money Grandad and I have left. Forty pounds? Maybe not even that. 'And Christine would like to speak to your mum as soon as possible.' Dawn watches me closely.

'Fine,' I say, smiling. 'She can speak to Mum tomorrow because she'll be dropping Elsa off.'

Dawn clearly isn't expecting this. 'Well … She wanted to speak to her today.'

'Sorry, Mum's got an appointment at the hospital.'

'Well, that's great!' says Dawn, and her smile is firmly back in place and so is mine. 'So pleased she's back on her feet.'

'Me too,' I say, and I give Elsa a wave and walk down the path.

Knowing Mum's coming back today makes it hard to concentrate at school and during lunchtime in the library I get totally confused by light and atoms and

Beer–Lambert, or, to be precise, how I can calculate absorbance from the equation $A = 2 - log_{10}$ %T. I work at it for twenty minutes, but in the end I give up and go and get some food.

I'm walking out of the canteen with my cheese baguette when I see Ed sitting with Bella and Raj and the rest of their friends. The thought crosses my mind that I could ask him to help me with the equation and then, before I really know what I'm doing, I'm winding my way through the crowded tables until I'm standing behind him.

Bella looks up and sees me standing there. 'It's Meg!' she announces, loudly, and everyone stops talking and turns to look at me, including Ed.

Quickly, I say, 'Ed, can I ask you something?'

Bella's eyes grow wide. 'Oh, wow …'

'About Beer–Lambert,' I add, then I thrust my notebook at Ed.

He studies the equation. 'It's hard,' he says, raising his eyebrows, 'but obviously not too hard for me!'

Bella groans, 'God, you're an idiot.' Then she shuffles along the bench until there's a small gap between the two of them. 'If Ed is about to impart his wisdom, you'd better sit down. It'll take a long time.' Because everyone is still staring at me, I feel I have no choice but to squeeze in between them.

Ed says, 'So, this equation lets you calculate absorbance from transmittance data, right?'

I nod.

'Then I think I get it.' He takes a pen out of his top pocket and starts to scribble down figures. After watching him for a few seconds, I unwrap my baguette and take a small bite. His friends get bored of watching me and start talking again. Only Bella keeps her eyes glued on me.

'Do you like this dress?' she asks, showing me her phone.

I look at the short lacy dress. I have absolutely no opinion about it except that the hexagonal lace looks like a diagram of a molecule. Usually I'd say, 'It's nice,' or something equally vague in the hope that she'd lose interest in me, but I'm sitting in the canteen eating lunch with Ed and Bella, the king and queen of Year Ten, the Jupiter and Saturn of the solar system! If I was brave enough to walk over and talk to Ed, then surely I'm brave enough to tell Bella what I think about a dress?

'I have absolutely no opinion about it,' I say with a shrug, 'except that the hexagonal lace looks like the diagram of a molecule.'

She grins. 'I love the stuff that comes out of your mouth, Megara. It's priceless.'

I sit up tall. 'Thank you,' I say, then I take another bite out of my baguette.

'I'm wearing this molecule dress to the dance,' she says, then she gives me a nudge. 'Got anyone to go with yet?'

'Shut up, Bella,' says Ed, his pen still scribbling across my notebook.

'The thing is,' I say, 'I don't like dances. I don't like discos. I don't even like dresses. I like stars and planets and sums. That's why – with or without anyone – I'm definitely not going to the dance.'

She blinks at me. 'Seriously? You don't like dresses?'

I shake my head.

'Huh,' she says, then she pushes a packet of Quavers towards me. 'Crisp?'

'OK,' I say, and because I want to do something to celebrate the amazing moment when I found the courage to show Bella Lofthouse just who I am, I don't take one, I take two! Still holding my head high, I turn back to Ed, but he's stopped working on the equation and is staring at the TV screen in the corner of the canteen. I follow his eyes and the triumph I'm feeling drains away from me.

A music video is playing, but Ed's watching the live news feed that's scrolling along the bottom of the screen: *Breaking news: massive earthquake strikes Myanmar. Thousands feared dead.* The words loop round and round, never ending.

'What's the matter with you two?' says Bella.

'Nothing,' says Ed, and at the same time he wraps his fingers round mine. 'It's nothing.' He squeezes my hand as icy fear fills my body from my scalp to my toes.

'I've got to go,' I manage to say, then I wriggle out from between them and walk towards the exit.

'Meg, you forgot your baguette!' Bella shouts after me, but I keep going, shoving through the double doors.

I've got to get out of here.

I find Annie in the sensory room, lounging on a beanbag and staring at blobs of light floating across the ceiling. She raises her head. 'What are you doing here?'

I walk straight up to her. 'I need you to write me another of your letters.' I pull my pencil case out of my bag. 'Make it about my teeth again, a follow-up appointment.'

She sits up and I thrust my planner and a pen at her.

'What's wrong?' she says.

'Nothing.'

She stares at me. 'Obviously something's wrong, Meg. I get that you've got all sorts of secrets and you're not into sharing, but you look like you're going to puke. Why don't you just go and see the nurse? She'll ring your mum and you'll be able to go straight home.'

I feel my shoulders rising. Why can't she just write me the note? I have to get round to Grandad's and find out if he's heard from Mum. I've already tried his phone but, of course, he's not answering. 'I can't talk to the nurse ...' I pause and stare at the floor. '... Because if I do, I might ...' I press my fingers into my eyes.

'*Cry?* Oh, God. Don't do that. I don't do crying.' She pulls the lid off the pen. 'I guess whatever it is, it's bad.'

I nod. 'I'll tell you if you like.' I don't think I can keep quiet about this any longer, and Annie has this strength about her. Maybe she can make it better.

'OK, but only if it's got nothing to do with boys, kissing, or girls being mean.'

I shake my head. 'It's to do with my mum ... and an earthquake.'

Her eyes go wide and she puts down her pen. 'Hot damn,' she whispers.

FORTY-SIX

I tell Annie everything, about Mum leaving, how they're getting suspicious at Elsa's nursery ... I even tell her about the competition on Saturday, although I feel like I shouldn't be worrying about that now.

Annie describes my situation as 'bleak, but not without hope', then she writes me a note to get me out of school.

It works, and I spend the afternoon with Grandad, checking our phones, watching the news and trawling the internet for information on the earthquake. Grandad rings the embassy, but they say they'll have no information for forty-eight hours. They take Mum's details, though, and when I hear Grandad describing her two tattoos, I have to hug Pongo to me really tight. In the end, Grandad resorts to his homebrew to 'take the edge off things', and soon he's lying flat on the sofa, snoring. He'd planned to come and get Elsa with me, but I can't bring myself to wake him up – I'm pretty sure he won't get much sleep tonight – so instead I write *Gone to get Elsa. Come round for dinner* on a Post-it note and stick it on his chest.

After I've handed over twenty pounds for the lunches, Dawn gives me Elsa. It's like a trade-off. 'Remind your mum to come in tomorrow,' she says as we set off for home.

'I will,' I say, hoping with everything inside me that Mum will be waiting for us at home.

She isn't. The flat is quiet and empty. I put Elsa down and drop our stuff by the door. Pongo bumps his head against my hand. He needs feeding and so does Elsa, but I just stand there, staring down the dark corridor feeling heavy inside. I don't think I've ever felt so close to giving up before.

Then Elsa pulls herself up my legs and stands there wobbling.

'Hungry?' I say. 'Let's see what we've got left.'

I'm feeding Elsa scrambled eggs when I see the message Ed's sent me on Facebook:

Where did you go this afternoon? I looked for you.
I know you'll only want facts, so I've found some out
for you:

1) The epicentre of the earthquake was in the north of the Myanmar and missed the majority of the tourist areas.

2) Even small earthquakes can disrupt all mobile phone and landline activity. It's likely that your Mum has no way of contacting you.

3) Myanmar has three international airports and one of them has closed because of damage to the runway. If your mum was planning to fly from this airport she would have had to travel the length of the country to a different one. Even if she has managed to change her flight, the flight itself takes over twenty hours, usually with two changes, so she would come back a day late. There have been reports of 180 fatalities. The country has a population of over fifty-three million people, and this doesn't include tourists. Using this data, the probability of your mum being one of the fatalities is roughly 1 in 294,000. This is an estimate, but I think you'll agree that the odds are reassuring.

See you tomorrow, Mega Knickers.

Ed.

After Elsa's bath, I take her for a sleepy walk along the seafront, leaving Grandad at the flat making dinner for us: spaghetti bolognaise with baked beans. It sounds revolting, but I doubt I'll be eating much. I wander along to the far end of the prom, well away from the pier, and scramble down the pebbly beach. While Elsa and I stare at the rolling, crashing waves, Pongo zooms around, stopping every now and then to sniff the air.

'Can you see Orion?' I ask Elsa, lifting my face to the sky and pointing. Elsa points too, copying as I trace the constellation. 'That star is Rigel and it's shining forty thousand times brighter than our sun.' Her hands close like she's trying to grab at the sky. 'And there's Betelgeuse. Get a good look at it because it's going to supernova soon … Well, sometime in the next million years.' Elsa's hand falls down and I see that her eyes are closing.

I start to rock from side to side. Ed's message helped. His conclusion – that statistically, Mum should be fine – was something I knew already, but his words meant much more than that. I'd been on and off the internet all afternoon and hadn't found out half the things he discovered. He must have spent a long time looking up those facts for me. And he wasn't the only one who was thinking about me. Annie sent me a picture of a galaxy with *Keep calm and look at the stars* written across it. The fact that it wasn't sarcastic, or a black hole joke, or a sarcastic black hole joke, meant a lot.

So that's why I'm out here staring up at the sky, waves

crashing down around me. My mission isn't over, it's just changed and I'm not giving up yet. When I get home, I'm writing a letter to Christine at the nursery and I'm going to fill it with missing capital letters and 'Namaste's and smileys so she'll be convinced it's from mum. Then Grandad and I will carry on looking after Elsa until Mum comes home. Because she *is* coming home.

'Come on, Pongo!' I call, then I turn my back on the beautiful cosmos and walk up the beach, my feet slipping on the stones.

FORTY-SEVEN

Christine herself comes to the door when I drop Elsa off at nursery.

'Where's your mum?' she says, peering over my shoulder like I might have Mum hidden behind me.

I shift Elsa to my other hip and make myself look directly at Christine's red glasses. 'She's got that horrible bug Elsa had. She's written you this.' I pass over the letter. 'Oh, and she said to say thank you so much for helping her out while she's had the slipped disc.' I pull a box of Ferrero Rocher out of my bag and hold them out. 'She's so grateful!' *These had better work*, I think. They cost five pounds that we really don't have.

Christine takes the chocolates and her face softens slightly. 'It's been hard work for you too, I imagine.'

'It's been fine,' I say with a shrug. 'I've not had to do too much.'

With this final lie, I give Elsa a kiss and hand her to Christine. I can hear Christine opening the letter and as I walk down the path I wonder if my sign off – *with love and energy* – was a bit much. 'So she'll be bringing Elsa in next week?' she calls after me.

'Definitely,' I shout over my shoulder.

I get through the morning by holding Ed's figure of one in 294,000 in my head like a talisman. When I get to Biscuit Club, Rose and Annie are already there and so is Mr Curtis. For the first time, they're sitting around a table and it's covered in books.

'What's going on?' I say. 'Where's Jackson?'

'Over there.' Mr Curtis points to the corner of the room where Jackson is sitting on his beanbag, playing on Annie's iPad. 'He's promised not to talk so that we can concentrate.'

Jackson waves at me, his lips clamped shut.

'Concentrate on what?' I sit with them at the table and notice that all the books are on maths, physics or astronomy.

'On your competition,' says Annie, not looking up from the book she's reading. 'Did you know that on the International Space Station they once tried to grow tomato plants on a pair of dirty pants?'

'I don't think Meg should mention that,' says Rose to Annie. She turns to me. 'Annie told us all about your problem.'

'With the competition,' Annie adds quickly.

'So we're going to help you,' says Mr Curtis.

'That's kind,' I say, and I know they're trying to help, but just looking at this enormous pile of books overwhelms me, 'but it's happening *this* Saturday and I know my speech isn't good enough. I think it might be too late to do anything about it.'

'Too late, Meg?' says Mr Curtis. 'How can you ever hope to become an astronaut if that's your attitude?'

Annie looks up from her book and shrugs. 'I might have told them about your whole astronaut-thing too.'

'It's so exciting!' Rose clasps her hands together.

'Rose, it isn't *happening*. The likelihood of me going into space is so infinitely small it's slightly embarrassing that I consider it a possibility.' I glare at Annie. '*That's* why I never tell anyone.'

'But it might be a little more likely if you win the competition and go to Houston,' says Mr Curtis. 'Haven't most astronauts worked towards their dream from a young age? Couldn't going to the Space Centre and meeting a real astronaut create a connection that might one day help you in some way?'

I blush when I hear him say this because the same thought has run through my head and it's one of the reasons I want to win so much. 'I suppose so,' I say. 'But where would we begin?'

'What's wrong with your speech at the moment?' he asks.

'What I've written is well researched and accurate, but it all falls apart when I try to say it out loud. I *hate* speaking in front of people: I talk too fast, and I get these red spots on my neck – see!' I point at the marks I can feel blooming on my skin right now. 'And even though I've crammed my speech full of incredible facts and statistics, my grandad says it lacks "passion and pizazz" – and he's right. Oh, and there's this muddled bit where I try, and fail, to change the subject of an equation by manipulating the fractional indices.'

Meg and Rose stare at me blankly, but Mr Curtis isn't about to be put off. 'And I assume you have your speech on you?'

'Always,' I say, and I pull my cards out of my bag.

Annie has picked up my card on rocky planets and their relationship with gas giants. 'This is like seeing into the mind of a maniac. You actually understand all this?'

I shrug. 'Of course.'

'Rose,' says Mr Curtis, 'you help Meg learn what's on

the cards because her speech will be much better if she's memorised it. Annie and I will –'

Annie laughs. 'Do nothing because we don't understand a word of it?'

'No. We will look at manipulating fractional …'

'Indices,' I say.

'Exactly!'

'Sir, this is definitely more useful than making origami elephants,' says Annie.

'Thank you,' says Mr Curtis. 'And in half an hour, all your hard work will be rewarded with some *whole* biscuits!' He pulls a packet of chocolate Hobnobs from his briefcase.

'Whoop!' calls out Jackson from the corner of the room.

'Quiet, you!' snaps Annie.

FORTY-EIGHT

I manage to memorise more cards during Biscuit Club than I have in the past two weeks. Rose teaches me this amazing technique called 'memory palace' and I have to visualise a different room that I know for each of my cards. At first I think she's making it up, but after I've imagined the Alpha Centauri B part of my speech in Grandad's hamster room and the bit on Beer–Lambert in my bedroom, I'm amazed to discover it actually works. Also, Annie solves the equation problem by ringing a friend who's some sort of mathematical genius. At the end, Rose highlights every word and phrase I get wrong and writes them up in a list headed 'What Meg Doesn't Know', so I can work on those parts later.

But the best thing is that for half an hour I'm forced to forget about Mum and the earthquake.

At lunchtime, it's too sunny to go to the library so

instead I sit in a corner of the field, as far away from flying footballs as I can get, and I work through Rose's list, rereading the sentences on the cards that I keep fluffing. Just as I'm trying to remember that the mass of Jupiter is double the mass of all the other planets combined, my phone buzzes, making me jump. As shouting and laughter drift across from the field, I stare at the little envelope on the screen. It's a text from Grandad.

'Meg!' I look up to see Ed walking towards me. He nods at my phone. 'Have you heard something?' He must have been playing football because his hair is slightly dishevelled and his sleeves are rolled up. He drops down next to me.

'I've got a text from Grandad, but I'm too scared to open it.' I feel the warmth of his shoulders as they brush against mine.

'He wouldn't text bad news!'

'He might,' I say. 'My grandad doesn't always think things through.'

'It'll be OK,' he says, nudging me, so I take a breath, and open the text.

I smile. It's good news. The *best* news! 'Listen to this,' I say. '*Alice just rang. The village she's staying in was hit by the quake, but she's fine. She's helping them out, then coming home. Phew!!! –*'

266

'Hang on, he actually wrote "phew"?'

'With three exclamation marks.' I read the rest of the message. *'She had to borrow a phone and she rang me as she could only make a quick call. Whoopy doop!!'*

'Whoopy doop?' says Ed.

I grin. 'Whoopy doop!'

'Ed!' comes a shout from the bottom of the slope. It's Raj and he's bouncing a football up and down. 'Come on!'

'I'd better go,' he says, but he stays next to me, pulling up bits of grass.

'Thank you for the facts,' I blurt out. 'They really helped.'

He shrugs. 'That's OK ... But I never did help you with that equation.'

'Annie's friend worked it out.' The sun is so bright, I have to shade my eyes to look at him.

'Right.' He sweeps the bits of grass off his trousers then jumps to his feet. 'See you later,' he says, then he jogs down the slope.

I look back at my list of what Meg doesn't know. I've got something else to add to it: What does Ed really think about Meg? Along with whether life exists on other planets and what the universe is made of, Ed's opinion of me is one of my top ten mysteries of the cosmos. But there is a difference. I'd love to find out that little green aliens are running around on some planet, but I'm not sure I want to know about Ed. There's something really good about this mystery. Who knew ignorance could be so enjoyable?

FORTY-NINE

For the rest of the week, two things dominate my life: money and the NASA competition. Grandad and I haven't got enough of the first and I haven't got enough time to do the second. Grandad's pension is coming through on Friday, but by Wednesday we've only got one sad little five-pound note left. I've counted all of Elsa's nappies and unless she eats something seriously dodgy, I shouldn't have to buy any more. Grandad and I both agree that the only thing we can spend money on is milk and fruit for Elsa.

So Grandad and I live off the food we already have. That night we have sweetcorn and mayonnaise toasties, on Wednesday we have pasta cooked in soup and Thursday sees us eating our worst dinner yet: rice and baked beans. Grandad covers his in chilli powder and claims it's delicious.

But on Friday – pension day – when I walk into Grandad's house with Elsa, I'm hit by an amazing smell.

'Curry!' shouts Grandad from the kitchen. I find him pulling cartons out of a plastic bag. 'Tonight we eat like kings, Meg!'

I start peeling back the cardboard lids; steam bursts off saffron-specked rice and crisp pakoras. 'Are we celebrating having money again?'

'No, we're celebrating you completing your mission.' He bangs plates down on the table. 'Your mum rang. She's at the airport about to get on a plane.'

I look up at him. 'Seriously?'

'Seriously.' He pours Coke into a glass for me. 'And we're celebrating you beating all those other kids in that competition tomorrow and going to Houston.' He looks up at me and gives me a quick smile. 'You know your mum won't make it back on time to watch, don't you? She's got two changes to make.'

'I know. That's OK.' Mum's managed to ring a few times throughout the week, but always when I've been at school. It's hard to believe she's actually on her way home. I look up at Grandad. 'Actually,' I say, trying to sound as casual as possible, 'I've got some friends coming.'

'Have you now!' Grandad's intrigued.

'It's not that big a deal,' I say, laughing, although of course I know it is a big deal. I don't think I've mentioned a single friend since Harriet left. 'You know how I told you about Biscuit Club? Well, they're all coming – Annie, Rose, Jackson, even my teacher Mr Curtis.'

'Meg, that's brilliant,' says Grandad. 'And you'll have me and Elsa too, watching you up on that stage, cheering you on.'

I was starving a second ago, but now I feel slightly queasy. 'Maybe we shouldn't talk about it, Grandad.' I sit down. 'I ran through my whole speech today with Rose ...'

'And?'

'I remembered every word.' Rose has spent each lunchtime this week helping me build my memory palace.

'But that's good news!' Grandad says.

'I was like a talking textbook ...' I say. 'Are my hands shaking?' I hold them out in front of me. 'They are!'

Grandad puts Elsa in her high chair and gives her a bowl full of curry and rice. Her hands plunge straight in. 'I've got the answer for that.'

'Really?'

'Clench your buttocks. It's almost physically impossible

for your hands to shake if you tighten your thigh or buttock muscles.'

I can't resist trying it out. 'Hey, it works!'

'There we go.'

'But I'm still nervous; you just can't see my physical symptoms any more!'

'Tell yourself it isn't nerves, it's *excitement*.' He pulls a naan bread out of a bag and tears it in half. 'You're excited because you're about to do something amazing.'

'No, I'm fairly certain I'm just really nervous because tomorrow I'm going to have to walk on to a stage –' I pause here to take a breath '– look at a room full of teen-agers and adults and deliver a complex speech ... from memory.' I shake my head. 'It's so –'

'Exciting!'

'Terrifying!'

Grandad has to be one of the most optimistic people in the world. As we eat, I go obsessively over our arrangements for tomorrow. The competition starts at two, so I'm going to spend the morning relaxing with Elsa and Pongo (ha!) then drop the two of them off at Grandad's after lunch so I can get to school early. Grandad and Elsa will come along just before it starts.

'I'm not sure about Elsa coming,' I say. 'I won't be able to concentrate if I can hear her crying.'

'Don't worry. I promise I'll take her straight out if she makes a fuss.'

The curry is delicious, but after a few more mouthfuls I put my fork down.

'Look,' says Grandad, 'you're so excited you can't eat!'

FIFTY

'**C**ards, phone, water, nappies, Annie's paper poo bear ...' As I walk to Grandad's, I run through everything I need, even though I already checked and double-checked my bags at the flat. 'Elsa, Pongo ...' I mutter, gripping the pushchair a bit tighter and checking that Pongo's lead is still wrapped around my wrist. He saw a squirrel a minute ago and nearly pulled us over trying to get at it.

In an unexpected role-reversal, last night Elsa slept the whole night through, but I woke up every couple of hours. This morning I took it easy. Elsa and I had a mammoth *Peppa Pig* session then we took Pongo for a quick walk at the rec. I didn't look at my speech once. I thought it would only make me nervous.

One thing I must remember to do at Grandad's is go to the toilet. When Yuri Gagarin was on his way to the

274

space shuttle – all suited up – he made them stop the bus so he could do a wee at the side of the road. All cosmonauts leaving from Baikonur do this now and I can see why Gagarin started the tradition: doing something 'exciting' makes you want to wee. Simple as that.

Grandad's front door is unlocked as usual. 'Grandad!' I shout. There's no answer, so I pull the pushchair inside and shout again. I stick my head in the front room, but he's not there. The house is eerily quiet so I run upstairs then check the garden. Where is he? Worry prickles through me, but I tell myself he must have popped to the Co-op or gone to visit a neighbour. There's no way Grandad could have forgotten what is happening today.

I decide to see if he's left a note for me somewhere. There's nothing in any of the usual places – on the fridge or the kitchen table – so I go to look in the front room. There's no note, but tucked behind the door I see a huge white cone. I run my hands over the peeling paint. I know what this is: it's the top half of the rocket he made me. I trace my hands over the words *MEGARA 1* and for a moment, I forget that Grandad's missing ... I even forget about the speech. Grandad gave me the rocket years ago and I spent hours in it, playing and dreaming ... I didn't even know he'd kept it. I pick up the cone to see if my mission notes are still scribbled on the inside, and that's when I see a tiny glass bottle filled with amber liquid sitting underneath it. *Meg's Rocket Fuel!* is written on a label tied on with string.

I smile. Russian cosmonauts always drink a sip of real rocket fuel before a mission; it's supposed to bring them luck. I don't know what Grandad's put in the bottle, but I'm guessing he was going to get me to drink it before I went to school. But why was it sitting under the cone? I slip the bottle in my pocket and go back into the hallway where Elsa's squirming in her pushchair.

And that's when I notice Grandad's bike is missing.

He wouldn't have gone for a bike ride, would he? Not today …? I ring his mobile, but it goes straight to voice-mail. 'Grandad's gone for a bike ride,' I say to Elsa, hardly believing the words myself. 'What shall I do?' I go to the front door and peer up and down the road.

'Da!' she shouts.

I go back inside. 'You're right,' I say. 'We should wait. I've still got loads of time until I need to be at school. Wherever he's gone, he'll be back soon. He knows how important this is.' I undo the clips on her pushchair and she wriggles out on to the carpet. 'Actually, this is good. Now I can read through my cards one last time.'

But I can't read through my cards. I try to, but every few minutes I keep jumping up to look out of the window, searching for Grandad's yellow helmet. After half an hour, I realise that I can't wait for him any longer.

'OK,' I say to Elsa, pushing her arms back into her coat. 'I don't know what Grandad was thinking, but I guess I'm just going to have to take you with me. The Biscuit Club will have to look after you.' I put her back in her pushchair.

'Na, na!' Elsa makes herself go rigid so I can't get the pushchair straps round her arms.

'Bend, Elsa!' I tickle her tummy until she doubles over and I manage to get the clips done up. But now I've made her mad, and she's screaming.

And that's when Grandad's landline starts to ring.

'Be quiet!' I say to Elsa and I snatch up the phone, covering my free ear to block out her cries.

'Meg?' The voice is crackly, distant.

'Grandad? Is that you?'

'Meg, thank goodness I caught you! But shouldn't you be at school by now?'

'Yes! The competition starts in twenty minutes! Where are you?'

'Ah, I'm in a spot of bother. I was out on my bike –'

'Grandad!' I shout this so loud that Elsa stops screaming and stares up at me. 'Why did you have to go on a bike ride today?'

'Well, it wasn't a bike ride exactly. I was so excited last night that I couldn't sleep and then I remembered that I still had your rocket up in the attic. I thought it would be brilliant if you walked into the house and saw it sitting there, in all its magnificence! I've even made you some rocket fuel and I was going to hide the bottle inside the cone –'

'I found the cone and the bottle,' I say, interrupting him, 'but what's that got to do with going on a bike ride?'

'Ah, that's what I was getting to. I discovered that the bottom of the rocket – the box you sat in – had been eaten – possibly by hamsters, possibly by rats – so I decided to go and get another one from the supermarket. They gave me a real beauty, Meg. It's even bigger than the original one. Anyway, I was cycling back through the woods, holding the box under one arm, when it happened.'

'What happened?'

'I hit a root. When I came round, my ankle was the size of a football. I'm having a bit of trouble walking.'

'When you *came round*? Grandad, where are you?'

'I'm at the bottom of the quarry – you should have seen me fly down it, Meg!'

'So you're not too far away –'

'Don't worry about me. You get down to your school

278

and win the competition.' The line crackles and for a moment I can't hear what he's saying. The reception is terrible on the Downs. 'Come and get me later ... Maybe bring a friend or two. I'm going to need a couple of people to lean on.'

I press the phone against my ear. 'If you've had a head injury, I can't leave you up there.'

'It was a tiny head injury! I've got a Lion Bar and a Fruit Shoot, so you can stop worrying about me. You are going to blow their minds about space, Meg, and you are going to go to Houston. That's your new mission! *Poyekhali*, Meg! *Poyek–*'

Then he's cut off.

I take a deep breath, fighting the panic that's rising inside me. This is unexpected, but I can work the problem, as long as I stay calm. Should I do what he says and go to school, do my presentation and then go and find him? No. I can't do that. What if he slips unconscious again, or if he was lying about how badly he was hurt? But how can I possibly go and get him without anyone to help me, and what should I do with Elsa?

Just as I'm considering ringing 999, my mobile rings and I snatch it up. 'Hello?'

'Where are you, you nutter?'

'Annie!'

'Rose and I are sitting here, the hall is full, the contestants are all here ... well, except you, of course. Meg, your massively important life-changing competition is about to start!'

'I know, but listen, I've got a problem.' Quickly, I explain that Grandad has managed to get stuck in a hole. 'Do you think I should call for an ambulance?'

'No, if you get involved with all that you'll definitely miss the competition.'

'Annie, what sort of person leaves an old man with a head injury up on the Downs just so they can try to win a free holiday?' My throat feels tight and I swallow to stop myself from crying.

'Get a grip, Clark,' says Annie. 'Your grandad's not an idiot. If he was that badly hurt he'd have rung for an ambulance himself. Just tell me where he is.'

'He's at the bottom of the old quarry, the one by Paynters Lane ... Why?'

'Because I'm going to get him out of there. Well, not me personally, but don't worry about that. You just get to school. I can look after Elsa while you do your speech.'

'No, he's my grandad. I should go and find him.'

'Meg, I'm your captain, or whatever it's called –'

'CAPCOM.'

'That's it. I'm CAPCOM Demos, and you're going to do exactly what I say. I'm going to talk you through your launch, got it?'

I nod. 'Got it.'

'Right,' she says. 'Get your arse to school.' Then the line goes dead.

FIFTY-ONE

'**W**here have you been?' Ms Edgecombe meets me in the foyer outside the hall. 'And why have you brought a *baby*?'

'Long story,' I manage to say, hanging over the handles of the pushchair to catch my breath. Running with a pushchair is hard, but at least all the jiggling has sent Elsa to sleep. 'Have you seen Annie Demos?'

'She's in the hall somewhere,' says Ms Edgecombe. 'But don't worry about your friends, Meg. It's about to start!'

She ushers me into the noisy, packed hall. Little brothers and sisters are darting around, grandmothers are sitting with handbags clutched on laps; there are so many people some are having to stand at the back. Up on the stage, I see a row of chairs, and in front of these a microphone with a spotlight shining down on it. My head is already spinning from the run, but I still feel a wave of anxiety sweep through me.

'I need to speak to Annie,' I say, desperately searching through the crowd.

Miss grips my arm. 'You're not going anywhere until you've registered. Come with me.'

She guides me down the centre aisle, right through the heart of the audience. 'Here's Meg Clark,' says Ms Edgecombe, delivering me to a table set up at the foot of the stage. 'Better late than never!'

'You're just in time,' says the woman, her eyes flicking over Elsa. She hands me a sticker. 'You're contestant number fifteen. Please stand with the other contestants so that we can begin.' A group of teenagers are waiting at the foot of the stage. Most are wearing uniforms but some, like me, are wearing their own clothes. Right at the back of the group, I see Ed, in a shirt and tie of course. His arms are folded and he's watching me curiously. He gives me a wave and I manage to smile back.

I have to find Annie, but Ms Edgecombe insists on leading me straight over to the other contestants. 'Right, you stay here,' she says, depositing me next to Ed. She nods at Elsa. 'What are you going to do with the baby?'

'That's why I need to find Annie; she's looking after her.'

Just then, I hear 'Meg!' bellowed from the other side of the hall, and then I see Annie, Jackson and Rose weaving through the crowd towards me.

'Good,' says Ms Edgecombe. 'For a moment I thought you were going to ask me to mind her, but I'm filming all the speeches.'

I turn back to look at her. 'You're doing *what*?'

'Filming the speeches.' She laughs. 'I didn't tell you about it earlier because I didn't want you obsessing over it – I knew you'd freak out. They're all going online.' Ms Edgecombe gives me a final pat on the shoulder. 'Good luck up there,' she says. 'You too, Ed. Show these other kids what a bloody amazing science teacher you've got!'

'*Miss!*' I say.

'I know, I know, I'm swearing.' She grins and walks back across the hall towards the judges.

'What's going on?' says Ed.

I shake my head because Annie, Jackson and Rose have arrived. 'I'll tell you in a minute.'

'Hey,' says Annie, abandoning her crutches and taking the pushchair from me. 'She's asleep. Bonus!'

I shrug off my coat and take a quick gulp of water. 'So who's gone to get my grandad?'

'Ah,' she says, 'about that …'

I stare at her. 'Annie, please tell me someone's gone, because if they haven't, I am out of here!'

'They're *about* to go.' Then I notice that Jackson and Rose are each holding a hockey stick and that Rose has a length of rope slung over her arm. 'This is your grandad's mountain rescue team,' she says, nodding towards Jackson and Rose. 'The only problem is his team consists of two unusually small people.'

'Hey! I'm *stocky*, not small,' says Jackson.

'I'm definitely petite,' admits Rose.

'Whatever you both want to call it, you're short,' says Annie. 'Meg, does your grandad happen to be one of those tiny wizened old people?'

'No!' I say, panic rising inside me. 'He's tall and he mountain bikes, so he's got muscles … and he eats too much curry!'

'Right, that's what I was worried about,' says Annie, looking critically at Jackson and Rose. 'I don't think these two could get a bike out of a hole, let alone a curry-stuffed man.'

'We'll be *fine*,' says Jackson. 'I know exactly where he is – gone down that hole myself a couple of times on my bike …'

'And I've done a first aid course,' adds Rose.

'But it's no good if you can't get him out!' I say. This is

silly – they're never going to get him out by themselves and I'm *not* going to abandon my grandad. 'I'm coming with you. Three of us will be able to do it.' I reach for my coat.

At that moment, there's a round of applause and all the talking in the hall fades away. I turn round and see a man wearing a white shirt, trainers and jeans walk on to the stage. He adjusts the microphone then leans towards it. 'I'm Professor Hayes,' he says, 'and I would like to welcome you to Reach for the Stars, where teenagers tell us what space *really* means to them!'

Wide-eyed, I turn to Annie, who's tugging my coat out of my hands. 'It's OK,' she whispers. 'I'll think of something. I've rung a couple of friends and I'm waiting for them to get back to me.'

I look back at the stage. I've been dreading walking up there, but now I've come this close, it's suddenly all I want to do.

Professor Hayes continues. 'Each of these young men and women will have just five minutes to convince us of their passion for space and astrophysics. Then we'll pick one lucky winner, who will jet off to America this summer to visit the Space Centre at Houston!'

Applause and a few 'whoops' break out across the hall.

'It's not OK, Annie,' I hiss, turning back to her. 'He's already been in that hole for too long.'

'I'll go,' says a voice behind me.

I spin round and see Ed standing there.

'But you can't,' I say. 'You'll miss the competition.'

'It doesn't matter,' he says, giving me a smile and a shrug. 'I heard what you were talking about. I understand the problem. I can help.'

'Please give a warm welcome,' says Professor Hayes, his voice booming out of the speakers, 'to our contestants!'

Applause rings out and the contestants start to walk up the stairs that lead to the stage.

'Right,' says Ed. 'Let's go to the PE cupboard. There's a first-aid kit in there and I know how to break in.'

He starts to walk away.

'Ed!' I grab his arm. Half of the contestants are on the stage now. 'This is *my* problem. You can't just walk out of here and give up on your chance of winning the competition.'

'Yes I can,' he says, like it's the easiest decision in the world. He looks straight at me. 'Just show them Mega Knickers and you'll blow them away.' Then he turns and walks out of the hall.

After a moment of hesitation, Jackson and Rose follow him.

'They're waiting for you,' whispers Annie, pushing me forward.

I stare up at the stage. Two seats in the row of chairs are empty. 'He gave up his chance to go to Houston for me.'

'I know,' says Annie, smiling. 'What a loser. Now get up there!'

I touch Elsa's head. 'Thank you,' I say to Annie.

'No worries. I believe this is what friends are for.'

FIFTY-TWO

As I walk across the stage, I feel the eyes of everyone in the audience following me. My mouth goes dry and then my hands start to shake, but I force myself to keep going, clenching my buttocks all the way. I walk past Ed's empty seat then sit down.

One of the judges comes to the foot of the stage and has a whispered conversation with Professor Hayes. They glance up at Ed's seat and suddenly I feel so sick I have to look away.

Professor Hayes goes back to the microphone. 'I'm afraid one contestant appears to have dropped out. That still leaves us with fourteen wonderful speeches to hear, though, so let's not waste another moment!'

I can't believe that this is happening, but I don't have time to think about what Ed's just done because already, Professor Hayes is talking and explaining the rules of the competition. 'A buzzer will sound to indicate the start of each contestant's five minutes,' he says, 'and it will sound again at the end, when the speaker must stop talking.'

One of the judges presses down on a button on the desk to demonstrate and a loud buzz rings through the hall. Nervous laughter ripples along the row of contestants.

'Now,' continues the professor, 'it's always intimidating to go first, so please give a warm and encouraging welcome to Scarlet Bedu from East Hoathly Girls' School!'

The audience claps politely as a girl in a bottle green blazer walks confidently up to the microphone. She stands staring out across the hall, a thin plait falling straight down her back. The buzzer sounds.

'Stars,' says Scarlet Bedu, lifting her chin, 'are the fundamental building blocks of our galaxies, and space is the grand stage on which the drama of their birth, evolution and death are played out!' Scarlet's voice rings out across the hall, clear and assured, and as she talks, she looks at different members of the audience. I see them smile back at her. She's not holding any sort of cards or notes, and she doesn't hesitate as she describes how space has allowed her to 'reach for the stars'.

Suddenly, the buzzer sounds and applause fills the room. Scarlet does two quick bows, then turns on her heel and walks back to her seat, unable to hide her smile of satisfaction. Her speech was delivered perfectly, and she knows it.

I take a deep breath, trying to stay calm. Scarlet's performance was so polished and accomplished, it's taken me by surprise.

After a few words from the professor, the boy sitting next to Scarlet goes to the microphone. He explains that, to him, space means fun, and that space exploration has led to all the best things in life: satellite TV, laptops, even air-cushioned trainers. He isn't word-perfect, but his enthusiasm is infectious and he bounces around the stage and makes everyone laugh.

And then the buzzer sounds again, and I listen to speech after speech about stars, black holes, new technologies, space exploration. Each time I hear the buzzer my heart beats a little faster and sweat prickles my skin because we are moving closer and closer to the moment when I will have to stand up.

Then there are just two students left, and then one, and then there's applause and the boy from Highbury Boys' School is returning to his seat next to me. Professor Hayes stands at the microphone. 'Please welcome our final contestant,' he says, stretching his arm towards me, 'Meg Clark!'

There is a new burst of clapping and all eyes turn towards me. I stand up and take a deep breath. I feel slightly dizzy, but I make myself walk towards the microphone. As I cross the stage, I tell myself that today might have started disastrously, but I'm here and I'm ready for this. All I have to do is stay calm, speak loudly and clearly, and remember every single word of my speech. I clutch my cards in my hand. I know I don't need them, but I have to hold them, just in case.

I reach the microphone.

This is it.

FIFTY-THREE

I stare out at the audience and the buzzer sounds. The cards shake in my hands and Professor Hayes smiles and nods encouragingly. I glance at my first card, reassure myself that I know the words, then look back up. 'To me, space means freedom,' I say, and I hear my shaky voice echo round the hall, 'because space exploration gives us the chance to leave planet Earth to explore the wonders of the universe.' I take a breath, and that's when I see someone slip into the back of the hall; it's a woman with white-blonde dreads, loose trousers and a rucksack slung over her shoulder. She sees me on the stage and a smile spreads across her face.

And, just like that, Mum steps back into my life.

In an instant, anger and hurt sweep through me and I'm taken back to the moment she rang from the plane. But my heart lifts too. It's just so good to see her. My fingers tighten on the cards that I know I don't need, and I force myself to carry on. 'Scientists believe that a planet capable of supporting life might be orbiting Alpha Centauri B, and that within centuries we may visit that planet ...' My voice trails off. I feel my heart thudding in my chest. Somewhere in the audience there is a cough, followed by a whisper.

I look back at the words written on the cards. With sudden and total clarity, I see that my description of space as my ultimate escape is *completely* wrong.

'Sorry,' I say, shaking my head, 'but I can't do this speech ... The words on these cards aren't true.' My voice is a whisper, but the microphone still manages to pick it up. 'I mean, they are true, but they don't come close to explaining what space really means to me.'

Now the silence in the hall is complete. I look at my precious cards that have taken me weeks to write and memorise, then I put them down on the floor. My heart beats hard in my chest as I stand back up and stare out across the audience. Several seconds tick by and my heart pounds and my skin prickles. Can I do this? Can I show them who I really am?

I know I can.

I take Grandad's bottle of rocket fuel out of my pocket and pull out the tiny cork. I lift the bottle to my lips and down the contents in one gulp. It's sweet and spicy. I put the bottle back in my pocket and my now empty hand curls into a fist.

I raise my fist into the air. '*Poyekhali!*' I say. *Let's go!*

Down in the audience, eyes widen with surprise and giggles break out, but I keep my head held high.

'When people look at the night sky they can feel tiny ...' My voice is still too quiet so I step closer to the microphone. '... And insignificant ... and I do get that.' I pause, trying to find the right words. 'Our galaxy, the Milky Way, is made up of one hundred billion stars, but there are one hundred billion *other* galaxies in the universe.' My words are slowing down, becoming clearer, louder. 'Each of these one hundred billion galaxies also contain billions of stars. I mean,' I shake my head, 'that's a lot of stars ...'

The laughter from the audience takes me by surprise and gives me the courage to carry on. 'If you could look at a map of the universe, Earth wouldn't even feature. You couldn't draw a dot small enough.' I wrap my hand around the microphone. 'But when I look into space, I don't feel scared or little, I feel ... reassured.' I feel my shoulders relax because my words are coming easily now, and I can tell they aren't going to stop.

'I guess I feel reassured because space is logical and it obeys the laws of physics.' I pause, remembering when I was up on the Downs the night after Mum left, and how soothing it was to see that the stars were exactly where they were supposed to be. 'Sometimes I think the movement of the stars are the only reliable thing in my life.'

I shake my head. 'No, that's not true. I *used* to think that. To be honest, in lots of ways space makes more sense to me than life on Earth, which is why I was planning to talk to you about how amazing it would be to leave Earth and find a brand new, human-free planet.' I pause. 'But looking at space has never been enough for me. I want to visit space in the same way people want to visit Disney World. I want to walk in space. I want to spin around the Earth at seventeen and a half thousand miles an hour. I want my feet to touch the surface of another planet!'

I'm smiling now and I see people smiling back at me.

'I thought the only way I could get to space was by working ridiculously hard. By myself.' I look around the room. 'Other people – human beings – *never* came into it. I didn't want their help and I just thought they got in the way. My baby sister screamed and stopped me revising, students at school seemed to care more about making each other laugh than lessons, and my mum forced me to plant carrot seeds on her community allotment when really I wanted to be doing my homework.' I remember how grumpy I was, how I planted a few seeds then made up some excuse and left.

'But a few weeks ago something happened.' My throat feels tight. I look right at Mum and she holds my gaze; I need her to know that I'm saying this to her. 'I had my very own big bang – and it changed everything. For the first time in my life, I felt lost in the universe … I was scared and I couldn't cope on my own. Then I discovered my Earth crew.'

I look back across the hall. 'To put one astronaut in space requires years of training from thousands of highly educated, unbelievably skilled people. I had a bunch of teenagers – Rose, Jackson and Annie – and they lifted me up and got me here today.'

From somewhere at the back of the room a loud 'Whoop!' rings out.

'That's Annie,' I say. 'No matter where I am, Annie is ready to help me work the problem. She's calm and collected and has the sort of brain that can cope with any mission contingency; she would definitely have got Apollo 13 back to Earth.'

'And I've got Ed – we sit next to each other in science. For a long time, I thought Ed was someone I had to compete against. But I got that so wrong. Everyone knows that Buzz Aldrin and Neil Armstrong were the first people to walk on the moon, but they could never have got there if Michael Collins hadn't been waiting for them in orbit. Ed is my Michael Collins. He put my mission first, which is why there's an empty seat on the stage behind me.'

'Before I met my Earth crew, I thought I could get to space just by studying – mathematics, physics, computing … I've even started to learn Russian –'

Laughter bursts out from the audience.

'No, really,' I say, then to prove it, I add, *'Ya mogu govorit' po-russki!* I forgot that an astronaut needs more than knowledge. They also need to reassure others and put others first. And they need to trust their team.

'Sir Isaac Newton said, "If I have seen further, it is by standing on the shoulders of giants." Yuri Gagarin, the first human to reach space, got there because throughout history, human beings, from Aristotle to Einstein, used their brains in crazy, incredible ways. Neil Armstrong could only take one giant leap for mankind because a crew of thousands stood behind him. I've realised that space isn't an escape from the chaos of human beings, it's something I have *because* of the chaos of human beings.'

I think back to that afternoon when Elsa was ill and suddenly see so clearly what Grandad was trying to say. 'Nietzsche said that we need chaos inside ourselves,' I press a hand against my chest, 'if we are to give birth to a dancing star.' My eyes find Mum's again. 'And I have two particularly chaotic human beings to thank for filling my mind with curiosity and encouraging me to look up in the first place. My grandad gave me my first pair of binoculars and taught me how to use them. He made me a rocket that took me to the moon on a daily basis. My mum painted the Milky Way on my bedroom ceiling. She put an arrow on it pointing to Earth and wrote next to it, *You Are Here*. Mum said that Earth was just my starting point. She has always believed I could go anywhere.'

'I'm still planning to visit space,' I say, my voice steady and certain. 'A countdown to lift-off is running through my life, like a heartbeat. This countdown started when I first looked at the moon through the binoculars Grandad gave me, and I can't imagine it will stop until the day I leave Earth.

'When I hold my baby sister in my arms and show her a twinkling star, I'm showing her where she came from. We come from elements that were formed at the heart of stars. The stars exploded, stardust was scattered across the universe and eventually formed this planet. Stardust made my sister. It made me and you. I don't need to leave Earth to see the wonder of space because I am living the wonder of space.'

I smile. It seems so obvious now that I've said it. 'And *that,*' I say, 'is what space means to me.'

Applause sweeps across the hall and I do a weird half-bow thing that I instantly regret, and as I walk back to my seat, I feel so light and free that I could be walking on the moon.

FIFTY-FOUR

Ms Edgecombe grabs me as I walk off the stage. 'Meg, you gave me goosebumps on my *face*!'

'Is that good?' I say.

'Definitely. The only other time it's happened was when I saw Benedict Cumberbatch at Luton airport.'

Mr Curtis joins us. 'That was an awesome – if slightly nerve-racking – improvisation, Meg.'

'Sir! I forgot you were coming.'

'I wouldn't have missed it for anything, although I'm slightly disappointed that I learnt how to manipulate fractional indices for nothing ... Maybe it will come in handy one day.'

'Sorry,' I say. 'I didn't mean to waste your time. It was a spur-of-the-moment thing.'

'Don't apologise. Your speech just proved, once and for all, that Biscuit Club is not a waste of time.' He passes me the box of broken biscuits. 'Here. You deserve these. Go and celebrate with Annie.'

I push through the crowd to the back of the hall, and find Annie sitting next to Elsa's empty pushchair.

She smiles up at me. 'You just made me utterly happy,' she says. 'But for the record, it's you, Jackson and Rose who are in *my* Earth crew.'

'I know that,' I say. I open the box and take a handful of broken biscuits. Suddenly I'm starving. 'Biscuit bits?'

She peers into the box. 'An entire *corner* of a Bourbon cream? Yes please!'

'So I have a question,' I say. 'What have you done with my sister?'

'I gave her to a small, sunburnt hippy. I assume she was your mum.'

'Sounds about right,' I say. 'Did she have *Poyekhali!* tattooed on one shoulder and a badly drawn Dumbo on the other?'

'That's the one.' Annie goes back to rummaging around in the box. 'So the big news is your grandad's fine. He's sprained his ankle but he's back home and being cared for by Rose, Jackson and Ed.' She looks at me. 'Bit weird?'

I try to imagine the three of them squeezed into Grandad's house. 'Just a bit …'

'Oh, and your mum is waiting for you outside.'

'Right.'

Annie catches the look on my face. 'I gave her a piece of my mind,' she says. 'Told her she was selfish and irresponsible and didn't deserve an A-grade daughter like you.'

'You didn't!'

'Course I didn't! To be honest, she was kind of quiet. Your big speech almost certainly made her cry, plus she has just survived an earthquake.'

'I know.' I say, but I still don't move.

'Well, go on!' She gives me a shove. 'You might as well get it over with. There's a reception in the drama room so I'm going to go and eat crisps and talk to geeks.'

'That sounds good,' I say wistfully.

'Go!'

I walk out of school and blink in the sunshine. It's quiet out here so it's easy to spot Mum sitting at the edge of the field. Elsa's on her lap and Mum's holding both of her hands and talking to her. Annie's right, she does look shaky. Even though she's smiling, her eyes are tired and somehow she looks pale under her sunburn.

I walk over to them. 'Hey,' I say.

'Meg!' Mum jumps to her feet and pulls me to her in a fierce hug. She smells sweaty and of suntan lotion, but

I can just get a trace of sandalwood incense. 'Sorry,' she says, letting me go. She stares down at her dusty clothes. 'I know I'm a mess. I came straight from the airport.'

'It doesn't matter,' I say, and then we stand there, Mum holding my arm and Elsa wriggling between us.

Mum stares at me. At least her nose stud is still sparkling. 'I didn't know a lot of those things you said, Meg … or maybe I did, you know, deep down.' She doesn't take her eyes off me and I start to feel hot. Part of me wants to run away, but I force myself to stay exactly where I am. 'The earthquake was bad,' she says. 'Not when it happened – I was so far away I only felt tremors – but how I felt afterwards. It shook me up inside.'

'I'm glad you're OK,' I say, making myself look at her. 'I saw all the pictures on the news. It was terrible. You had to help.'

She nods, but she still looks uncertain. 'I went to this temporary shelter and gave out food. One day, I got talking to this boy. He was all on his own, trying to look after his brother who was ill. When he told me he was fifteen, I felt so strongly that this was wrong: he should have been playing football with his friends, not worrying about how he was going to get medicine for his brother.' She looks at me. 'Then I realised he was the same age as you, Meg.' She holds on tight to my arm. 'I should never have left you.'

'No,' I say, 'you shouldn't. Not the way you did.'

'I thought about it for hours when I was on the plane. Even if you had gone to Grandad's, it wouldn't have made what I did OK.' A tear runs down her cheek, but I still can't bring myself to comfort her. Elsa puts her arms round my legs and holds on to me. After a moment, Mum says, 'Are you angry with me, Meg?'

'I was,' I manage to say.

She stares down at the ground and I have this weird feeling that she's the child and I'm telling her off. 'I guess I just told myself that Grandad would be looking after you ...'

'He tried to,' I admit, 'and we could have gone there, but I wanted to be at home so much.' I laugh and shake my head. 'I think I wanted to prove that I could do it on my own, teach you a lesson or something.'

She looks up at me. 'But I thought you both loved being with Grandad?'

'We do,' I say. 'But we want to be with you more.'

'Really?' I nod and she laughs. 'Sometimes I don't think you like me very much ... Or need me. We're so different.'

'I know.'

We look at each other and even though we're standing together, and Mum's hand is on my arm, I'm still holding back from her. 'I'll change,' she says. 'I'll stop the campaigning and the volunteering –'

'Mum,' I interrupt, 'don't change. Stay the same, just … stay here.'

Sometimes the smallest, simplest things are the hardest to do. I step closer to her and put my arms around her, then I rest my head against her, just like I did when I was little. The sun shines on us and I feel safe inside. Mum's probably always going to drive me mad, and I'm never going to be the daughter she imagined having … But that's OK. I only have to look at the stars shining in the night sky to know that beautiful things can come from chaos.

Honestly, it's not a great hug – Elsa is stuck between us and the beads in Mum's hair are squished into my face – but it's definitely one small step for Meg and Mum.

Elsa's muffled screams make us step apart. 'I guess we should go and see Grandad,' says Mum. She picks Elsa up and goes to put her in the pushchair, but Elsa wriggles and says, 'Beb, Beb!', reaching towards me.

'I'll carry her,' I say, and I pick her up. Mum grabs her rucksack, then the three of us walk out of school.

FIFTY-FIVE

When we get round to Grandad's, I leave Mum in the hall, sorting out the pushchair, and follow the noise coming from the front room.

A surreal sight meets my eyes.

Grandad's lying on the sofa, a pile of pillows propping him up, Nina Simone is blaring out of the hi-fi, Jackson's simultaneously dancing and fiddling around with the home brewery system, and Ed is bandaging Grandad's foot.

Ed King is bandaging Grandad's foot!

'Meg!' Grandad cries when he sees me at the door. 'I was just telling the boys all about fermentation ... Tell me how it went!'

He looks at me eagerly, but I can't speak. I'm still frozen with horror at the sight of Ed winding a bandage round and round Grandad's gnarly foot.

'Did you blow them away?' he adds.

'Ed, you don't have to do that,' I manage to say.

'I've finished now,' he says, looking up. 'I got my first-aid badge when I was a scout. It's good to finally use my skills. Rose was going to do it, but she disappeared.'

'Well, OK, just … wash your hands.'

Jackson turns up the music and I look around the room, trying to take everything in. 'Where is Rose?' I say.

'With the hamsters,' says Grandad.

Of course, I think. … And then lots of things happen at once and Grandad's tiny living room suddenly gets very crowded. Mum appears with Elsa, making Grandad leap to his feet in delight – and then crash back down on the sofa, I discover Jackson necking Grandad's Badger Foot ale, Rose creeps in with a pregnant hamster, Pongo barks and Elsa starts crying.

'This stuff is *lush*,' says Jackson, sipping at his mug of ale. 'You're right. It does taste of biscuit and burnt raisins!'

'I've got a keg of Diabolo stored under the stairs,' says Grandad. 'Why don't you go and find it, Jackson? It's a bit strong, but this is a celebration: Alice's home!'

'No,' I say, shaking my head at Jackson, but he darts out into the hallway anyway.

Mum is down on the floor whipping Pongo into a frenzy, saying, 'Who's missed me? Who's missed me?'

308

Ed comes over and joins me at the door.

'So,' I say, surveying the scene, 'you've met my family.'

He nods. 'But I haven't met the chickens.'

There is so much I need to say to Ed, but I don't know where to start. Then Ed does one of his half-smiles and I suddenly realise that it's not an arrogant smile. It's a shy smile, and I wonder why it's taken me so long to realise this.

'Ed,' I say, 'would you like me to show you the chickens?'

'Yes,' he says, nodding his head.

I take him out into Grandad's wild garden and we sit on the bench under the holly tree. Chickens peck round our feet and the sun finds its way through the canopy of leaves.

We sit like this for a while, with me swinging my legs and Ed telling me about their rescue mission. He's just describing how they had to drag Grandad out of the hole then wheel him down the hill on his bike when I interrupt him. I can't wait another second.

'Thank you –' the words burst out of me '– for giving up your place like that … It was the nicest thing anyone has ever done for me.'

He looks at me and smiles. 'That's all right.'

I'm not sure what to say next, so to cover my

embarrassment I pick up a chicken, but she just flies out of my hand with a burst of clucking. 'Can you do your speech another time?'

'Nope,' he says. 'I met Ms Edgecombe outside the hall and she made it very clear that it was now or never.' He laughs. 'I don't think my mum's going to be too happy.'

'I'm so sorry,' I say, shaking my head. 'What a disaster. Will you still be able to go?'

'Go where?' he says, like he's forgotten why we were even entering the competition.

'To Houston on the NASA trip. Your mum and dad could pay for you, couldn't they?'

He laughs. 'Meg, do you know how much the trip costs?'

'But I thought …' I trail off. What did I think? That Ed's family had so much money he was doing the competition for fun, or just to try to beat me?

'When I told Mum about the trip, she said if I wanted to go, I'd better win the competition.'

'So you just gave up your chance of going to Houston …'

'… For you.' He looks right at me as he says this.

'But, Ed, I might not win!'

He shrugs. 'I don't care. You deserved the chance more than I did. I've watched you working towards this for years, plus I've seen your bedroom.'

310

'Oh ... that.' We both fall quiet and look across Grandad's messy garden. 'It is pretty spacey,' I say, and we laugh.

'Oh, there was one other reason why I did it.'

Something about the way Ed says this makes me look down at the ground. Our hands are close together. 'Yeah?'

'I did it because I like you.'

And I know he means *like* like, because as he says this, he takes my hand in his, and there is no way this is an accidental touching of fingers. This is a total hold: palm to palm, fingers wrapped around fingers, and it feels like all the billions of atoms in our hands are bonding and joining. I look up at Ed. 'I like you too,' I say.

'*You do?*' He sounds slightly amazed.

'Yes ... I do.'

Then he says in a rush, 'Good, because I want to ask you out next Saturday.'

Down at my feet, a chicken scratches at the soil and a warm breeze blows my hair. 'The night of the dance?'

He nods. 'I know you said you'd never go out with me, even if every other person on the planet had been fried by a meteor –'

'*Asteroid*,' I correct him, then I carry on nervously, 'a meteor is a much smaller rocky particle that vaporises when it enters the Earth's atmosphere –'

'Right,' he squeezes my hand, 'so I know you said you would never go out with me even if every other person had been fried by an *asteroid*, but have your feelings changed, Meg?'

I look up at him. Even though we're sitting so close together and I know what he did for me this afternoon, I can't help remembering the gleeful look on Bella's face when she announced that Ed wanted to ask me to the dance. 'You're not joking this time?'

'Meg, I was *never* joking! That lunchtime on the science trip I was planning on asking you out – Bella had even made me rehearse it because she knew how nervous I was – but you seemed so angry with me about the whole Mega Knickers thing that I couldn't go through with it.' He laughs. 'Asking someone out is really difficult. It's probably more difficult than understanding relativity.'

'Relativity isn't that difficult to understand,' I say. 'You just have to remember that the laws of physics don't change and –'

'Meg!'

'Yes?'

'Next Saturday. Date with me. Yes or no?'

'Yes!' I say, and I nod as well so he knows I really mean it and to convince myself that this is actually happening, that I, Meg Clark, am about to boldly go where I have never gone before: on a date.

Actually, scrap the 'boldly' …

But I'm definitely going on a date … and I might be going to Houston. I can't quite bring myself to look at Ed right now, but I want to show him how happy I feel so I go with squeezing his hand back.

'Oi!' A shout from the back door makes us look up. Annie is standing there with Rose. 'Are you two *holding hands*?'

'Yes,' says Ed, holding our linked hands up in the air and gripping tight so I can't let go. 'Yes, we are!'

FIFTY-SIX

And then the party moves to the garden, because that's what it's become: a party.

Mum gets fish and chips for everyone and we put Grandad on a deckchair in the sun. A combination of Diabolo, strong painkillers and the chips makes him fall asleep, and then Mum decides she should go home and have a shower.

Elsa's loving having so many people give her attention and she's walking around handing out presents like stones and screwed-up flowers. 'It seems a shame to take her with me,' Mum says, watching as Rose pulls Elsa on to her lap.

'I'll bring her home later,' I say.

Mum's tired face brightens. 'Really?'

'I might take her for a walk first,' I say. For the past hour, Mum's done everything for Elsa – fed her chips,

314

picked her up when she's fallen over and cried, changed her nappy. Although it's been great handing over the responsibility, it's been strange too. I feel like I want Elsa all to myself again, just for a while.

When Mum's gone, the five of us just hang out in the garden, talking over Grandad's snores and the distant sound of Nina Simone, and even though I could never imagine us doing this in school, right now, in Grandad's garden, it seems like such a natural thing to do. Annie describes a conversation she had at the reception with a boy called Alistair. 'He couldn't stop staring at my crutches, and I thought, maybe he's from a boys' school and doesn't get to talk to girls very often and doesn't know what to say, but then he went, "Did you know that the memory foam on your crutches was developed by NASA?", then he walked off!'

'He's right,' I say. 'It was: it was to improve seat cushioning and crash protection.'

'That's enough from you,' says Annie. 'You've had your moment.'

'So how did it go?' asks Rose. In the chaos of Mum being back and getting the fish and chips, we've barely talked about the competition.

'Ah …' I glance at Ed. 'I kind of scrapped my entire speech and made up a new one on the spot.'

'*What?*' Ed stares at me. 'I gave up my chance to do my, frankly, amazing talk on space and the environment, just so you could *make something up?*'

'You should have heard it, though,' says Annie. 'She mentioned all of us.'

Ed's eyes narrow. 'Really … What did you say?'

'You'll have to wait and see,' I say. 'They're going to put the speeches online.'

There's a ring of the doorbell and Ed jumps up. 'That'll be my mum,' he says. Earlier he arranged for her to come and pick him up.

'No!' says Annie. 'You can't go now; it will ruin the party.'

'Sorry,' says Ed, 'but I've got to face the music. She's about to give me hell for dropping out of the competition.'

He looks at me, and I look at him, and an awkward silence falls across the garden. Annie rolls her eyes. 'See him to the door, you idiot,' she says.

Ed follows me through the house. When we open the door, there's no one there, but then I see a very ordinary-looking blue car parked at the kerb with Ed's brother's cheeky face peeking out of the back. The lady sitting in the front waves at us. She doesn't look like she's going to give Ed hell. She looks like she's going to give him a lovely dinner.

'So …' says Ed, turning to look at me.

How do you say goodbye to someone when they've just asked you out … and their mum is watching you? 'So … Bye,' I say. Bye … *bye?!*

He nods. 'Call me later?'

As he goes to get in the car, I shout out, 'Thank you!', and he does this sort of salute which I love because it is exactly the sort of thing Buzz Aldrin might have done. In fact, the more I think about it, I realise Ed does have the air of a man from the 1960s. I feel a smile spread across my face. Somehow I've managed to get myself a date with a boy who looks like a retro astronaut.

I literally dance back out into the garden and the other three look up at me.

'Yeah, he's hot,' Annie says. 'Congratulations. Now wipe that smile off your face. It's making me feel queasy.'

FIFTY-SEVEN

O nce the others have gone, and I've persuaded Grandad that a soak in the hot tub isn't 'just what he needs', I take Elsa down to the seafront and push her along the prom in her pushchair.

It's getting late, and the darkening sky is reflecting on the still sea. We stop at the park at the foot of the Downs and I sit on a swing with Elsa on my lap. 'So, Mum's home,' I say.

She cranes her neck back to look back at me. 'Mamama,' she says.

'That's right.' She smiles at me and makes a grab for my face. 'Ow! I need to cut your nails.' Then I realise that Mum will do that ... and give Elsa her dinner and do up all the poppers on her Babygro tonight. Elsa turns back to face the sea and I push off with my toes and start us swinging. She laughs and I press my nose into her silky hair and smell a mixture of bubble bath and Weetabix. Rose is right. This is the best smell in the world.

I point up at the sky. The moon has just started to appear, a pale orange disc sitting low in the sky. 'That's the moon,' I say. '*Moon.*'

'Beb,' she says.

'No, not Meg, *moon.*' But she just bangs back against me, trying to get me to swing higher. 'Nearly fifty years ago,' I say, 'two men walked on the moon for the first time. Did you know that the moon has a smell? When the astronauts got back into the lunar module and shook the moon dust from their clothes, it smelt of gunpowder. They could even taste it.' Elsa settles against me as we float up and down. 'Then they discovered the switch that they needed to leave the moon had broken so Buzz Aldrin made a new one by sticking a pen in the control panel.' I breathe in the evening air and stare at the luminescent lump of rock that has been pulling me closer all my life. 'I think that the moon is the most beautiful thing in the world,' I say, 'except for you.'

'Da,' she says, then she blows a raspberry, then she says, 'moo'.

'There are no cows here,' I say. 'Only seagulls.'

'MOO!' she says, pointing up at the pale sky.

I follow her finger and see that she's pointing right at the golden moon. 'Moo!' Elsa says again, 'Moo!'

My heart lifts. 'That's right,' I say, 'that's the moon.'

FIFTY-EIGHT

'**S**tand close to the mirror and tilt your head back.' I do what Annie tells me. We're talking on Skype and she's being my CAPCOM again, helping me get ready for my date with Ed. She wanted to come round here, but I didn't trust her not to say anything embarrassing in front of Ed. Having Mum around is going to be bad enough.

'And why exactly am I doing this?' I ask her.

'You're looking for out-of-sight boogers that might drop down later … See any?'

'God, *yes*!' I get a tissue and blow my nose.

Annie says, 'Right, now growl at yourself. You're checking for bits between your teeth.'

I bare my teeth in the mirror. 'Grrrr … No bits.'

'I think you're ready. Nervous?'

'Want to puke.'

'Yeah … don't do that. Right, now show me how you look.'

I prop my phone on my desk and take a last look in the mirror. I'm actually wearing a dress. I've never been to any of our school discos, but if I've learnt anything from Bella this week it's that some sort of special outfit is expected tonight. It's been a strange week at school. Ed and I have done a lot of talking and hanging out together, but no more hand-holding. I've even wondered if somehow I've got it all wrong – if he's asked me to the dance as a really good friend – but Annie said I was just taking insecurity to a whole new, pathetic level.

Mum got me the dress from Brighton. I run my hands over the full skirt. I'm fairly confident that no one else will be wearing a dress with the planets printed all over it. 'I look like me in a dress,' I say, turning round. 'I look weird.'

'Not weird,' says Annie. 'Cosmic.'

The doorbell rings. Pongo starts barking and Mum runs past my room. 'Hurry up!' she calls.

'Oh, God,' I say, staring at my phone. 'He's here!'

I can see Annie sitting on her bed wearing a bright red dress. Her white rat, Alice, is curled up on her shoulder. 'Wow.' Her eyes go wide. 'This is it, mate.'

'Wish me luck.'

'No way. You don't believe in that rubbish.'

'You're right. Wish me a logical outcome.'

'And what would that be?'

Up on the wall, Valentina Tereshkova gives me her sternest look, reminding me that good things happen when I tell the truth. I look back at Annie and say, 'A kiss.'

'Then go get that kiss, space girl!' she says, then her hand reaches forward and she disappears. Annie doesn't do goodbyes.

'*Come on!*' Mum calls from the hallway.

I take a deep breath, check my nose one final time, then leave my room. Out in the hallway, Mum holds Elsa and Pongo back while I open the door.

And there's Ed, standing there and smiling at me ... and looking *very* casual. He's wearing jeans and a sweatshirt along with his big parka. Slung over his shoulder is a sports bag.

'Wow, Meg, you look ...' He frowns down at my dress.

'What?'

'Like you might get cold.'

'I've got a cardi.' I grab it off the hook by the door. Mum's grinning at Ed and I know she's bursting to talk to him. I need to get us out of here before she asks what his star sign is or tries to touch him to check out his energy.

'But we're going to be sitting outside for hours,' says Ed. 'The asteroid doesn't pass by until eleven.'

'The asteroid? But what about the school dance?' I look at my nails. I actually let my mum paint them red to match Mars on my dress. She was in heaven. 'Why didn't you tell me?'

He grins and shrugs. 'Romantic surprise? Plus, you told me I was never *ever* allowed to mention the dance to you.'

'I think you took that a bit literally.'

'Probably, but I'd never take you to the dance. You said you hated them.' He pats his bag. 'I thought we'd go on the Downs. I borrowed Raj's fishing shelter, I've got food and we can make a fire.' He hesitates. 'Was it a stupid idea? I thought you liked it up there.'

I actually have to stop myself from hugging him. 'I *love* it up there. I'll get changed.' I go to my room and while I'm pulling on leggings under my dress and finding my warmest hoodie, I hear Mum chatting to Ed, offering to lend him sleeping bags and cotton wool to light the fire.

Soon I'm ready. Just before we go, I ask Mum, 'What time do I need to be back?'

'Any time you like, as long as you look after each other.' OK, I'm starting to see the benefits of having a mother with no boundaries. 'Enjoy it *not* being the end of the world!' she adds.

'Moo, moo!' says Elsa, and they both wave goodbye to us.

'Hey,' says Ed, giving me a nudge as we walk down the wee stairs. 'How are you?'

'I'm very good,' I say, as our shoulders brush, then, before I can change my mind, I slip my hand into his. Ed's fingers curl round mine and he squeezes my hand.

FIFTY-NINE

We walk across the Downs for over an hour to get away from the light pollution of town, then set up our asteroid-spotting camp. While Ed puts up the shelter, I find twigs and make a fire.

'That looks a bit professional,' Ed says, when he sees my pyramid of kindling.

'My mum loves making fires on the beach … or in parks. Basically, anywhere where she's not supposed to.' I put a match to the bit of cotton wool I stuffed in at the bottom and the fire crackles to life.

'Look at that!' says Ed, as flames lick along the twigs.

'We'll have to let it die out in a couple of hours, or we won't be able to see the sky properly.'

We collect a pile of dead wood then sit in the shelter, shoulders touching, and we toast marshmallows. It's cold because it's such a clear night. Beyond the glow of the fire are the dark shadows of trees. It's quiet too. Every now and then we hear a squeak or a scuffle in the leaves.

'You don't wish you were at the dance?' I say.

He shrugs. 'No, I don't need to go. I'll hear every single detail about it tomorrow from Bella.'

Bella's making a big effort with me at school, and I guess I'm making a big effort with her. Yesterday, we were doing an experiment and I asked her if I'd measured a wavelength correctly. She stared at me, open-mouthed, and said, 'Megara, did you just ask *me* a question? What is going on with the world?'

I take a look at Ed. His hood is up and it's hiding his face. 'I bet you'd have enjoyed wearing a suit,' I say.

He smiles. 'Yeah, but I don't need to go to a dance to do that.'

I stare up at the sky. The moon is beautifully clear. I pass Ed my binoculars so he can see the craters. Somewhere across the hill, a fox barks. 'A couple of weeks ago,' I say, 'I couldn't have imagined doing this.'

'I could,' says Ed.

'What, you imagined us sitting in Raj's fishing shelter on the Downs?'

'The fishing shelter I didn't anticipate,' he says. 'I just imagined being with you and looking up at the sky.'

A shiver of excitement runs through me and to break

the silence, I say, 'Look,' and point up. 'That's the Andromeda Galaxy.'

It takes Ed a second to find the galaxy with the binoculars and I have to lean close to him to point it out. 'How far away is it?' he asks.

'About two and a half million light years.'

'And I'm looking at it ...' His voice is filled with wonder.

'You're not looking at it *now*. You're looking at it two and a half million light years ago.'

'So if a little alien was on a planet over there, looking through a telescope at Earth, it wouldn't see us?'

'It wouldn't even see human beings. They came along two hundred and thirty thousand years later.'

Ed lowers the binoculars and looks at me. 'But here we are,' he says.

Our faces are centimetres apart. 'Here we are,' I say.

He nods, and to prove the point he leans forward and kisses me, and that spark that's been pulling us together for days, weeks, maybe even years, bursts into life. His hand draws me close and I hold on tight to his coat and kiss him back. I can taste marshmallows and his lips feel totally alien, but at the same time like something that belongs to me. I kiss Ed King and he kisses me, and I really love my life on planet Earth.

SIXTY

'Open it! Open it!' Mum, Elsa and Pongo have piled on to my bed. Elsa is waving an envelope up and down. A thick, white envelope with *NASA* printed in one corner. Mum pulls it out of Elsa's hands and passes it to me.

I run my hands over the smooth surface. 'I don't think I won, Mum. It feels like bad news.'

'Look how thick it is,' she says. 'How many words do you need to say, "Bad luck, you didn't win"? Not many. But if you have to include information about flights and hotels ...'

'You really think so?'

'I do, but there's only one way to find out.'

Elsa jumps up and down, my planets spin on their threads and the fifty-nine female astronauts smile down at me. I pull open the corner of the envelope then stop.

329

'I really want to go,' I say, 'more than anything in the world.' I think Mum knows I don't just mean to Houston. 'But if I haven't won, I won't give up. This is just the start.'

Mum nods and puts her hands over her eyes, like she can't bear to watch.

I take a deep breath, then carefully peel open the envelope. I pull out the folded sheets of paper and smooth them out on my lap. '*Dear Megara*,' I read, then I stare at the next sentence. I read it again and again.

'Lift-off?' Mum says.

I look back up at her. All I can do is smile.

ACKNOWLEDGEMENTS

I'd like to thank the staff at the Physics and Astronomy department at the Sussex University who were so helpful during my research visits. Walking round the PhD research lab was an incredible experience and one I will never forget. I'd particularly like to thank David Daniels from the schools lab who runs inspiring workshops very like the one Meg attended and who so patiently answered all my questions.

Meg's beloved science centre is inspired by The Observatory Science Centre at Herstmonceux in East Sussex. It's a brilliant place and the staff there are passionate about space and physics. The domes exist. The huge telescopes exist. The tea room exists. Go and visit them!

FALL IN LOVE
WITH THE WARMTH, WIT, ROMANCE AND FIERCE FRIENDSHIPS OF BEA, BETTY, KAT AND PEARL'S LIVES IN

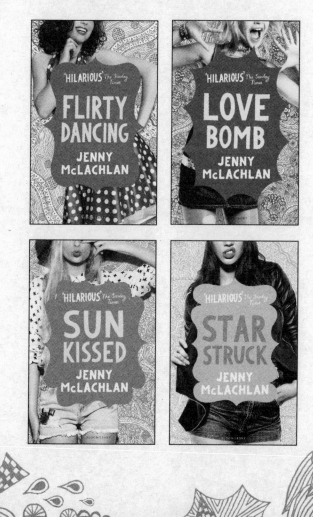

SEE BEA STEP INTO THE LIMELIGHT IN

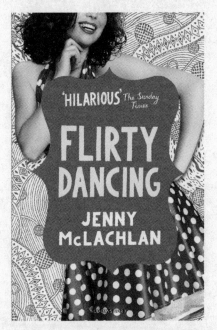

Bea Hogg is in deep trouble. She entered a TV dance competition with a mystery partner . . . who turns out to be the unbelievably hot Ollie Matthews. Boyfriend of the school's meanest girl.

Now Bea must prepare for the fallout as national humiliation beckons. And at school she faces something far worse: Pearl Harris.

Bea is *sooo* dead.

TURN OVER FOR A SNEAK PEEK

ONE

A small naked person is licking me. I don't panic – this happens a lot. The naked person starts kissing my face. I smell Marmite and banana and . . . hang on . . . the person is not entirely naked. It's wearing wellies. *Wellies?* This is new. And *totally* unacceptable.

I grope for my phone . . . 5.34 a.m.

5.34 *a.m*!

'Bea!' Emma cries. 'Happy birthday!'

'Go away. It is *not* my birthday.' I try to push her out of my bed, but she resists and we start to scuffle.

Mistake. For a three-year-old, my sister's a mean wrestler. I briefly consider being grown-up, but before I know it we're having a proper fight.

'I got you a present!' comes her muffled voice from somewhere around my feet.

'Present later?' I could probably sleep with her down there. It's not so bad, quite cosy and –

'PRESENT NOW!' she screams.

She's clearly in one of her extra-special moods, so I say what I always say when I want to get rid of her. 'Did you hear that, Emma?'

'What?'

'I heard Dad's voice . . . He's home! Dad's home!' (He isn't. He's in Mexico.)

'Daddy!' She shoots out of my bed and down the stairs, leaving me to roll over and snuggle my face into something warm and squidgy. A forgotten bit of banana, perhaps?

I sniff it. It's not banana.

Two hours later, Emma's come to the door to see me off to school. Headbutting me in the stomach, she shouts, 'Love you, frog-nose!'

Birds fly off our neighbour's roof.

'Love you, botty-breath,' I say, pushing her firmly back into the house. I walk down the path. Now is the time *the shyness* sweeps over me and I leave Real Bea at home and take Shy Bea to school.

Already, as I walk to the bus stop, Shy Bea is making me hunch my shoulders and stare at the floor. The further I get from my house, with Emma's broken slide sitting on the patch of tatty lawn, and our red front door, the less I feel like me.

'Though she be but little, she is fierce!' I whisper under my breath as I approach the Year Elevens who hang out on the wall outside the Co-op. I sit in my usual spot away from the others and get out my phone. One of the boys throws an M&M at me. It bounces off my head and lands on my lap. He laughs and watches to see what I will do. I stare at it. It's blue.

Though she be but little, she is fierce, I think.

Eat the M&M, Bea! Go on, EAT IT!

I brush it to the floor. Not my fiercest moment.

I've pretty much made myself invisible by the time the bus arrives, and when I drop down into the seat next to Kat she doesn't even look up. She's staring into the tiny mirror she always carries somewhere about her person. At first, I think she's just checking out the perfectness of her blonde, blonde hair, but then she grabs my arm and pulls me closer, hissing, 'Look behind us!'

I peer back through the bus, 'What?'

'It's *him*: Ollie "The Hug" Matthews. Oh, God. Don't look! Look! No. Don't look. OK. Look now. Soooo hot!' I sneak a sideways glance at her. Just as I suspected, her mouth is half open and her eyes are all big and puppy-like. She's doing her 'Sexy Lady Face'. She looks like Emma when she's doing 'a big one' on the potty.

'Don't look at me,' she says. 'Look at *him*.'

And so I look. For once, I can see what she's getting at. Ollie Matthews has got these kind, brown eyes, sort of tousled hair and shoulders that look a bit like *man* shoulders and his hands are . . .

'Bean, are you listening?' Kat snaps her mirror shut. 'I think I need to be more realistic and forget about Year Elevens and focus on Year Tens. Also, well, maybe he's *the one*? There was "The Hug", after all.'

'What? He said *that* was an accident.'

Kat snorts, 'It didn't *feel* like an "accident"!'

'He thought you were his sister. You've got the same coat . . . that one with the birds on it.'

'He. Is. So. So. Hot. Don't you think?' says Kat, ignoring my little slice of REALITY.

The Hug is listening to his iPod and looking out of the window in a, you know, *hot* type of way, with his eyes, which are open (**sexily**), looking at trees . . . **hot** trees covered in **sexy** green leaves. 'Yeah, Kat,' I say. 'Ollie seems —'

'Say it!' Kat is gleeful. 'Go on, say it. Say Ollie Matthews is HOT.' I shut my mouth. 'Say it say it say it!'

'OK. I can see, from your point of view, that he could be described as . . . hot.'

'Yes! He *totally* is.' She grabs my arm. 'Now tell me *everything* you know!'

I have a great memory. 'Year Ten.'

'I know that.'

'Was in *Bugsy Malone* last year.'

'Who was he?'

'Bugsy.'

'That's good, isn't it?'

'Yes.'

'More,' she demands hungrily.

'Rugby team.'

'Mmmmm.'

'Captain of the rugby team.'

'MMMMM.'

'Sang that song at Celebration Evening with his band.'

'What song?'

'*Do ya think I'm sexy?*' I sing under my breath.

'Bean. Don't.'

'OK. Sorry.'

'More?'

I look back at The Hug. 'He rolls his sleeves up, you know, all the time, and his arms are . . .' I trail off. I refuse to use *that* word again.